GUARDED TREASURE

BY

Mae Lovette

For my Mom

Thanks for hiding that box of
romance novels under your bed.

CHAPTER ONE

THE OFFICE OF Ronald Pimsley had the familiar nature of a traditional English study but was stuffed almost to brimming with an impressive collection of rare Egyptian artifacts. There were shadow boxes of jewelry: a lapis scarab brooch; a turquoise and gold broad collar; a fiery carnelian and copper ring depicting the Eye of Horus. A curio cabinet contained vases of terracotta clay, creamy ivory, and turquoise faience. On the west wall hung a four-foot ankh that portrayed a serpent encircling an obelisk in bronze. A small fig wood window box displayed several scraps of linen labeled for which mummies they had allegedly come from and held space for future additions. The wall behind his desk featured a giant sculpture of the goddess Isis, showing the massive span of her raptor wings.

Edith considered the irony. Isis was the protector of women and children. It was unlikely Pimsley recognized that virtue considering his penchant for treating a grown woman like a child.

Her career as a female in Egyptology thus far had been an exercise in placating an endless parade of insufferable men just like the one she sat across from now. Suppressing a smirk, she stirred the tea his secretary had set before her. He sat behind his desk in a wingback chair with his hands folded in front of him, head tilted in curious fascination. The look on his face was that of a man who considered himself exceedingly patient and magnanimous.

She already disliked him.

The secretary served him tea as well, before turning to leave. He shamelessly ogled her rear as she walked out, not returning his attention to Edith until the woman's backside was out of sight with the door closed behind her. Edith had to dig her nails into the palm of her hand to resist a full panoramic eye roll. Pimsley's worship of Isis likely began and ended with her bare breasts, she surmised.

"What a lovely replica of the canopic jars of Ptahhotep." Edith smiled tightly as she gestured to the gleaming ceremonial jars on a bookshelf behind him. The alabaster lids were carved to depict a baboon, a jackal, a falcon, and predictably... a man. The jars represented one of the most distinctive elements of the mummification process, a ritual that was among the many aspects of ancient Egyptian life and lore that had fascinated the world. The containers were designed to hold the organs of the Pharaohs for safekeeping in the afterlife.

"Replica, indeed," he chortled. Edith narrowed her eyes suspiciously at his implication before she could think better of it. Certainly, any real canopic jars belonged in a museum, not on the bookshelf of a slimy newspaper mogul. Out of habit, a well-crafted argument began to stack itself in her mind, but as things were, she wasn't in a position to be disagreeable.

Ronald Pimsley was the heir of the Near East Publishing Company, the crown jewel publication of which was the Alexandria Gazette. It was founded by his father in the late 1800s. Not only did it offer English-print reporting to British expatriates, it was also the premier source delivering Egyptian current events to Western newspapers.

Walter Pimsley had been a journalist and editor abroad, and the Gazette was his proudest accomplishment; the culmination of an impressive career. His son Ronald, on the other hand, had only ever served in the capacity of a shareholder. He enjoyed all the advantages of being a tycoon and did not trouble himself overmuch with the pesky business of running a news outlet.

Since living in Cairo, Edith had come to know he was notorious for his collection of Egyptian art and ancient trinkets. This being the first time Edith had ever met with him or seen his office, the reputation that preceded him was shockingly accurate.

"There's no need to mince words, Miss Taylor. I know we do not wish to waste each other's time," he chuffed in his clipped King's English accent.

"Certainly not. As I said, I do apologize for arriving earlier than expected." She polished up her own English accent, which had relaxed over her years living abroad in Egypt. She assumed mirroring would be an effective strategy in her pursuit to win over Ronald Pimsley, and she certainly wasn't above switching on her nobility if the occasion called for it.

"You see, I am quite eager to secure the position," she said.

"That's all very good, Miss Taylor, but you see, I'm not quite sure you understand what you're asking."

"Mr. Pimsley, I think you'll find I'm a rather well-educated and intelligent woman, and you might be surprised how much I understand the things I say."

His brow furrowed quizzically at her meaning, but he nonetheless dismissed it as a pleasantry.

"Yes, you're certainly very well educated. Your letters of recommendation are high praise, and I can see you read history at Durham." He leaned over to the stack of papers beside him, reviewing any details that could be gleaned from the top sheet. "I'm aware that your brother is lecturing at Oxford. He's quite well, I hope?"

She set down her teacup and joined her hands in her lap.

"He's very well, thank you," Edith said, working to unclench her jaw.

"I'm not doubting that you are sufficiently knowledgeable in the subject matter at hand," he said, offering his palms up in a gesture of graciousness. "You see, it's just that the site of an archeological dig is hardly the place for a woman of gentility such as yourself. Don't you agree?"

"On the contrary, as it happens… a man once told me that Dame Maud Cunnington is one of the foremost archeologists in history."

"Well," he lifted his eyebrows, "sounds like a very good sort of fellow, indeed. I'm sure he knows his history."

Edith pursed her lips and held her breath. It was becoming more and more difficult to stop herself from smashing the teacup over his bald head.

"The fact of the matter is that we are now in the year 1930. The conditions that would allow the involvement of ah, Miss Cunnington, were the early days of archaeology. That was before the field was legitimately professional," he said, slowly and quietly, as he might speak to his grandchild.

"What I mean to say is that archaeology has become a much larger and more complicated endeavor than it used to be. Additionally, being entrenched in such a well-known legend, this dig site in particular is very likely to draw an excess of attention and press. It will be a very masculine environment, and a rather crowded one at that."

Pimsley took a moment to stir his tea, considering how to continue.

"I understand that you are not satisfied to act as the translator for the team via correspondence, but that you are demanding to be granted access to the tomb itself."

"Exclusive access, yes."

"Ah, yes. Exclusive access," he repeated after her, very troubled. "My misgivings are not limited to the concerns I've already raised. Argo, that is, the city itself, is a city without luxuries. It has been plagued by misfortune for centuries. Of course, local folk tales would point to the curse as an explanation for that. But the logical source of the area's depression is a geographical one. Without a freshwater source, they're mired in a constant battle with the distillation of the oasis. And aside from the very small amount of tourism the tomb itself draws... why, the city is mostly a maze of destitute slums, you see."

She disagreed.

Instantly she knew Pimsley had come by his assessment of Argo due to his narrow mind. He would have been the type to assume a city without luxuries and comforts was a city of miserable impoverished degenerates. Edith had been in Egypt for many years and had studied the region many years before that. Her love and respect for its people was unwavering. Pimsley would probably judge the worthiness of an entire city by whether his lunch setting included a bouillon spoon.

Edith knew better. What rural Egyptian towns lacked in comforts and commerce they more than made up for in culture and community, and their way of life was no lesser for being different. In fact, she found it much richer in affection than her own British upbringing had been.

"Mr. Pimsley, I appreciate your words... beyond what I am able to express at this moment," she stated carefully. "You know me to be a member of the aristocracy in England. You know that my father is a gentleman, you know that my brother lectures at Oxford. But what you may not know — that I did happen to mention in our correspondence," she glanced at the stack of papers beside him, "is that my mother is Egyptian. Here in Cairo, I am not known as a lady of the aristocracy, I am simply Edith Taylor, a scholar, well respected in my field for my knowledge of Egyptology. Aside from the fact that my heritage naturally inspires a deep connection with the rich history here, I have lived and worked in this country for many years."

"As a librarian," he grunted.

"Yes, a librarian. At the Egyptian National Library and Archives. Furthermore, I have been to archeological sites before, I have been in tombs before, and I have been in male-dominated environments before. I have simply never been given the opportunity to work in them before. What I hope to convince you of here today is that I am capable of doing so… and I would very much like for you to give me the job I have asked for, according to the terms I've requested, so that I may prove it."

Taking a deep breath, she sat very straight, immensely proud of herself. Take that, she thought. Edith Taylor was here to prove she was a poised and capable professional; that she wouldn't back down from any man.

Suddenly Edith squealed, flailing in her chair as the double doors behind her were flung open with a thunderous clamor.

"Pimsley!" a deep, booming voice called, as she turned around to see a wall of a man standing in the doorway. He was covered in a thin film of dust and it was clear he had barely wiped his face with the bandana tied around his neck. She was alarmed to notice two pistols in a brown leather shoulder holster that matched his belt. Underneath he wore a white linen safari shirt and khaki trousers. His brown hair fell across his sweaty brow, and he was bearded with many days of stubble.

The shock of his startling arrival instantly gave way to irritation as she deemed him obnoxious, disheveled, and to her dismay, devilishly handsome.

The giant man's boots thudded heavily across the floorboards as he took wide strides toward the seat next to her.

"Ben!" Pimsley cheered, as he stood. Ben accepted Pimsley's handshake as his other hand clapped his shoulder companionably.

"A pleasure as always," Pimsley beamed at him.

Ben took the empty chair next to a small brunette woman he assumed was a new typist.

"Sorry I'm late. If you're dictating a letter or something, I can always hang back in the lobby." He leaned over in his chair glancing back the way he came in to wink at the leggy blonde secretary.

Edith wondered if she actually glowered, or if she had managed to conceal it within herself. He was American, she gathered, and she swiftly judged him to be an uneducated one at that, as he mustered all the formality of a stray dog. He was certainly no gentleman.

"Not at all, my dear boy. Ingrid, the doors please." Pimsley gestured toward the lobby before once again taking his seat.

"Hey, thanks, Toots," Benjamin Brooks said to the secretary as she closed the doors on her own beaming smile.

"I'm not taking dictation. As it happens, Mr. Pimsley requested an appointment with me especially to discuss very important business." The woman beside him spoke in a soft voice with an English accent but was distinctly on edge.

"Yeah, me too," he smiled brightly while turning to her. His smile fell slightly when he really saw her for the first time.

Her ankles were crossed beneath her smart mid-length skirt, and she wore dainty flat loafers. Some interesting curves were hidden in her demure outfit, he suspected, despite her narrow waist cinched by a thin belt. The neckline of her boxy blouse revealed only a stingy glimpse at the glowing olive skin of her throat, tied with a prim kerchief underneath the collar. Wild curls the color of coffee were swept into a tidy bun at the nape of her neck. Surely against her best efforts, small winding tendrils sprang free around her face. Behind large frame glasses, her light green eyes gave him pause. Though she seemed slight sitting there, the impact she had on Ben was colossal.

When his gaze returned to her face from all the places it had roamed, those light eyes were shooting daggers at him. She didn't seem to appreciate being examined. Whipping off her glasses, she swept another tendril loose from her knot of hair.

If she was trying to look fierce and dissuade his attention, it didn't help. His heart had skipped a beat at first glance, but upon locking eyes with her, it skidded to a full stop.

Pimlsey cleared his throat when he noticed that Ben was staring at Edith, agape, and she seemed on the verge of clawing his eyes out.

"It's just as well you should meet, as you're about to be hired as partners."

Their heads both snapped to Pimsley so swiftly he wondered that the papers didn't fly off his desk with the force of it.

"Allow me to introduce—"

Ben went to stand, reaching to button his jacket before realizing he hadn't worn one. Edith sat up as if she were going to stand out of habit, but had reconsidered.

"Yes, yes, that's quite alright," Pimsley flapped his hands, gesturing for him to sit back down.

"Benjamin, this is Edith Taylor, sister of well-known historian, Elliot Taylor. She is a librarian and has arrived quite early for her appointment. Miss Taylor, this is Benjamin Brooks, entrepreneurial expeditionist world-renowned for his discoveries in the east… who has arrived very late indeed." Pimsley reached to pat the pocket of his double-breasted suit, and looked down curiously to find nothing there, then shrugged.

"No matter," he mumbled. "You're here now, so we can get down to brass tacks."

"Yeah, let's start with the word partners," Ben said, squaring his shoulders, just at the edge of fury. His face had transformed from a dazed stare to a dangerous scowl in record time.

"Well, not quite partners. Miss Taylor has negotiated into her contract that in addition to acting as the translator on this project, she will also be given exclusive access to the tomb as the head excavator."

Ben sat back, considering for a moment.

"Are we all on the same page here?" He turned to Edith. Her eyes were alight, her lips pressed tightly to quell a burgeoning smile. The young woman had been looking pretty sour when he walked in, but now she was suddenly beaming. He was pleased for her, as she was clearly delighted to be heading her own dig… but he needed to be certain it wasn't his dig.

"Do you know what site we're talking about?" Ben asked her.

"Yes, the burial site of Isfetheru," Edith crooned.

"Ah, well that clears up the confusion. I'm on the Weeping Viper job." Ben looked back at Pimsley.

"Yes," Pimsley's lips curled into a grin beneath his handlebar mustache. "The Cursed Tomb of Argo," his eyebrows tipped wickedly and Ben could almost see dollar signs flashing in his eyes.

"Sounds like all three of us showed up to the wrong office today," Ben said, grimacing a bit at Pimsley.

"Gentlemen," Edith said, drawing the attention of both men. "Isfetheru, colloquially known as the Weeping Viper, is buried beneath the oasis outside the city of Argo. Due to centuries-old lore, the archeological site is unofficially known as The Cursed Tomb of the Weeping Viper in Oasis Argo. Or, abbreviated for newspapers," Edith gestured to Pimsley, "The Cursed Tomb of Argo. We may be coming from different career fields and…" she shot a sidelong glance toward Ben, "levels of knowledge and education. But, yes Mr. Brooks, we are all talking about the same dig."

"A dig where you have just been hired as head excavator," Ben said to Edith, as she broke into a full smile that distracted him, her chin tipping with a curt nod.

"Congratulations, Miss Taylor," Ben said softly, taking a long beat to ensure she understood he was being genuine.

The intensity of his sustained eye contact stirred unease in her chest.

Abruptly he turned back once again to bark at Pimsley.

"So, I've been fired," Ben raged.

"No, you're still on the job…" Pimsley assured him.

"So, I've been demoted," he said with equal fervor.

"Not exactly..." Pimsley squirmed in his seat.

"Look Pimsley, are you going to start talking, or do you plan to let Miss Taylor break all the bad news?"

"I can assure you I know quite as much, or rather as little, as you do. I'm only just now hearing I've been hired at all," Edith said, blinking at him.

Ben realized that's why she'd suddenly changed her tune moments ago and appeared to be suppressing a full-body celebration. She had only just found out she'd been given the job when Pimsley mentioned it to him. What it meant to her was written all over her face. It struck him as an inconsiderate way to announce it; as an afterthought in the midst of a misunderstanding.

"Miss Taylor, I mean no disrespect, but... are you aware what you're taking on? This worksite is going to be crawling with—"

"Ben," Pimsley hissed, pulling a long face and shaking his head discreetly.

Edith was nearing the end of her patience. She reminded herself to proceed with caution. If handling these two egos was all that stood between her and the career opportunity of her wildest dreams, she was more than equal to the task.

"Believe it or not, I'm well aware of the conditions on an archeological site, and the environment they typically encourage, as well as the high-profile nature of this tomb in particular. As an academic who has devoted the entirety of my adult life to the study of Egyptology, the benefits of this opportunity far outweigh the risk it presents to my apparent sensibilities."

"Look, no one's questioning the extent of your studies, but I think what I'm hearing is that I've been demoted in favor of someone with zero experience in the field?"

She narrowed her eyes at him and shifted her angle.

"While we're reviewing each other's credentials, an important distinction was notably missing from your otherwise glowing introduction. Am I right in assuming that you are not, in fact, a proper archaeologist, and thereby arguably less qualified for the role than I am?"

"I don't think you can argue that anything you've read in a book can prepare you for what I've seen with my own eyes, Miss Taylor."

"What I see is a man who thinks swinging a pickaxe is a reasonable substitute for a decade of research, Mr. Brooks. Furthermore, I imagine the former is much easier to pick up than the latter."

"Oh really? You don't look like you could swing a pickaxe if your life depended on it. But if you really think being armed with knowledge is all you need to tangle with a mummy and make it out alive, you should look up all of the proper archaeologists who've died on jobs I was hired to finish."

"That's not what I meant!" Edith shouted.

Her voice had gradually raised, as did the color in her cheeks, while Ben remained calm.

"Honey, I think you've got your hanky knotted a little too tight there if you think you're proving you can stay cool under pressure."

Edith's jaw dropped.

"Well, I never!" she scoffed.

Ben smiled and swept his upturned palm toward Pimsley, a silent expression that he'd proved his point.

"Exactly. You never. And if you think that's bad, just wait till you meet my crew. They'll be catcalling about a lot more than your little hanky," he said, letting his eyes roam over her suggestively once more.

"And that is where you come in Benjamin," Pimsley interjected, convinced this conversation had no chance of being resolved before his tea went cold.

Edith turned away from Ben in abject horror. Swept away in the heat of debate she had forgotten Pimsley was there.

"If you decide to stay on the job," Pimsley continued, "at the same rate as we discussed earlier, you will be accompanying Miss Taylor in a capacity… much like a bodyguard."

"Bodyguard?!" they repeated in unison, whirling on Pimsley again.

"Honestly, will the two of you stop with the hysterics?" Pimsley griped.

"Those are n-not the terms outlined in my contract, I—" Edith stammered, unraveling quickly despite herself.

"I'm sorry, but doesn't the fact that she needs a bodyguard take her out of the running? How can she manage a crew she needs her own body guarded from?" he shouted, scorched with instant regret over his own phrasing.

When they had sparred in competition over who was more qualified, Edith had prickled and Ben had relaxed. He enjoyed the battle immensely. It was so rare to find a woman equally matched and ready for a fight. But when the debate turned to imagining how Edith would hold her own in a crowd of sweaty scoundrels, Ben became red faced and angry in the blink of an eye.

"I'm so glad you've asked Ben," Pimsley replied with a smug grin. "But I believe you've both laid out a rather undeniable argument all on your own. A decade of academic study and a decade of hands-on experience. The brains and the brawn. I must admit, when the gold is in my safe I will insist it was my idea, rather than the handiwork of an underqualified, over confident librarian."

Eyes wide, Edith shook her head at the carpet, at a loss for words as she tried to parse the compliment within the insult.

"It's a bit underhanded that you didn't mention any of this before," Ben shot back at Pimsley. "If I wasn't summoned to meet at the last minute, I'd be halfway to Argo by now, and my crew is already there. I've been packing the rest of the gear into trunks since dawn, and I just stopped by on my way to get them on the barge."

"Well," Pimsley sat back with a contented grin as he pulled a thin envelope from his breast pocket. "You'll have plenty of time to get used to the idea on the train, which departs in an hour."

He set the envelope at the edge of the desk between them, as their eyes clung to it.

"I've gotten you both tickets in the same compartment so you may get to know each other a little better. Arrangements have been made for your lodging at the Hotel Argo."

Pimsley hooked his thumbs in his vest pockets as he sat back, clearly pleased at his own maneuvering. He knew neither of them wanted to turn down the job, and introducing the sense of urgency would seal the deal at once. It was a delightful added bonus that they clearly despised each other; something he would certainly use to his advantage in future negotiations.

Edith and Ben's eyes lifted from the ticket to meet in a shared expression of wary disappointment.

CHAPTER TWO

EDITH GLARED ACROSS the compartment at Ben as the train gently jostled her in the stiff leather bench seat. He was no more dressed up than he had been a few hours ago, other than adding a waistcoat. Though, it seemed he had washed up a bit.

When he looked up from his newspaper to meet her gaze, she turned up her nose and looked out the window. She couldn't believe she had a gun toting caveman tagalong for the most consequential assignment of her career. Or worse yet, a spy, all too eager to relay any missteps she might make. A long suffering sigh escaped her lips, and she looked at the desert landscape whizzing by.

Ben folded his paper and leaned casually on the armrest of his seat.

"Congratulations again on getting the job. Back at the office you seemed to barely contain your excitement," Ben offered, clearly picking up on her aggrieved mood.

A brief wave of sympathy swept through her, remembering that she got the job because he didn't.

Don't you dare feel sorry for a man, she scolded herself. I got the job because I am more qualified by a mile. She instantly tried to replace her compassion with smugness, brushing off her nagging self doubt about having no experience in the field.

"While you, on the other hand, were completely void of excitement to contain."

"Can you blame me?" he smiled playfully while cocking a brow. She looked away again. He was so damned good looking, she thought. His smile made her feel things she had absolutely no plans to acknowledge.

"I went from having the mummy of the Weeping Viper in my charge, to... well..." he shrugged, gesturing toward her.

"To having me in your charge? A very important professor's sister. What a disappointment for you."

"I'm not discrediting your credentials. It turns out a woman was the better man for the job," he offered amiably.

Her eyes widened. She couldn't believe he'd said something so ... right.

"Still, what it means is my job description just went from being hired as the boss of this work site to being hired as the boss's nanny."

"Ugh," she groaned. He couldn't have said something more wrong.

"What? It's a fact. If you can manage to keep up at all, you'll just be getting in the way. Translators usually examine hieroglyphs from rubbings off site. You could be sunning yourself at the oasis, letting a bunch of filthy men like me do the grunt work, and reading all the mummy comics as they come out of the tomb to your heart's content."

"How tiresome it is to never be taken seriously," she mumbled to the dunes beyond her window.

"It's dangerous," he snapped, the levity suddenly drained from his voice. "It's because I'm taking it so seriously that I don't think you should be there."

"I can hold my own."

"Oh please," he said with a laugh. "I had to help you get your suitcase into the luggage compartment."

"In that case, you'll be glad to know my job description doesn't require heavy lifting and I have no intention of swinging a pickaxe. As a historian of antiquities, it follows logic that I should be the first explorer within the tomb, as I have the most advanced ability to identify artifacts and the most comprehensive knowledge of how they must be preserved."

He couldn't argue with that. But, it still didn't solve the mystery of Edith Taylor.

"So, where did Pimsley find you? You must have quite the reputation as a historian of antiquities for him to scout you for this job, knowing that it's your first."

Edith considered a moment, separating what she would and wouldn't say. Perhaps it would be best to give him just enough information so that he'd stop sniffing around, while certainly not giving the game away.

"I found him," she replied, honestly. "I've always felt I had a deep connection to this tomb in particular, and the legends within it. Pimsley is a well known figure in Cairo, and he brags too much to keep any of his projects secret for long."

"What are you getting out of this?" he said, eyeing her curiously. "This isn't exactly the ideal project to get your feet wet with."

Edith's eyes darted from her lap to the window. The explanation was on the tip of her tongue, of course, but she didn't know if there was any benefit to spilling her life story to someone like him.

"Come on, it's going to be a long couple of months if you only talk to me when you're spitting mad. You already got the job, you said it yourself. I'm just the muscle of the operation. So, what gives?"

Edith looked him straight in the eye now. She could tell him part of the truth.

"I'd like to be introduced by my own accomplishments. Not as someone's sister."

"Ah, so it's a family rivalry type deal. I get it. That's pretty juicy."

"Not a family rivalry per se… I don't blame Elliot, he's dear to me. It's more so… me against the world, I suppose."

"Well that makes sense," he laughed, "you've been sore from the jump. No wonder you feel your kindred spirits with the Weeping Viper."

"Laugh all you want," she spat back "You have no idea how hard it is for a woman to make her own way, in academia, in archaeology, or just about anywhere. Just listen to the way Pimsley introduced us. He dismissed me as a librarian, where he all but trumpeted your arrival as an adventurer known throughout all the land." She waved her hands in exaggeration. "Even you just said working with me would make you a nanny, which means as far as you're concerned, I'm nothing more than a child."

"Well, that's just another thing you've got wrong," he said, letting his gaze roam over her. "I'm more than aware you're a grown woman."

She peered at him warily. Was he making a pass at her? Before she could wonder further, the mischief in his eyes vanished as quickly as it had surfaced, and she decided to ignore it.

Ben continued, "I wasn't insulting you, I was pointing out that I'm not normally hired as a chaperone, and I'm not crazy about the idea. It doesn't help that so far, you've done nothing but sneer at me. As it stands, you're unwilling and I'm uninterested. Why are you offended that I don't want to do a job you also don't want me to do?"

"I resent the implication that I require supervision. As much as you are disinclined to be my bodyguard, you still seem to insist that I need one."

Wrong again, he thought.

It was the thought of her being anywhere near the tomb at all that he hated. But, if there was no way to stop her from going to Argo, and she required a bodyguard to do so, Ben wasn't about to let any other man get the job done.

He knew better than to mention that out loud. There was a new impulse rearing its head that he couldn't explain to himself, much less to her: he wouldn't be letting Miss Edith Taylor out of his sight any time soon.

She briefly closed her eyes and shook her head, dismissing the topic of conversation as inconsequential. "To answer your question, although I'm just as intelligent as my brother… I was rejected by Oxford, while he not only attended, but went on to lecture there. I belong in that tomb, and I'm going to prove it."

That was the root of it, and she knew she had shown her entire hand, the emotional aspect of it anyway, just by the pain she heard in her own voice. She had blatantly admitted she had something to prove. When she looked up, he was still searching her face.

"Yeah, maybe that explains why you wanted the job," he suggested, "Which was already obvious. Succeeding at this would undoubtedly make your entire career, as it would anyone's. But it doesn't explain why you'd demand to be the first one down there in the dirt."

"Well… why should you get to see all the action?" she shrugged, feeling a little embarrassed — and desperate to move on now that she'd spilled her heart out.

"Oh, so it's action you're looking for? That can be arranged…" he said, and his wicked smile was back on his face.

He was making a pass at her.

It had taken her a while to add it up. Usually men were either saccharine and complimentary to a level that was clearly a farce, or arrogantly displayed overt vulgarity. In a lifetime of presumptuous, drooling suitors, Ben's way had caught her off guard.

In general his demeanor was courteous. Affable, even. When he made these leading comments, they cruised along almost undetected, consistent with his pleasant nature... but with just the hint of something underneath. His suggestions seemed to be intended as an offer, rather than a plea, or demand. He was charming, from a purely objective standpoint, of course.

"You know you shouldn't speak to your boss that way," she said coldly, despite the warmth she noticed rising inside of her.

"You're not my boss, Pimsley's my boss. You're my..." he leaned toward her "assignment..." he said, bouncing his eyebrows.

How is it that he was speaking so plainly and making her stomach flutter as if it were salacious? It wasn't what he was saying, but the way he said it. She felt herself flush and realized she was getting in over her head and couldn't afford to be distracted, not for a moment, not even for a smile like that.

"And what about you?" she said, her self pity evaporated, burning off in the heat of her anger, humiliation, and an inconvenient attraction she'd have to talk herself out of later.

"What about me?" he answered.

"You never answered my question in Pimsley's office earlier," she said, staring him down. "Are you an archaeologist... or not?"

He leaned back in his seat, resting a hand against the front of his vest, a teasing smile returning to his lips.

"I deal in private antiquarian... acquisition," he finally said.

"A tomb raider," she spat.

"A treasure hunter," he countered.

"A grave robber. Stealing significant ancient discoveries that belong in a museum." She was relieved to find disgust had begun to take the place of the butterflies in her stomach. As a historian herself, his chosen profession made him her arch nemesis.

"It's just like a librarian to get caught up in semantics, but my line of work is simple. People tell me what they're looking for, and I find it."

"You're despicable," she said, scowling fiercely. "I can't be expected to tarnish my career by working with someone like you. A gentleman would have the decency to resign and let me run the project myself."

She noted he was stifling laughter, and seethed.

"First of all, believe me when I tell you, you cannot do this job without me. Not that you're incapable. For the half a day I've known you, one thing I can say for sure is that you have no trouble speaking your mind. But you are en route to meet up with my crew. Without me, there is no job. Not to mention the reason we're going there at all is because the Cursed Tomb of Argo is the most famously inaccessible and dangerous tomb in Egypt."

Ben found that, once again, something about thinking of Edith getting anywhere near that tomb filled him with instantaneous and uncontrollable rage. It choked out the common sense bidding him to remain friendly, and left him with very little willpower to avoid snapping back at her.

"Besides, it sounds like without this job you have no career to tarnish."

Edith's jaw clenched and she wanted to scream.

"This is ridiculous, I'm getting my own seating arrangements."

Just as she got to her feet, the train went around a turn that rocked the cabin and sent her tumbling into him. His hands caught her around the waist as she crashed into his lap. A hard intake of his breath rushed past her cheek as she felt her body press against his. To her horror, she realized too late that she had instantly curled into him before she could stop herself; her back arched slightly, pressing her side into his chest and her backside into his lap. Lightheaded at the feel of his hands, her eyes squeezed shut as embarrassment washed over her.

Her poorly thought out attempt to take a stand, literally and figuratively, had backfired. Subconscious urges were screaming at her to sink further into his arms, to rake her fingers through his hair. She couldn't believe what she was thinking.

"This is the seat you wanted, is it?" he whispered against her neck. It was more of the wisecracking she was beginning to understand as his default style of communication, but he didn't say it with humor.

She opened her eyes and turned to face him intending to reply with what she hoped he would come to know as her razor sharp wit. But when she tilted her face just an inch her lips were nearly on his. Looking straight into his brown eyes caused her to experience an unfamiliar sensation… speechlessness.

Frozen like that, she felt his hands slide, slowly, from her waist to her hips. Then, she was being dragged across his lap and dumped onto the seat beside him.

"I know the boss said we should get to know each other but I don't think that's what he had in mind." He was smiling again, but she didn't think it was her imagination that his breathing had become heavy.

His hand rose to sweep an unruly lock of hair behind her ear. When he glanced down to her lips, she leapt from her seat without a care for the consequences. Before she was even fully standing, Ben had shot up beside her, reaching one hand on the railing above them, and the other clamped around her elbow, and they swayed together as the boxcar wobbled again. It raised ire in her to know that if he hadn't stood up to steady her, she would have toppled over again.

"This train is full," he said sharply, his jaw clenched. "It was lovely of you to drop in, but sit the hell down, will you?"

Gazing up at him, she took her seat again slowly. Staring back at her, he sat down just as slowly. They were squared off like opponents brandishing pistols at dawn.

Partners, indeed.

He combed his fingers through his hair in an effort to compose himself. It worried him how quickly his control over his thoughts about Edith had snapped. He hoped that shoving her off of him like a sack of potatoes had been taken as chivalrous rather than what it was — panic. No sooner than she'd fallen into his lap, he was fighting off the urge to draw her closer, to dig his fingers into her hips, to feel her ass tucked snuggly against the crotch of his pants. As the thoughts raced across his mind again, he shook his head as if he could physically dislodge the event from his brain.

He had thought Pimsley's office smelled of iris, but he'd been wrong. It was her hair. Just now he'd been close enough to bury his face in it. When he first saw her an odd thought had popped into his head. Back then, he had imagined her tame updo unraveled more as the day wore on. He was right about that. Now it was twisted up slightly lower than it was this morning, with even more tendrils springing free. He looked back at her now, thinking that as long as he kept his thoughts tangled in her hair, he was safe.

Wrong again. Looking at her, the way her chest rose and fell with her quickened breath, he realized that he had an effect on her, too. It only had him thinking of unraveling that twist of hair himself and then untying the scarf around her neck. He thought she looked like a startled doe staring down a shotgun. She didn't seem to like his sense of humor, but he wanted to break the ice anyway, for her sake. At least that's what he told himself.

"Don't be too broken up about sharing a compartment. Pimsley's incredibly cheap." Edith smoothed her skirt as she watched him pull a feminine mother of pearl cigarette case out of his waistcoat pocket. She wondered if he had a wife and was disappointed in herself for not considering it before now, since her subconscious seemed so determined to size him up by his body rather than his ambiguous resume. He pulled a gold pocket watch out of his waistcoat to check the time.

Was she seeing things? Her mind worried over the events of the morning as she was quite sure she had seen Pimsley with the very same gold Persian pocket watch, and then it wasn't there when he went to reach for it later on in the meeting. Maybe she was mistaken and it was Ben who had checked his pocket watch. But Ben wasn't wearing a waistcoat this morning. He was wearing guns.

You're dizzy, Edith, she thought to herself as she rubbed her forehead. You're letting a man make you positively dizzy.

He held the cigarette case open to her in offering and she waved it away.

"Luckily, he's not too cheap to pay for two head excavators. That's an awful habit," she said, absently looking back out the window not knowing how much longer this trip would take, or if she would make it unscathed. Wondering if it would be long enough for the tingle he'd left on her skin to finally subside. Hoping she would eventually stop thinking of sliding back into his lap.

"Right," he chuckled, stamping out the cigarette. "At least for your sake, it probably didn't take too much convincing for him to give you the job. He'd have to pay a man three times as much."

She whipped her head around to glare at him, her jaw hanging open. Color rushed to burn her cheeks as she thought of herself there in Pimsley's office, flattering and fawning, practically groveling for the job, prepared to beg, just before a dirty barrel chested thug exploded from the doors behind her.

It was apparent to Ben that she'd not been hired for her competence, but for her economy, suggesting that it would also be apparent to everyone else on the work site — the dig that she was supposed to be running. Benjamin Brooks had made her certain of one thing—sure, a man had never made her this hot and bothered before, but he could be counted on to make her blood run cold just as quickly.

CHAPTER THREE

THE OMNIBUS KICKED up a crispy cloud of dirt as it sped off, leaving Edith and Ben at the gate of a small military hotel on the outskirts of Argo. Exhausted and irritable, they momentarily set aside their differences to share a look of dread before embarking up the dirt path. He was carrying his own duffle as well as her suitcase, which was so heavy he wondered if she'd brought a collection of decorative anvils.

"What in the world do you have packed in this suitcase, bricks?"

"Books."

"Ah."

"I said I'd carry my own suitcase," she mumbled, wanting to avoid making a habit of being indebted.

"Nonsense, what are man servants for?" He looked at her with clear eyes and half a smile.

She let out a breathless giggle she was too tired to conceal. It was unsettling to find herself worried for him. On the train platform, she had witnessed him bump into a middle aged woman who was quarreling with a ticket collector, but the platform wasn't even crowded. It was as if he'd walked straight into her, and clumsiness seemed so uncharacteristic of him. In the short time she'd known him, Ben seemed to move as intentionally as a panther. Ever since leaving the station she had kept a close eye on him, but he had shown no further signs of being out of sorts. Dismissing it as her own hypervigilance, she reasoned perhaps his leg had fallen asleep on the tiresome journey.

Edith took in her surroundings as they approached the hotel and she was not put at ease as they got closer. There was a sparse gated courtyard with a few small tables and chairs. No attempt at landscaping had been made in at least several decades. A stingy patch of shade ran along the building beneath a tattered awning. The exterior was plain, notable for the lack of flourish so common in Egyptian architecture. The only archway was to the main entrance, and all of the windows were rectangular and joyless. The sign, almost entirely bleached by the sun, faintly read "Hotel Argo."

It was late afternoon and she had never been so hungry, thirsty, or tired. They stood in the lobby for the briefest of moments, looking on as the only bellhop at check in was being told off by one of the officers. Without bothering to wait at the front desk, they took a seat in the lounge. A waiter brought them glasses of water, then lingered as they drained them. Unprompted, the waiter filled their glasses again.

"Bring us the four most popular dishes on the menu and a Glenlivet, neat."

"We only have three dishes on the menu," the waiter said blandly.

"We'll take one of everything. Thank you."

Sitting up in her chair, Edith began to examine the place, considering that she may be taking all of her meals here for the next few weeks, or possibly months. It was little more than an officers' club. The chairs had been crafted out of whiskey barrels, and it was devoid of the whimsy and flair of any other hotel she'd stayed at in Egypt. It was a dark room with a low ceiling, unembellished once-white walls, and a dusty concrete floor. There was an arched doorway from the lobby, a bar on the far wall, and a few tables.

Withdrawing a compact from her bag to tidy her hair a bit in the reflection, she showed no signs of whether she noticed the shouting that had broken out from somewhere on the floor above them. When regrettable thoughts of what the bedrooms might look like popped into her head, she doubled her resolve to think of the imminent success of her future rather than the shortcomings of her current surroundings.

She refused to be precious about it.

It wouldn't do at all for her to spend the entire day insisting that she could rough it with the rest of them, and go on to spend the entire evening remarking at everything she found subpar.

When she looked at Ben, he didn't seem to share her optimism. As her bodyguard, he was a man at work, peering around the room suspiciously.

"Taking stock of your surroundings Mr. Brooks?" she asked brightly.

"Not much stock to take," he said looking past her into the lobby.

While he was absorbed in his survey of their new home, she indulged herself in a lengthy appraisal of his strong jawline, though his displeasure was obvious by the set of it.

"I think it's … rather interesting. Very rugged," she said cheerfully, peeling her arm off the table with some effort, and placing her hands in her lap.

His impatient eyes bore into her at that.

"It's a flophouse, Miss Taylor," he quipped without his usual mirth.

"Oh, it's not as bad as all that," she waved him off.

Their spirits rallied when the food arrived. Edith took a bite of a bean patty with dipping sauce, and quietly moaned. She sank into her seat with delight, forgetting that a moment before she'd been careful to not let her shirt touch the back of it.

"I imagine we'll get used to it once we've stayed a few days."

"More like a few months," he grunted with his mouth full.

As if he'd pulled a drawstring between her eyebrows, he watched the worry fall over her face.

"How familiar are you with the physical challenges of this project?" he said, narrowing his eyes at her.

"I know the history and the legend, but I haven't been briefed on the site at all."

"Well, I don't know much about legend. But I do know the facts. No one from around here will actually work the site, and foreigners are too spooked by the King Tut team dropping like flies."

He cleared his throat, noting the grim look on her face, and wondered how delicately he should be delivering this information.

"We're working with a skeleton crew, made up mostly of characters who needed to get off the beaten path where no one would think to look for them. So really, no one working on this project knows much about the history. But I have been to Argo before. I can catch you up to speed on the site itself."

"How could you not know one of the greatest unsolved mysteries of ancient Egypt? As a tomb raider, isn't it your job to know?"

"I don't care much about all that," he said, taking another bite of flatbread. "I know they're dead and they won't be needing any of their gold."

She rolled her eyes at his disregard for culture and history.

Ben then watched her transform as she straightened in her chair. A moment ago she had been Edith; exhausted, disappointed, eating a meal with unfortunate company. Now he sat before Miss Taylor, the Egyptologist, professional to a fault with a light burning brightly in her eyes.

"It was long ago..." Edith said, sweeping her hands apart, "during the reign of Ramesses II, or as history would come to remember him, Ramesses the Great—"

Ben let out a hearty burst of laughter, overwhelmed by amusement at her theatrical retelling of a subject that bored him to tears. She dropped her hands and scowled at him.

"I thought I was the nanny on this trip, and here you are telling a bedtime story," he said, mopping up sauce with the rest of his flatbread.

"Oh, do shut up. Nevermind," she said, tugging at the kerchief still tied tight at her neck. Ben thought she must be ridiculously uncomfortable and hot, as his own shirt front became more undone as the day wore on.

"No, please continue. Regale me with fables of an ancient cat fight."

She threw a date right at his face, but he intercepted it and tossed it in the air to catch in his mouth. Ben was bringing out a side of her she was not at all acquainted with. Never in her life had irritation collided with attraction so intensely, and so often.

She continued anyway, because, as they both knew, she told the story for her own love of telling it, whether he learned anything or not.

"Long before she became known as the Weeping Viper, Isfetheru—"

"Bless you," he quipped, and she ignored him.

"—was the mistress of the Pharaoh Ramesses. It was said by many to be true love, but ambitious greed began to stew in the heart of Isfetheru—"

"Gesundheit,"

"Okay," she said, unamused by his antics. "Is. Feather. Oooh. Isfetheru. Now you say it."

Slumped in his chair, he looked around to make sure no one was in earshot.

"Isfetheru," he grumbled.

"High marks!" she said, clapping her hands together.

He couldn't help but smile. She hadn't even been halfway this happy since they'd met this morning. That already felt like ages ago. It was clear she had a passionate connection with history, and though he didn't share it, he did admire it.

"Now, where were we? Isfetheru was jealous of Ramesses' wife, Nefertari."

"If Isfetheru was Ramesses' one true love, why didn't he marry her?"

Caught off guard, Edith blinked at him for a moment. She'd never given it thought before.

"Well, I assume it was for political reasons. As I said, Ramesses is generally regarded as one of the greatest rulers of his time, and his first great royal wife, Nefertari, is one of the most beloved queens in ancient Egypt. She had to be of the correct lineage to marry him in the first place, but she was also equal to the task. She was highly educated, literate, and diplomatic. She was truly a well suited partner to rule beside him, which was important. As a nearly egalitarian society, women in ancient Egypt had almost equal standing with men, which would demand a great deal of responsibility. Isfetheru was… an almah. She would have been an unqualified and unpopular candidate to rule alongside him."

"An almah?" he asked.

"A… well, a belly dancer," she said. It wasn't historically accurate, but she grasped for the closest approximation.

"Well, now you've got my attention" he said, grinning mischievously.

"Oh, don't be vulgar," she said dismissively. "As I was saying, Isfetheru couldn't see past her own interests enough to agree that Nefertari was a better wife for practical reasons. So, she devised a plot to have Ramesses assassinated. She believed that she could rally support and have her son Cepos rise to the throne. But ultimately, the attempted assassination failed, and Isfetheru was put to death."

"Uh oh," he said, "a curse that starts with a woman scorned never ends well."

"Ramesses did truly love her though, so he attempted to secretly build her a tomb that reflected how much he cared for her. That's why it's all the way out here in the middle of nowhere. She wouldn't have been permitted burial in the Valley of Queens. But also, Argo is closer to where Ramesses lived. Apparently, he wished to keep her close."

She tilted her head and she dropped her librarian voice briefly. "This is the part that may interest you most. It is said she was buried with a humongous load of riches. It was his symbolic way of granting her the royal status in death he could not give her in life."

"This is the part of the story I already know," he said.

"Oh?"

"Yes, it isn't everyone's first day on the job. I've been preparing for months. A professional acquaintance, a historian, has been working closely with me to decipher what fortunes might be in the tomb."

"Why isn't your colleague going on the dig with you?"

"Because he's staying in the library, where you belong."

It struck a nerve for Ben to tell her where she belonged—not because it was irritating, though it was, but because she actually never felt she belonged anywhere. She hadn't felt she belonged in the library any more than she felt she belonged in England as the wife of a duke. Brushing aside old wounds, she cut off the doubt that made her feel as if she'd chased belonging all the way here.

"He could have been the translator on this job and worked via correspondence like you already suggested."

"He wouldn't take it. No one would. That's why you're here. As of our arrival, this job has taken its place as the most doomed archeological dig in history."

Edith's eyes fell to the table. She was crestfallen. It hadn't been her accomplishments that had gotten her this job, but the simple fact that no one else would take it. Not only that, it was beginning to dawn on her really for the first time that for all of her bravado, she may have actually gotten herself into a very dangerous situation.

Dangerous and barbaric, she thought, looking around the dingy bar. For a moment, she felt the tiniest sting in her eyes but instantly thought better of letting herself wallow. She pressed her palm to her chest and resolved that she wouldn't let herself minimize this opportunity in any way.

The truth was, she wouldn't have gotten hired at an archeological dig for her accomplishments regardless. It wasn't for lack of trying, or a lacking background. It was beyond her control that society was stacked against her. She refused to lament that she could never take a man's way through the world. Instead, she would celebrate her triumph for making her own way: by seizing an opportunity and making it a success.

Ben looked at the shattered expression on Edith's face. She had been such a spitfire from the beginning, it hadn't occurred to him that something he said could have any reaction that didn't lie somewhere on the road between mild annoyance and fury. She had sworn up and down that she could handle anything you throw at her.

Now it looked like the excitement was wearing off. Sitting in this officers' club across from the likes of him was throwing into harsh perspective what her day-to-day life was about to become. Everything Ben learned about Edith on this day pointed to the same conclusion: as far as she was concerned, her whole life was riding on this job.

He already knew Edith was equal to the task. Although he'd teased her about it, she could have gotten that suitcase in the train storage if it came to that. After so many years in the field, Ben knew when someone was hard as nails.

He hadn't particularly cared for how Pimsley spoke to her during their interview, or rather, what he gathered from interrupting the very end of it. He was familiar with what he saw in her then. There was no chance in hell she was backing down.

Edith was going to be a great asset to the team, and a formidable presence on site. Ben knew it. The problem was what he'd just seen flicker over her face. For a split second, she didn't know it.

"Aren't you going to finish your bedtime story?"

"What?" she said, coming back from far away.

"You were saying, about the tomb… the story of Ramesses and Feathery. What do legends say about the curse?"

Edith shooed her self pity away and found comfort in moving forward. Ben was glad, as it had been his intention to guide her back to her happy place: boring history.

"Well… despite his efforts to keep it all a secret, not long after the burial was completed, an oasis sprang up around the tomb. That's why she is known in the legend as the Weeping Viper. Partly because, as you can tell, Isfetheru doesn't quite roll off the tongue. So, Viper because of her misdeeds — unlike cobras, vipers were not a revered animal in Egyptian symbolism, they were seen as a nuisance. Weeping, because it is said that Oasis Argo is made up of her tears."

"…and that's the explanation for why the oasis is brackish?"

"Yes, it's over a source of fresh groundwater, but even when they try to drill a well, the water is still salty when it comes to the surface. I suppose the modern explanation is that perhaps they are mistaken and it's saltwater down there," Edith shrugged.

"No, it's a mystery because Oasis Argo, and all other oases in the Sahara are from the same source. The Nubian Sandstone Aquifer. It stretches from Libya to Sudan, so it isn't possible, for any scientific reason, for any oasis from the same freshwater aquifer to be salinated," he said while folding his napkin and eyeing another patron entering the restaurant from across the room.

She narrowed her eyes at him.

"What?" he said, before tossing back the last of his scotch.

"What did you say your background was again?" she asked.

Just then the waiter walked by placing the check on the table, refilling their waters for the fifth time, and continuing on to the next patron. Edith set her purse on the table to pay the bill.

"What are you doing?" he asked.

"Paying my bill, of course," she said, still rummaging in her purse.

"Absolutely not," he said curtly, with mild amusement on his face.

She blinked a few times.

"You're not paying for my dinner, don't be ridiculous. This is not a…" she shook her head slightly, searching for what to say, "… social arrangement."

His eyes widened as his grin morphed into feigned shock.

"What are you implying Miss Taylor? As if I'd let any woman on earth pay for a meal with me. I've got quicker ways to get you into bed, believe me. I wouldn't have to pay for it."

"You will not be paying for anything! Not my meal or—" she said, thinking it would sound more affronted, but she heard it come out as a nervous stammer. She couldn't bear it if he realized that his off-handed comment had made her involuntarily plunge back into thoughts of sitting on his lap with his hands around her waist. In the course of this entirely too hot, too dry, too eventful day, she'd never wanted to loosen her kerchief more than right now, as she felt heat rising from her collarbone to her cheeks.

"Social arrangement," he snorted, reaching into his waistcoat to pull out his wallet. But when he did so, she saw behind his lapel a corner of oxblood embossed leather.

Suddenly something clicked within Edith's mind. Scenes throughout this endless day flashed back to her now. The cigarette case. The pocket watch. This very distinctive wallet.

The dots connected and Edith's face contorted with disgust.

"You unbelievably vile scoundrel!" she hissed at length.

"Is this how you treat all men who buy you dinner?" he said, counting bills as his waistcoat shifted back into place concealing the glimpse of leather. She shot across the table to reach behind his lapel feeling for the wallet. His breath hitched as her hand searched his chest, just before she pulled it out of his pocket, brandishing it like damning evidence.

"I saw this wallet. It belongs to the man who was arguing with the bellhop when we came in." She leaned in to whisper, "You're nothing but a third-rate pickpocket."

"Miss Taylor," he said, enormously offended, "you don't know me." His mock disdain melted into a mischievous grin as he leaned in to match her, and whispered "I'm a first rate pickpocket."

She snatched the wallet from him and stuffed it in her purse.

"He might still be in the lobby, I'm giving this back to him." She snapped the kiss lock clasp shut and stood. "You should be ashamed of yourself," she whispered harshly as she marched by him.

Ben laid bills on the table before strolling out behind her.

The officer was in the lobby reading the newspaper on a shabby tufted loveseat. Her hasty gait slowed in an attempt to approach him civilly. Ben came up from behind to fall into step with her, and placed his hand on the small of her back.

She was trying to appear nonchalant, but the broad steps she had to take to keep up with Ben had her purse knocking between them with each step she took. His words were bad enough, but now his proximity rattled her even further.

If she was lucky, her anger would conceal the fact that she was still flushed to her hairline from his threat to take her to bed.

"You're overreacting. Have you seen his signet ring? A misplaced wallet would hardly break him," he whispered in her ear, making them appear like any other couple in the lobby.

"What if this wallet is a gift, or an heirloom? You don't think he'd notice his wallet is missing?"

"I didn't say he wouldn't notice." Then he stepped in front of her and extended a hand. The officer had seen them approaching and folded his newspaper, standing to accept Ben's offered handshake.

"Hello, officer. Pardon me, I was wondering if you knew whether Captain Bernard is in Egypt, or abroad?" Ben said, shaking one hand, and clapping him on the shoulder with the other.

"Hello, yes he is in fact. In Egypt, that is," the officer said, with an amiable smile. "Do I know you?"

"Excuse me, officer," Edith interjected, coming from behind Ben. He wasn't going to get away with it that easily.

"Yes, and I'd love to catch up if you'll just excuse me for one moment. I have to make a phone call." Ben brushed by Edith walking toward the telephone at reception, and she gaped after him.

"Ah yes, Miss, you were saying?" the officer said to Edith.

"Yes..." she said, breaking her stare from Ben to return her attention to the officer. "I... why, yes sir..." With a shake of her head she attempted to get back on task. "I believe you dropped your wallet."

She unsnapped her purse, while the officer looked puzzled and reached into his jacket pocket.

"I do believe you're mistaken," he said, just as his hand emerged from behind his lapel.

In it he held the oxblood wallet. Sure enough, when she looked down into her purse it was gone. She stared at the wallet in shock.

"Miss, are you quite alright?" the officer said, his face twisted in sympathy for Edith, whom he must have seen as a very confused woman.

"Oh, what a relief... Well, I'm so sorry to bother you."

Humiliated, she scurried out of the front entrance of the hotel as fast as she could.

CHAPTER FOUR

BY THE TIME Ben strided out of the hotel, she was still fuming on an entryway bench. He walked right by her without stopping, hefting his duffle bag and her suitcase.

"Come on Taylor, let's make tracks," he barked over his shoulder as he sped by. Once she was up from the bench she nearly had to run to keep up with him.

"Where are we going?"

"To our hotel."

"This is our hotel."

"No, it's not."

Edith glanced back at the shabby building and decided she wouldn't argue. It was unlikely where they were going could be any worse than where they'd just been.

Just then he glanced down to see her tiny loafers shuffling madly, and he slowed down. There was no reason to rush, he supposed, as they fell into step with one another. Even as eager as he was to get her away from the officers' club and lodging, it was clear that she was determined to make the best of it, and that her pride would prevent her from letting on if she was miserable. While he admired her for it, he wasn't about to let her stay there.

"Who is Captain Bernard?"

"Someone who owes me a favor."

"Where is our hotel?"

"Somewhere that owes him a favor."

"I just bet you know all the right people, don't you," she said, sneering at his underhanded way through the world.

"And I just bet you're used to keeping everything above board," he said, smirking down at her, not minding the way she glared at him. He kind of liked it. "Well, you've got a filthy lowdown bodyguard now, Miss Taylor. Get ready to live."

She looked away, rolling her eyes. Children were playing in the street, and a woman was sweeping her stoop. Two men sat at a card table. The city itself didn't seem in disrepair as much as it seemed to have never developed past this point. Everyone stared at them as they walked by, and she understood the onlookers would know exactly why she and Ben were here.

Although Edith was enormously proud of this project, and her career in general, she felt the familiar pang of longing that she'd always be a spectacle when she walked down an Eastern street. It wasn't quite that she knew she could never truly belong in Egypt like a native. But rather... She did wish she felt she belonged somewhere.

The flophouse had been on the very outskirts of town, only surrounded by other buildings in a similar state of disrepair, beyond which was nothing but desert. As they continued to walk the main road approaching the center of town, she noticed more and more lush vegetation, and eventually, palm and date trees. Then, as they neared the top of the inclined path they took, the slight elevation leveled off culminating in the town square, an open area with clear sightlines to where the city limits met the vast expanse of the desert beyond.

And that's when she laid eyes on it for the first time. It was there, right in the center of the oasis.

The Cursed Tomb of Argo.

The oasis sparkled against an endless backdrop of mountainous undulating sand dunes that repeated for miles. Blinding shards of light reflected off the rippling water lapping at its long rectangular stone platform, an angular contrast to the meandering shoreline crowded with verdant palm trees and shrubs.

The tomb itself was constructed of giant square slabs of limestone and stood at the very end of the quay, preceded by three massive pylon gateways. The last pylon, at the entrance of the tomb, was guarded by two statues of Anubis.

As the potent cocktail of pride and anticipation flooded her, it mingled with something else. Something new. A tingle swarmed at the tips of her fingers, and behind the ringing in her ears lingered a rustling sound, though she felt no breeze.

Ben only made it a few steps before realizing Edith had stopped dead in her tracks. A look of awe was displayed candidly on her face as she stared at the tomb.

Originally the temple would have been inaccessible in the middle of the water, she noted. The delineation in the color of the bricks indicated a point at which the original quay ended, and a more recently constructed pier began. While the original pier had been built for the Weeping Viper, the walkway that connected it to the shore had been built for tourists.

"Did you know?" Ben asked, as Edith looked at him in bewilderment. "That it was underwater?"

"Every time I've told the story, I said 'an oasis sprang around the tomb,' I didn't realize the tomb was actually submerged in the oasis."

"One more reason why we're the only two who would take the job."

She sent him a grim look and tentatively started walking again.

"So here we are," Ben said as she joined him again and they fell back into step. "The ambitious librarian with something to prove and the petty scoundrel with nothing to lose."

They continued to walk until he made the final turn that brought them out of the winding streets to where the town ended and the clearing of the oasis began. Once they'd emerged, a magnificent building of gleaming white stone came into view. It was several stories high, and the entrance was elevated at the top of a grand imperial staircase. Two flights divided from a platform sweeping to the ground in a wide curve. A wide, luxurious terrace wrapped around the entire building, with sheer white billowing curtains wafting out of each door and window along the uniform row of rooms on each floor.

Edith's eyes widened in awe but she didn't let herself wish that this would be where they'd stay. Surely some elderly woman ran a modest inn around the next corner.

Floating on anticipation, she adopted a causal affect as she glanced at Ben. He was already watching her with his teasing half grin. Her senses were so heightened by the gravity of this day that his deep voice raised a wave of goosebumps across her skin.

"This is the Oasis Hotel. If it's alright with you, this is where we'll stay for the remainder of our time in Argo."

If he was any other man she would have kissed him right there. But Ben was growing on her, and she liked that idea a little too much to actually do it. Especially on the very first day of their working partnership that, so far, had been precarious to say the least.

Edith tried hard to keep her feet from skipping as the dusty street beneath them gave way to the paved and landscaped grounds of the luxurious hotel. Ben stopped at the foot of one flight of stairs and motioned for her to take them.

"How on earth..." she mumbled to no one in particular as she watched her footfalls land on a gorgeous red carpet that enrobed each step. Then, as she ascended, her eyes swept back over the simple desert town.

"Tourism is the only industry of note here. This hotel is the best kept secret of starlets and politicians. As far as getaways go, it's a hidden gem."

Once they'd arrived at the top of the stairs, a young man dressed in white robes and a red fez and sash introduced himself as Masuda, and took their bags. Somewhere in the back of her mind, Edith filed away that Ben had given him an unusually large tip.

When she entered the lobby her eyes darkened to adjust to the indoor ambiance by contrast to the burning desert sun, and it only added to the sensory drama she was experiencing. As her pupils dilated, the splendor surrounding her revealed itself like a blooming flower.

Diamond-shaped gold and cream tiles interlocked beneath lush coordinating carpets that anchored the center of the cavernous room, and runners in front of various service desks. There were several conversational arrangements of velvet tufted chairs and benches with black lacquered arms and legs. Elaborately carved ivory columns extended from the expansive floor to the soaring ceiling, which held a dizzying crystal chandelier. Another elegant staircase led to the rooms. On opposite sides of the lobby, twin archways lead to a bar on the left, and a restaurant on the right, featuring a grand piano and a big band stage, respectively. Towering tropical plants with vast fronds fanned out of hammered copper pots everywhere she looked, adding life, color, and dimension to the space.

Mindlessly, she followed Ben to a counter where he began to speak while she remained awestruck at the exotic palatial splendor around her.

Edith had been raised in an ostentatious level of grandeur due to her father's socioeconomic rank. However, only ever in a stuffy British setting which was a comfort to her, but hardly dazzling. Drizzling, yes. But not dazzling.

Her own choices had led her down many paths that had acclimated her to a more humble life. Too pragmatic to seek luxury, she was simply a woman singularly focused on academic pursuits. Not that she denied herself, it just simply didn't occur to her. She always had so many other things on her mind, that when it came to booking accommodations for travel, she never considered anything more upscale than absolutely necessary. When it came to any utility in fact, from her clothes to her food, and so on, aside from safety and efficiency, luxury didn't factor into her choices at all.

She hadn't been aware of that until this moment. If she'd come on her own (which, if you'd asked her yesterday, surely she would have told you that's exactly what she wanted) she may have seen the flophouse on the outside of town and decided that she'd be better off finding a small apartment instead. She'd never have presumed to hope for lodgings this marvelous.

Enveloped in splendor, feeling her body react to the promise of comfort, she wondered why she hadn't rewarded herself with more experiences like this as the architect of her own permanently single adult life. Stopping just short of considering a change in lifestyle, her mind went completely blank to luxuriate in the moment. Unabashedly dumbfounded, she stood still as Ben gathered their keys from reception.

Upon looking at her face, Ben's thoughts were running completely parallel to Edith's. An awestruck expression played across her face and he was sure that she never would have picked this hotel for herself, but appreciated every square inch of its posh glory nonetheless. He could tell from the clothes she wore.

High enough quality to last, but not enough to draw attention. The expensive well-worn suitcase he carried for her probably held six more identical outfits.

Relieved beyond measure that she didn't appear to be spoiling for a fight, at least not at the moment, Ben let himself feel a satisfaction that bordered on triumph. The gratification of getting her away from the flophouse, and tucking her into the Oasis Hotel fulfilled some sort of primal urge he didn't want to examine too closely. Like the way it felt to make her laugh, but multiplied.

She was safe. She was happy. She was excited.

She was walking up the stairs. She was tugging at her collar. She was letting her eyes drift along the walls.

He was bewitched. Thank heaven she'd suffer any brand of torture before asking him for even the most insignificant of favors, or they'd get into trouble fast.

She'd been a stranger this morning.

But now?

There might be nothing on earth he could bring himself to deny her. If she asked for the moon, he'd search for a ladder.

Before he knew it, it was time to act as though he hadn't been staring at her in order to meet her eyes again.

"This is your room," he said, as she turned to face him.

"I'm sure you'll want to settle in after the day we've had. We'll tour the worksite tomorrow."

He held the key out to her, its copper tag dangling between them, mingling with the air of what went unspoken.

When she'd turned around Ben's presence hit her like a wall. She must have driven him from her thoughts, maybe on purpose, as she sailed away on her peace of mind upon crossing the threshold of this place. He'd done everything to check them in, guiding her along, as if she'd been in a trance. Of course, she probably was. Ever since Ben had said the words "Oasis Hotel," the high stakes alert she'd been on the brink of all day had dissipated, and she let herself disconnect from calculation and worry.

Facing each other in an empty hall, about to go their separate ways, it felt as though she'd emerged from this trance to find herself face to face with a different man. He was the same though, of course. It was Edith who had changed. Or rather, he was never the man she thought he was to begin with. Standing here now, to Edith, that guy was gone.

Dropping her gaze to search the carpet beside her, she recognized she needed to speak to avoid embarrassment. But her feelings didn't neatly match up with words.

An unwanted reminder invaded her thoughts that not long ago she had scolded him, making accusations that his way of doing things was underhanded. Now look at her.

She decided to let the silence speak. She placed her hand over the key, letting her fingers drape over his, and looked up into his eyes. Wetting her lips, she drew in a breath as if to say something, but then hesitated. Part of her wanted to apologize for the wallet debacle… but she was not quite grateful enough to swallow her pride.

"Thank you, Ben," she said finally.

It wasn't quite an apology, he thought. But he wouldn't change the look she gave him for anything else in the world. It was a look that said this is as close to an apology as I am willing to extend at this time. Although they'd just met, he already knew how sentimental that was by Edith Taylor standards.

Luckily, she disappeared into her room and slammed the door behind her, or he might have flattened her back against it and made her indignant all over again.

He pictured her doe eyes, her wet lips, the golden flush of her cheeks, and felt tension course through his veins.

He blew a ragged sigh as his eyes opened again.

"How will I think straight," he said absently as he turned to walk toward his own room.

When she closed the door behind her, she flopped on the bed and let out a moan of ecstasy. It was enormous and had crisp white linens and big fluffy pillows. The sunlight glinted off the wallpaper's golden damask print. There was a lacquered black desk with an upholstered chair and Tiffany lamp. Through French doors and gauzy curtains was a spacious balcony that curved around the courtyard. Beyond the banister was a stunning view of the oasis.

She undid the knot of her kerchief and unbuttoned and discarded her shirt and skirt, undressing as she looked out the window.

The sunlight glittered off of the silver chain around her neck that disappeared beneath the neckline of her satin slip dress.

Feeling the sun bake her chest and shoulders, she liberated her curls from their pins and massaged her scalp for a moment. Her discarded loafers remained with her rumpled pile of clothes as her stocking feet carried her back to the bed again where she lowered herself, slower this time, feeling every inch against her back as her hands slid out across the bedspread taking in the sensation.

It wasn't just the room, or the sights, or the sumptuous feel of the bed that she took in. She basked in the symbolism of the moment. Tomorrow was the first day of the career she'd been working toward as long as she could remember.

She recalled what Ben had said. No one else would take on this project. But it didn't dampen her mood a bit. She was grateful to Isfetheru for being so notorious... otherwise Edith may never have made it here. Grateful to Ramesses for being so romantic. Grateful to Pimsley for being so cheap. And grateful to Ben for... well, a lot, now that she thought about it. Too long of a list to dwell on at the moment.

When she recalled witnessing the morally reprehensible act of stealing, her heart sank. He was such a quandary of a man. So far, he seemed so brash and unruly, vulgar and calculated. But he was also generous, passionate, and capable. And humorous. And... something else. There was something about him that belied a different sort of man underneath. There were times when she knew — somehow, she knew that he was thinking something he wouldn't say.

She could certainly thank him for this room. Now from the comfort of her luxurious bed, she could let herself openly admit that she would be repulsed to sleep on a cot back at the officers lodgings.

A deep breath filled her lungs to capacity as her eyes drifted shut, lying still; but to her dismay, what she immediately saw in her mind were Ben's brown eyes and how close they were when he pulled her into his lap. The feel of his broad hands sliding from her waist to her hips. When her eyes popped open her hand was covering her mouth.

What was she thinking? She couldn't be fantasizing about Ben. They hadn't yet known each other for an entire day. To say nothing of the fact that she'd seen him rob three people in that small expanse of time. Or, rather curiously… she hadn't seen it, even though each time it had happened right in front of her.

Edith flung open her suitcase and set a book on the desk, then selected a nightgown to change into before drawing a hot bath.

As she sank into the water, it wasn't Ben's brown eyes she was thinking about.

It was his smile.

CHAPTER FIVE

GLANCING BACK AT the hotel the next morning from the very edge of where the white hot desert sand gave way to the lush greenery of the oasis, it seemed she'd just traversed another dimension somehow.

It couldn't possibly have taken as long as it felt to cover the distance from there to here.

Edith put it out of her mind when she stood before the work-site, which was situated at what she suspected to be a superstitious length from the outstretched fronds that encircled the water.

She turned away from her last look at the hotel to stare down between the two rows of white tents she'd seen from her terrace the night before.

As a life-long early riser, she was dismayed by awakening to the knowledge that Ben had already left for the day. The only reason she knew that was by the note he'd sent with her breakfast from room service.

The harsh noise and commotion pummeled her senses as she walked by open tents filled with luggage and equipment. Next to a worn steamer trunk was a towering pile of dirty pith helmets, where new additions heaped on top tumbled to the bottom. A bouquet of pick axes leaned against a beat up steamer trunk. A camel's leather saddle was burdened with an incredible amount of food from town. A few men floated on the water in boats lazily nearing the outer walls of the tomb. The shaky hands of a man with no eyebrows filled an array of empty bottles with gunpowder as he squinted intensely. The smell of tobacco and sweat was staggering.

Men, everywhere. Shirtless. Toothless. Tall and broad, short and scrawny. Tall and scrawny, short and broad. Every shape, size and color. Every language she knew, and a few she didn't, murmured all around her. In fact the only thing all of these men had in common is that not one made eye contact with her — except one little boy from town who's beautiful black eyes bore into her with a look that could be desperation or disgust, she couldn't be sure.

At the end of the row stood the only tent with canvas walls. It was much larger than all the others. She hoped she would find Ben inside, because she hadn't seen him along the way and it seemed no one was willing to speak with her.

When she parted the split canvas panel to step inside, she saw Ben and was hit with a wave of relief. If someone had told her two days ago she'd feel that way to see him standing there, she wouldn't have believed it.

The papers in his hand fell to the table as his eyes skimmed over her. His teasing smile didn't reach his lips right away. For a moment he just stared.

"Good morning," he said, breaking the silence.

She'd only just seen him last night, but it felt like a surprise to be reacquainted with the sound of his voice — its deep, smooth timbre.

"Yes, it looks like it has been."

He rounded the small cluttered table that served as his desk, and came to stand before her next to a larger empty table in the center of the tent.

"Did you enjoy your breakfast?"

"Yes," she said dismissively. "When did you get here?"

He looked puzzled.

"Hours ago. Why do you ask?"

"I didn't think I was sleeping in. Is the crew very upset that I'm late?"

"You're not late, the crew starts early, when it's cool, before midday when the sun is the highest."

He was reassuring at first, then scowled.

"Why would you think the crew is upset?" his brows furrowed, but he didn't break eye contact as he took what seemed to be a subconscious step in the direction she'd just come from.

"No one would look at me. Not one, and there must be two dozen men out there."

His frown vanished, replaced by his full dazzling smile. Something she said had amused him.

"Yes, they've been debriefed."

She bristled instantly.

"Ben, have you told the crew not to look at me? Why on earth would you say such a thing?"

He stood with his hands in his pockets, regarding her.

"I didn't tell them not to look at you. I told them what would happen if they did. It sounds like they chose to conduct themselves wisely."

"I thought I needed to be tough enough to withstand their catcalling about my little kerchief, and so on."

She saw his forearms tense as if his hands were balled into fists within his pockets.

"I was trying to talk you out of coming. Now that you're here, you might as well know — there's not a chance in hell my crew will give you any trouble."

"Alright…" she mumbled, looking at the dry, cracked ground.

"And… you'll also be perfectly safe at the hotel."

"Yes, well, I suppose upon retrospect it's curious that Pimsley cared enough about my safety to demote his finest man to bodyguard status, but didn't seem to mind putting us up in a dump."

"Miss Taylor." Ben ignored her poor attempt at humor, and dipped his head to try and get her to look at him.

When she looked up his brown eyes were intent on her.

"Don't go into town without…" his jaw tensed for a moment. "Do not venture into town unaccompanied."

"By you," she clarified.

"That's right," he said, crossing his arms.

"Of course, I wouldn't want to be caught without a chaperone," she spat, turning to leave.

He snatched her arm, pulling her back to face him. She turned on him and tried to yank her arm back, but his fist was like a vice.

"Do you understand me?" he said calmly, despite the glare in his eyes.

She looked down at his hand where it was wrapped around her bicep and laid her fingers over his tentatively before looking up at him again.

"Yes," she whispered.

As soon as he'd felt her light touch he slowly released her arm. The space between them hummed with tension. Where she usually would have radiated defensiveness and resentment, the look in her eyes was earnest, genuinely intended to soothe the fear she saw behind his anger.

Something told Edith that this was about more than job security for Ben.

"Well, this is a fine way to begin my first day on site — with everyone afraid to look at me. For pete's sake," she said lightly, rubbing her arm. "What else did you tell them?"

"Nothing."

She eyed him suspiciously.

"Nothing?"

"I was waiting for you to get here. I didn't want to make an announcement without you." He gestured to the flap of canvas that led outside. "Shall we?"

A young man with glasses and slick, black hair rounded up the crew at Ben's order. She saw a formidable look on his face she hadn't seen before.

Slicing through the noise, a piercing hand-whistle sailed from Ben's lips over the crowd to hush the diverse range of voices.

"Gentlemen," he bellowed followed by a long pause. He let the word sink in, making the expectation in it clear.

"This is Miss Edith Taylor," he extended a hand to present her. "She is a historian from the Egyptian National Archives in Cairo, and an egyptologist specializing in the era of the New Kingdom. In addition to her work in the archives, she has done consulting on archaeological sites in the Nile Delta, and has made a dedicated study of this tomb in particular, and the legend surrounding it."

He paused again, scanning the crowd.

"She is the most qualified person in Egypt for this project, and as of today she will be acting as the Archaeological Director of this expedition. I am honored to have the opportunity to assist her, and I plan to learn as much as I can from her expertise."

There was a gruff whisper from the back of the crowd, but a sharp glance from Ben silenced it. Then, he delivered the speech again, in Arabic.

"Miss Taylor, do you have anything to add?"

Edith's jaw snapped shut when he addressed her, and she felt a fine mist over her eyes as she peered over the crowd. She took a deep breath, willing the lump in her throat to abide.

She felt a surreal surge of pride bloom in her chest knowing this is where she'd be reporting for work each day for the foreseeable future. Or, rather, where all of the men she employed would report to her.

"I look forward to working with all of you," she said, her strong, steady voice carrying all the way to the back of her crew.

"Selim, translate," Ben ordered the young man with glasses, and turned to open the flap of the tent for Edith to enter through. As they receded into the tent that would serve as Ben's office, they heard Selim begin to shout in French.

Inside the tent, Edith stared at him. Her throat was seized by so many feelings. Ben had introduced her to the crew with career highlights she hadn't mentioned to him. It meant he must have researched her past on his own.

Battling to remain professional in the wake of being treated with the most respect she'd ever gotten from a man at work, she lost the fight and flung herself at him. She crashed into him and reached her arms around his neck, burying her face there in an extremely inappropriate hug.

His arms came around her, lifting her against him as his hands spread against her back. Turning his head, he rested his jaw to the crown of her head. Discreetly he inhaled her scent into his lungs. It felt like he'd waited an eternity to sink his face into her hair, though it had been less than 24 hours.

Iris, he thought.

She hopped down abruptly, having fulfilled the impulse and ready to get back to work with a clear head.

Ben planted his hands on his hips and looked down at her.

"Thank you," she said.

"Don't."

"Yes, I do apologize. That was improper. It will not happen again."

"No, don't thank me for introducing you based on fact, how I would introduce any colleague. Now, as for what you did when you got me alone..." The stern look on his face gave way to the mischievous bouncing eyebrows she recognized.

"You can jump me anytime."

"I did not..." she scoffed at him. Her eyes rolled all the way to his desk, landing on the papers he'd been holding when she'd first walked in. It was her resume.

She bit her lip to conceal a smile as Ben reached past her to retrieve something off of a messy pile.

It was a large scroll that he unfurled across the table in the center of the tent. She searched the large sheet of parchment marked up in fine detail with intersecting lines, cross hatched shading, and small neat print identifying rooms, corridors, and architectural details.

It was a depiction of the tomb's layout.

"Treasure map?" she asked.

"Floorplan."

She recognized the segment of the temple that was visible above ground. The quay, the three archways, the two statues of Anubis, but that enormous monument was tiny on the map compared to the illustration of the catacombs that sprawled under the very ground they were standing on. The stories-high pylon gateways she would pass through tomorrow were only the tiny tip of a colossal iceberg underground.

"This rendering is based on a mixture of what we know, and what we can assume based on other tombs from this period in history."

Edith's eyes roamed over the map.

"Who did this?" she asked.

"Zakaria and Selim worked on it."

"Can I speak with them?"

At Ben's beckoning, both men filed in to stand across from her on the other side of the table. Their eyes skittered along the map until they looked up at Ben, who jerked his chin toward Edith.

Once they reluctantly met her gaze, she spoke.

"Hello. What made you choose this shape for the anteroom?"

"From the footprint that can be discerned from above ground, we based the layout on the tomb of Nefertari, but more on the size and scale of Ramesses' lower ranking wives, because it was the closest in rank to the Weeping Viper in that era, before her death."

"Are there any geographical differences between those burial sites and this one?"

Zakaria looked at Ben, and paused. When Ben nodded at him, Zakaria was taken aback for a moment before continuing.

"Sure… no, aside from the oasis, which of course presents its own issues. However, any drilling from previous excavations attempted on this site hasn't uncovered any obstacles underground. The burial site was clear and mostly subterranean."

Edith glanced at Zakaria.

"So, we are safe in assuming there would be no other variations from other tombs in that time period. What can you tell me about previous excavations? Where they have succeeded and … failed," Edith said as her eyes fell back to the blue prints.

Then Zakaria looked to Ben again, and this time held his gaze. Ben turned to Edith then and squared off.

"There have been four teams who've attempted to access the tomb, on record — countless others off the record. Mysterious circumstances surround all of these expeditions. There are theories that the archways initiate the curse. Once you've trespassed each of them, they say the curse is activated, like a timebomb."

"Sometimes crew members would drop dead on site," Selim piped up. "Sometimes it happens after they pack it in and leave. Some died before they ever made it here."

"Well, surely that can be dismissed as coincidence." Edith reasoned, "How could they presume to know whether it was related if the victim hadn't stepped foot in Argo?"

"Each death related to this site …" Selim said, "They weren't thought to be accidental like a lot of the casualties of King Tut's Curse. Everyone who died in relation to the Cursed Tomb of Argo died exactly the same way — of asphyxiation consistent with smoke inhalation."

"Miss Taylor…" Ben said, his voice grave, "in each case, in every single one… the first crew member to die has been the first person to pass though the archways, or attempt to breach the door. Even in cases where crew members died before arriving in Argo, the leader of the party is always killed first."

Edith solemnly took in the information she was being given, absently pressing her palm to her chest. For the briefest moment, she imagined feeling smoke filling her lungs.

"It's a wonder you're all brave enough to be here," she whispered.

"It will be more than worth our while, with Ben at the head —I mean… with Ben on the job."

Zakaria and Selim shared an amused glance before leaving the tent.

"Well, I learned early on that you wouldn't be here for the historical significance. What treasure have you promised all of these unsuspecting men?"

"Unsuspecting? You mean the men who just told you, in detail, what they understand to be the worst possible outcome of this dig?"

"Fair enough. I suppose they're aware of the legend. But would they take the risk if they knew there was no treasure to be had?"

"Ah, but that's where you're wrong," Ben smirked.

"Yes, there is a fortune of riches. But not for the taking. Maybe you've ransacked ancient artifacts in all of your past jobs, but that won't be how we conduct this dig. Every single flake of gold from this point forward will ultimately take its rightful place in a museum."

"Yeah," he exhaled.

She sensed the slightest hitch behind the word, and knew that wasn't all.

"Ben," she said coyly, with an unfair softening of her voice.

"Yes, Miss Taylor?" he groaned.

He didn't want to tell her. But he knew she needed only to ask.

"You could get gold anywhere. According to your admirers, anyway."

"Since when are you a flatterer?" he griped.

"... and everything you've shared so far suggests that you hate Pharaohs, mummies, and cursed tombs."

"Yes," he said, with a muscle twitching in his jaw.

He hated to even think about it. Especially in the context of Edith Taylor leading the way.

"So, I wonder why you'd be going after this gold. A treasure guarded by the most cursed tomb in known history. Where there's no guarantee you'll survive to walk away with any treasure at all."

"There's never a guarantee that I'll get to walk away, not from any treasure hunt I've been on in the past ten years."

"You didn't answer my question."

"The curse is the only reason why there's untouched gold left in this tomb. Ancient Egyptians pilfered most of their own graves centuries before England's Egyptian revival. Untouched fortunes are becoming more scarce every year."

She paused, waiting for him to admit it.

"Well, out with it," she said, placing her hands on her hips.

Untie that scarf and I'll tell you, he thought.

Ultimately he sighed, and relented.

"The Collar of Queens," he said.

Edith's eyes went wide, dropping to the blueprints again, her mind racing over bits and pieces of information filed away in her brain.

The Collar of Queens… could it be?

"You know of it then," Ben stated, watching her stream of consciousness scribble itself across her forehead.

"I know that there are depictions of a golden royal collar in some records of ancient Egypt. I know that it's called The Collar of Queens because it is made up of jewels harvested from the Valley of Queens."

Edith's hands were planted on either side of the map as she leaned over it. Ben was mirroring her.

"Each of the jewels were considered to hold the power of the family tribe they came from. The collar is said to combine the power of each of these queens to imbue the collar with… magic. Making it a sort of super powerful talisman. It was commissioned by Ramesses as a gift for his eventual heir, intended for protection, but it disappeared before it could be passed down."

She looked up to see him admiring her.

"High marks," he said with a half smile.

Her eyes slid back to the map to avoid lingering on his face.

"I've heard many theories about where it might be hidden, but can't say I'm familiar with the notion that it's buried with the Weeping Viper."

"Perhaps it was a gift from Ramesses. As a 'sorry I killed you for trying to kill me' sort of gift."

She laughed, and it lit up her face. As the days wore on she was forgetting to dislike him. He made her laugh so easily. Where she had to be careful was interpreting the look on his face whenever he'd succeeded in making her laugh.

"I don't think it would have been permissible. Ramesses went to great lengths to conceal how opulent Isfetherus' tomb and treasure room were. He never could have gotten away with giving her what definitely was, and still is to this day, the most rare and valuable artifact in the entirety of the Golden Age."

"To answer your question, yes. That's exactly what I'm hoping to get out of this dig, what you just said. I would have done the dig for a lot less, but making the most consequential discovery of my career is definitely a draw."

He noted that Edith's eyes no longer scattered all over the map as she got lost in her own thoughts. Now they were trained toward one spot in the tomb.

The treasure room.

"Anyway, we have a theory. Colleagues of mine have compared different findings and believe the timelines match up. As I'm sure you know, it is difficult to get details about the burial of the Weeping Viper because of the nature of her scandal. But, if you piece together the puzzle a certain way, the disappearance of the The Collar of Queens, and the sealing of this tomb, may coincide."

"So," she said, looking up from the map.

Ben crossed his arms over his chest and stared back at her.

"What's your plan?" she said.

Half a smile quirked his lips.

"What's your plan, boss?"

"I think …" she pursed her lips, summoning the courage to share her opinion. As the head of this expedition, she would have to find the nerve and hold on for dear life.

"I think there are three doors."

Ben's eyes were alight with adventure as he smiled upon hearing her share his own theory.

"... and they're all cursed," he nodded.

She stood up straight and stepped back from the table.

"Yes."

They pored over the map, swapping ideas and theories with shared fervor. At some point, Edith retrieved a pencil from her curly plait of hair and began to make improvements. Ben relayed some of what lies beneath in the catacombs of his past, and Edith buttressed his findings with historical data. Edith shared her educated assumptions of what they might encounter, and Ben offered his knowledge of the more concrete details.

When Zakaria came in much later, they were side by side, arms over lapping, chattering back and forth. Swept up in the rush of discoveries, they weren't aware of their proximity until they were interrupted, at which point their minds returned to the present with the force of a freight train.

He looked down to see Edith sprawled on the table, her loafers barely touching the ground as she reached to maneuver her pencil around a protractor somewhere near the second annex.

Towering over her, his hands were planted on either side of her as her hip grazed his groin. He'd been so intent on watching her revisions of the map, at the ready to fight her over any detail he thought was out of place, that he felt the warmth of her body there for the first time.

Edith's head snapped up when she realized Zakaria had entered the room to find her all but flattened on the table, knowing that Ben hovered over her from behind.

Ben inadvertently brushed his hands along Edith's hips as he stepped away from her, as if he needed to physically separate their bodies. Edith stood up straight, smoothing her hands down her shirtfront in a desperate attempt to regain decorum.

"Hey..." Zakaria said, startled at first by his awkward intrusion on — what, he wasn't sure.

"Hey!" he said again when he realized Edith was making changes to the map he'd spent ages perfecting, her curly, haphazard handwriting scribbled beside his neat print.

He shook his head, remembering at once the reason he'd rushed in here in the first place.

"Hey," he said once more. "You'd better come see this."

When they emerged from the tent, Ben and Edith turned to follow the eyes of the crew members who stared at the horizon.

There, on the crest of a faraway dune, stood an army of figures dressed in black robes, astride a team of black stallions.

"The Medjai..." they turned to each other and spoke in unison.

The Medjai were an order of royal guardians that went back as far as the Pharaohs themselves. When the Egyptian empire fell from power, the band of desert rangers went from being the official royal army to a band of vigilantes.

"What are they doing here?" Selim mumbled to another crew member.

"They are always nearby when they suspect outsiders might make entry to a tomb holding any wonders lost to Egypt," Zakaria said.

"The treasure? If they're here, that must be a sign that this tomb is filled with gold," Selim said, warily looking over his shoulder, avoiding any mention of what specific treasures presumably lay beneath their boots.

"No, not treasure. Not even rare, royal treasure," Zakaria said, sharing a discreet glance with Selim. "The Medjai specifically protect the secret sorcery of the ancient Egyptian priesthood. They would only be here now if they believed this tomb were to hold… any of the ancient scrolls, perhaps."

"Maybe this time they'll be right," Edith whispered to herself.

After a moment, Zakaria mustered the gumption to ask.

"Ben, will they come for her?"

Ben stared gravely at the horizon, his jaw set like stone, before taking a deliberate step in front of Edith in full view of the black fleet of desert rangers.

"No," Ben said, "They won't."

CHAPTER SIX

IN THE LOUNGE of the Oasis Hotel, tucked under elegant white table cloths, they sat in shallow round dining chairs of emerald green velvet with gold trimmed legs and hardware. There was an enormous chandelier of stamped copper hanging above them. Behind the bar was a man in a black tie and white jacket mixing drinks and speaking French to one of the guests. All of the waiters were wearing white tunics and a red fez with matching red sash.

She stared at Ben as he spoke to the waiter. The sweat and grime he'd accumulated over the course of their workday had vanished; his filthy stained clothes had been replaced by fine attire that included a sharp dinner jacket. His stubble was still many days past needing a shave, but his outgrown hair had been combed. As he ordered them champagne, Edith thought he must have seen the evidence of her celebrating in her room.

When he had knocked on her door, she opened it wearing a powder blue linen dress, much the same as her shirt earlier, buttoned to the collar, tied with a kerchief. Glasses framed her eyes as always, but her hair, freed from its usual restraints, cascaded down her back in big curls.

"Hello, Mr. Brooks?" she said, nodding to spur him on as he stood still as a statue.

"Ben," he finally said.

"You've been calling me Miss Taylor for two days."

"Call me Ben."

"Alright," she agreed. "You can call me Edith."

"Edith… would you like to join me for dinner?"

It occurred to her that he wasn't really asking her to dinner. He was informing her that it was time for them to go to dinner. As a colleague. As a professional acquaintance. As a man being paid to accompany her.

"I suppose it is time for dinner. Yes. Let me get my bag." Once she had turned away from him, she bit her lip to conceal a smile before joining him.

In the numbing afterglow of the first few glasses, she decided there was no harm in having another glass with dinner. Or two.

He ordered in the same way she'd seen him order before, by asking what was best on the menu. When the waiter turned to her, she said she'd have the same. She saw the merits of this dining strategy.

Over dinner they fell into easy conversation, as colleagues, regarding the discoveries of the day. They discussed the site, the crew, and the dangers that lie ahead. All of her logistical questions were answered with patience, no matter how many she asked. There was no condescension in his tone, nor did he use any inquiry as an opportunity to inflate his own intelligence, or insult hers. In his way, Ben cracked jokes around any grim news he was obliged to relay, and flirted his way around any topics he preferred to keep close to the vest.

As the champagne went to her head, she became intoxicated by how refreshing it was to enjoy a conversation as equals. Most of the time. Though, there was one area of conversation that always held an imbalance.

"You said they wouldn't come for me," she broached, during a lull in their conversation "but they will."

Ben looked up from his plate to study her. Then she watched understanding dawn on his face.

The Medjai.

"They won't," he said with finality.

"You can't be sure."

"Yes I can."

"You're so arrogant." A champagne giggle bubbled up with the insult she usually would have issued with disdain.

"Yes, I'm arrogant," he agreed, smiling at her. Unable to keep himself from smiling when she laughed. "About a lot of things. But on this subject, I'm also informed."

"How can you be sure they won't be coming for me?"

"I already told you. Because they'll be coming for me."

"You think they also believe The Collar of Queens is buried with the Weeping Viper?"

"Well, you saw them asserting their presence today. Their concern only fortifies my theory."

"Have you encountered the Medjai before?"

Ben burst into laughter, shaking his head.

"You could say that, yeah," he said when he regained composure.

"Well, of course you have," she reasoned. "If your reputation is based in fact, you would be their archnemesis."

"We have an understanding."

"Oh?"

"Yes. They understand that I get what I want, and they can't stop me."

"Well, as the vigilantes of the Sahara, I would think they'd be well within their duty to stop you from robbing the graves they've sworn to protect."

"It may be their duty to come after me. But they won't pull it off. And they certainly won't come anywhere near you."

Silence stretched out between them.

Edith basked in the heat she felt whenever Ben was protective of her. She found that her current state made the sensation even more enjoyable. When sober, she would have ruined it by reminding herself that he was being paid to protect her. Being tipsy, however, made it easier to pretend he was being possessive.

It dampened her spirits a bit when she considered there was a piece of this puzzle she knew that Ben didn't.

Ben sat across from her thinking the exact same thing.

Once the plates were cleared he leaned in, a hint of challenge on his face.

"So," he said, "Now that you've seen the tomb..." his voice dropped, playfully ominous. "How do you plan to get in?"

She smiled, looking away.

"I hope you have some good ideas, because like I said, there's a reason the only two people in Egypt crazy enough to take on this job are you and me. The crew can't dig around the tomb, because they'd be up to their ears in water. You can't blast it with dynamite, because it will flood. The door has long been thought to be a false door, but because it was built to look like a temple, the front door already would be a false door. So, it could be a false false door. Or, to the layman, a door. Is that your strategy?"

"Well, Ben, I have my ways," Edith said.

Aided by three and a half glasses of champagne (only because Ben had slid her fourth glass across the tablecloth and out of reach when she wasn't looking) she couldn't remember why it would be a bad idea to tell him.

After sneaking a look from side to side, thinking she was hidden behind a well placed potted plant, she touched the scarf at her neck, timidly at first. She watched Ben's face as he saw her untie it, revealing the neckline of her dress.

It took Ben a moment to realize what she was doing; dropping only the first and most superfluous bastion of her modesty. Watching her untie the scarf at her neck was having a more severe effect on his blood pressure than any burlesque show he'd ever seen.

"Miss Taylor..." he said with a warning tone as he saw her undo the top button of her dress, and reach for the next

"Tsk, tsk," she said, shaking her head sending spirals of her hair swaying.

"Edith."

She could undo three more buttons and still be the most demurely dressed woman in the dining room. And yet, for some reason, he discreetly shifted in his seat to block her from view of the rest of the dining room.

"I have something none of the other men who have attempted this dig ever had," she said, fluttering her eyelashes.

"You sure do," he whispered, seeing the first swath of her decolletage, and the light just catching the glint of a silver chain. He didn't know how torturing him would get her into that tomb, he thought, but he wasn't about to stop her.

She undid another button, flashing a rare and dazzling smile.

He leaned in so far that his elbow slipped off the table and he had to catch himself. Somewhere along the way they'd become huddled together conspiratorially.

Ben watched as she released another button and finally ran her hands up the sides of her collar, spreading her lapels apart. When he saw a hint of lacy satin, reluctance rose up within him. He looked up to glare into her eyes, but found it no less intoxicating.

She leaned in, resting her elbow on the table, angling her chest to give him a view straight down the front of her dress.

"See?" she said.

He let out a breath he hadn't known he'd been holding in. Despite his efforts to avert his eyes like a gentleman, he couldn't resist her beckoning him to look. The fit of her dress was as boxy as all of her other clothes, and the soft blue linen gaped away from her chest revealing an entirely unobstructed view.

His heart pounded as he saw the paltry strip of fabric attempt to hold the ample breasts her button up shirts never hinted at.

A soft groan rumbled in his throat.

"Ben..." she whispered, trailing her fingers down her chest.

"You've had too much champagne," he said, to himself.

"I have a key," her nose crinkled slightly when the admission spilled out of her and she pulled at the chain tucked between her breasts revealing a pendant.

The sight of the pendant hit him like a splash of cold water and Ben realized he was bracketing her into her seat, with one arm on the table and one hand on the back of her chair.

After all of his years on the job, he knew an ancient Egyptian artifact when he saw one. He knew their materials, their methods, their quality of work, and even their taste.

He reached for the pendant and the back of his hand brushed her chest sending a shiver down her spine. The tremor was sobering for a moment, and a part of her realized she was now leaning into Ben with the front of her dress halfway undone.

Even knowing how she'd gotten here, it was startling.

Ben examined the pendant, small and heavy in his palm. It was a lotus flower, with rows of layered filigree petals. The stone in the center was a smooth peridot. He searched her eyes and when he reached to remove her glasses her lips parted to protest, but the words stopped in her throat.

He studied her eyes again and looked back at the pendant. They were exactly the same color.

"Where did you get this?"

"I've always had it. It's a family heirloom. I've read that the false false door to the tomb is said to be missing a lotus shaped stone in the center. I think this is what's missing, and if we replace it, we can open the door."

"Why would your family heirloom be the key to this tomb?"

Edith leaned her elbow on the table, resting her head on her limp wrist.

"I don't know," she exclaimed with a sigh. "It could have been found by, or gifted to my family at any point over the centuries. Maybe someone in my lineage found it in a curiosities shop. Wouldn't that be the odd thing?"

An exhale rushed from Ben's lips as he pieced together what she was saying. It was a shock to think that the secret to unlocking one of the most notorious ancient mysteries in Egypt was hidden in Edith's bra. However, while his mind was clouded with what else was in Edith's bra, processing new information was difficult.

"That's fascinating," he said, clearing his throat.

Holding her gaze he lowered the necklace, dipping his fingers between her breasts to return the pendant to its hiding spot.

Her hand shot out to grip his knee when she felt his touch there, and he pulled a wicked smile. She withdrew her hand just as quickly as she'd placed in there, making it obvious that it had been involuntary.

Leaning close to her ear as he joined the halves of her dress over her chest, he added "… but I won't be able to hear anything you say until you put your dress back together."

She felt far less tipsy and couldn't seem to recall what she was thinking. He continued to stare into her eyes as her fingers worked slowly at the buttons.

"Are you flirting with me Miss Taylor?"

He sat back in his chair to put a safer distance between them, now that he was no longer using his body as a dressing room screen.

"You've been flirting with me for two days, Mr. Brooks."

Reaching across him to retrieve her glass from his custody, she didn't realize she was already smiling with the ease brought on by several glasses of champagne. If she had, maybe she wouldn't have taken the contents of her flute in a shot as a counterproductive attempt to clear her head. Contrary to her efforts, it only made her wonder why her hand wasn't on his leg anymore.

"Yes, I have. You didn't answer my question."

"No, I don't flirt, Mr. Ben," she slurred, "I'm just passionate about my work."

Pleased with herself, her palm found its way back to his leg.

The muscles bunched with tension beneath her touch. By now, he was rigid with need. There were things he wanted to do to her — things he knew they both wanted, that wouldn't be happening tonight. She had already celebrated too much.

The thought made an unwelcome rage cloud his ordinarily unshakable grip on composure. So far, the Edith he knew was probably the most uptight woman he'd ever met. Tonight he learned that it only took an adorable amount of champagne before she felt comfortable unbuttoning her top in public.

What if she'd been out to dinner with a lesser man?

The thought of it made him withdraw his hand from his own glass of scotch, lest it shatter in his fist.

Yet, there was one advantage to having her defenses temporarily inebriated, at least. She deserved it for how recklessly she tempted him.

"Despite how ... revealing you've been thus far," he said, with a grin that had now gone cold. "I still think there's some element of this you're not telling me. Of course, especially considering the pendant, I understand why you would fight to be on this team. But I still don't understand why you demand to go in alone. If any element of the curse is true... well, at risk of sounding unfeeling, I would think you'd want to send some lackeys down first before going in yourself. I'd rather see a few despicable grave robbers get haunted by a mummy than..." he looked her up and down, "you."

"I don't know what you mean," she said, leaning into him again, this time placing her palm flat against his chest, half flirting, half for balance. A tiny whimper escaped her lips. He clamped his hand on the arm of his chair to stop himself from touching her.

"Yes, you do."

Losing the battle, he lifted his hand and brushed his fingertips along her jaw. He tipped her chin up, encouraging her eyes to meet his.

"What do you want, Edith?"

"I just want what every librarian wants."

"Quiet?"

Her giggle started them both laughing, and the tension dissipated.

"You're so hard," she said with a dreamy grin, and looked at her hand against his chest.

"Jesus Christ," he sighed under his breath, and tugged at his collar.

Her comment was innocent. He wasn't. Immediately his mind filled with what he wanted to say to her, quick dirty demands that he would have shot at any other woman, especially when they were setting it up so blatantly.

But not with Edith.

He wanted to tell her just how hard he was. He wanted to grab her hand that was fondling his chest, and show her. He wanted to see the look on her face when he pressed himself into her palm. The look she gave him every time something he said aroused her, in spite of herself. The look on her face when her ass fell into his lap on the train. The look that said she was yearning, but scared. Frightened by her own desire. Afraid of how good it would be.

Not tonight. Not with Edith. He was scared, too. He'd never wanted a woman as bad as he wanted Edith right now.

That alone was enough to be worrying, but there was more. He'd never wanted to carry a woman's suitcase this badly. He'd never wanted to put a woman up in a luxury hotel this badly. He'd never wanted to take a woman to dinner this badly, and wanted it to be the best meal she'd ever had.

He'd spent his entire career making a name for himself as the man who gets people what they want. Powerful, rich, connected people. In all that time, he had never wanted to find anything as badly as he wanted to find what Edith was looking for, and he didn't even know what she wanted yet.

The conflict was written all over his face, in the tension she felt in the hard muscles of his chest. She could see that he wasn't joking anymore.

What about her?

"Want to see my necklace again?" she said coyly, wondering if her lips could reach his neck.

"Alright, time to get you to bed," he said nodding to the waiter as he removed her hand from his shirt and held it on the table, interlocking her fingers with his.

CHAPTER SEVEN

THIS FAR OUT in the Sahara, the desert played tricks with your mind. From the terrace of her hotel room it looked like the tomb was just beyond the courtyard. But now that she was walking, no matter how many steps they took, it never seemed to get closer.

And then finally, she was there. Once she'd made her way down the quay, Edith looked down at the bricks beneath her loafers. There was a line between the newer bricks that had been added for tourists and the original bricks that had been laid thousands of years ago. They'd been laid by the Egyptians she spent her life studying.

They were her companions for all those years. She never felt lonely when she spent time with them in the library, even if she was on her own. It occurred to her that so much of that time had been spent yearning for what she was doing right now.

Once she stepped over that threshold, between now, and what was then, her life would forever be divided by this moment. She stood in the era that was her entire life up until this moment, and she was about to step into her future.

What that future would hold she didn't know, but she knew it would be shaped by today.

Just then it occurred to her that she hadn't had a contingency plan for if she was wrong about the lotus. Ben had mentioned that you couldn't dig around it, and you couldn't blow it up with dynamite, you couldn't come at it from above or below. That no one who tried to open the tomb had ever been able to do so. And not only that… they all met an untimely death soon after.

If he were to have the audacity to repeat it in the light of day, she would tell him exactly why he would never use dynamite on this ancient site, or any other ancient site. It had very little to do with the fact that it would flood the tomb and everything to do with the fact that Edith wouldn't stand for it.

Quarreling with him wasn't an option last night because she was exhausted and … too friendly.

Her thoughts meandered of their own accord to last night, having champagne with Ben underneath a starry chandelier. Looking down to see their fingers linked while he paid the bill with one hand. In the harsh desert sunlight, the memory of the night before seemed like a mirage. She thought she must be remembering it wrong, because in her memory a stranger sat in her chair. Had she really said and done those things?

Then it nagged at her again… what if the lotus doesn't work? How would you access it? Would you try to crack through the top like a soft boiled egg, or burrow from underground beyond the oasis and live in this hotel for months, possibly years, before you even touched stone? All she'd come with was a family heirloom, and zero experience in the field.

No.

That wasn't happening.

She knew it.

In fact, she realized she wasn't actually wondering any of those things. She was imagining what she would wonder if she wasn't absolutely certain the lotus would work. But it simply couldn't take root in her mind. This was going to work. She would be inside that tomb today.

At the tents she could see many members of the crew busying themselves, casting conspicuous glances at her. Ben had been right, of course, as she was coming to realize he had been in certain categories. It was a rag tag team. It turned out to be true that no one from Oasis Argo was on the crew. So, that was just another obstacle, Edith lamented. No one here had the home advantage. It made it an altogether more clumsy affair.

She looked up from the crack in the bricks that had her considering the schism this day would leave between the two halves of her life. Down the long quay, through all three archways, she saw the first door… where Ben was waiting for her.

Strong legs carried her swiftly beating heart between each set of pylons, the first, then the second, then the third, finally passing through the giant onyx twin statues of Anubis, the jackal-headed god of the dead.

That's where she met Ben and saw the grim look on his face.

"I told them that it will just be us for now," he said, glancing back at the crew. "I'd ask if you're sure about this, but I won't bother."

She would usually take the bait of his teasing, but today she couldn't. Her heart was racing in her chest, and nerves fluttered in her stomach.

He could tell by the stark look on her face.

"Hey boss, don't forget to breathe."

"Everything's just a joke to you," she said, with no anger or bitterness, just stating it as fact. "All you see through these arches is another paycheck. No different than the last dig you came from, or the one you'll head to when you've gotten what you came for. I've worked my entire life for this moment. And..." she glanced over her shoulder, even though he'd assured her that no one would accompany them on the dig today, she couldn't be too careful about the information.

She looked up at him now, "you know now why it's so important, more than professionally, but personally."

"When it comes to you, is there a difference?"

A whisper started in the back of her brain that was just another worry that would have to wait until later... Why had she trusted Ben with this after all? He had to be privy to what he'd see by accompanying her, but she'd told him (and shown him) more than she needed to.

"There is not, in fact. It's all of who I am. It's my past, my present, and my future. It's my profession, my passion, my heritage, and my hobby. There are enough mysteries in the lifetime of one pharaoh alone to keep me busy for my entire career."

Edith turned to examine the relief of the door, or the false door, or the false false door, also known as a door. She wasn't sure yet.

But the first thing that caught her eye, immediately, caught the breath in her throat, clutched the very heart in her chest, was the cavity in the center of the relief.

The door was covered in an etched scene that she'd read about. A wave of goosebumps shot up her arms to see it in real life.

Two figures separated by the seam in the center of the door were framed by rows and rows of hieroglyphs telling the story of their love. On one side of the door stood the stylized profile Ramesses, arms outstretched, hands cupping the empty spot for the missing stone. On the other side stood the Weeping Viper, holding the same pose, hands open to receive what belonged there in the hollow shaped like a lotus.

As Edith studied the door, Ben studied her. She looked over at him when she realized she was being watched, only to see that he had retrieved both guns from their holsters. He cocked the hammer on both pistols, one then the other, just as she locked eyes with him.

She whirled on him furiously.

"What do you think you're doing?" she shrieked.

"Don't worry about it," he scowled, dismissing her as he kept his intense gaze fixed on the door.

"I absolutely will worry about it if you think you're about to shoot off a gun anywhere near a tomb that is over three thousand years old!"

He tore his eyes from the door of the tomb and now his fierce stare was locked on her instead. Just the look in his eyes made her blood run cold. Even with her fury muzzled considerably, she tried, in vain, to maintain a commanding tone.

"I won't let you go any further until you discard your weapons," she said in a timid whisper.

"Oh Edith," and the humor she teased him about only a moment before had vanished. It turned out everything was not a joke to him. Not this.

"I'd love to see you try and stop me," he said. "Let's get something straight right now. The next time you want to go on and on about your many years of diligent study, you'll want to remember this—"

Slowly, almost imperceptibly, he was moving toward her.

"All those years while you were curled up with a spot of tea in an English library, I was breaking into these tombs, deep underground, surrounded by dead bodies. While you were reading about curses cast by these ruthless pharaohs you're so fond of, I was in the desert, in the darkness, seeing and suffering what happens to the cursed."

He was close enough to tower over her now, and his face, usually lit up with charming boyish mischief, was unrecognizable. The horrors he'd lived through were surfacing.

"I'm sure you've taken the deluxe tour of every tomb in Egypt, starry eyed behind a velvet rope. But know this. I've seen what's beyond that door before it's cleared out for tourists," he said, with finality, "It's evil."

He softened when Edith wet her lips and looked away. She seemed distracted by his closeness, despite the urgency of his words. He realized his face was an inch from hers.

Ben stood up straight to see Edith had flattened herself against the arch, her palms pressed to the stone behind her. While the atrocities of nearly a decade of mummies played against the backs of his eyes like a film reel, he had all but cornered her. When he took a step back, her chest was rising and falling with her quickened breath. Her eyes were still wide with fright.

He took another step back to his place before the door, close enough to react, but no closer than absolutely necessary.

"You better believe I'll shoot anything that comes near you, without hesitation. I don't care if I blast the Rosetta Stone to gravel in the crossfire."

She took a shaky step forward, smoothing her shirt front with a huff, attempting to regain composure. Moments like these reminded her that the notion she had the upper hand was a farce they both entertained.

The truth was that Benjamin Brooks, in having the upper hand, amused himself by letting her pretend she was in charge. Edith knew what no clever contract could change. Ben was the man in charge of this expedition, and perhaps more troubling… of her.

She felt hot. Was it the sun? Or was she furious? Or was she afraid? All she knew for sure was that, outwardly, she didn't intend to let it show.

"You're taking this bodyguard business a little too seriously. I think you've let it go to your head. I'm hardly Greta Garbo."

Now she was the one cracking jokes to diffuse tension. His jaw flexed as he looked down, seeming to consider his response, but he said nothing.

Edith closed her eyes and took a deep breath trying to reclaim her moment. With her eyes still closed, she stepped forward and placed her hands on the wall. It was supposed to be a sentimental exercise, an attempt to return to the present, and what was important about the here and now, blocking out Ben and everything else.

But once her eyes were shut, her mind moved through the door. She saw the inside of the tomb, and her vision flew down a tunnel of stairs as clearly as if it was real. Her eyes snapped open as she gasped and jumped back from the door.

Ben had lunged forward, poised to catch her without actually touching her. He searched her shocked face when she stood blinking at him, before his eyes narrowed at the door again, and he stood back in his spot.

"I saw…" she said breathlessly,

Ben shook his head, breathing a terse sigh, still watching the door like a hawk.

She fumbled at her scarf and blouse buttons to retrieve the lotus, and it occurred to her that her attempts to ceremonialize this moment were actually just her stalling. Before she hadn't wanted to know if she turned out to be wrong, if the lotus was just a useless trinket. But when her mind had connected with the temple and seen past the door, she knew. Just like she'd always known.

It was real.

Ben glanced over his shoulder to see that, as per his orders, almost all of the workers had gone back to the city for the day. All that was left was a young local boy sitting by the water, who probably had nothing to do for the day now that the dig had been called off. Ben looked back at Edith just as she had removed the chain from around her neck, and was giving the lotus one last glance before she approached the door.

She lifted the lotus, the smooth peridot gleaming in the desert sun, and pressed it into the depression. It was a perfect fit.

Suddenly, the tomb seemed to inhale the pendant, as it clicked into place flush against the stone, and just then, the doors themselves shifted back and sand sprinkled out around it exposing seams of the doorframe.

Ben grabbed Edith's arm and yanked her back out of the pathway of the enormous stone doors just as they swung open, releasing a cloud of shimmering smoke that engulfed them. Ben and Edith coughed and rubbed at their burning eyes until the dust had cleared, and as soon as she could see again, Edith broke free of Ben's grasp to see down the tunnel stairs.

"This is what I saw," she exclaimed, "I just saw this when I touched the doors!" she turned back to him.

"Oh that's nothing," Ben scoffed, "It's about to get a lot spookier than that," he said as he looked into the abysmal darkness of the stairwell.

Edith clasped her hands at her waist in a nervous gesture.

"How does it feel," he said, his face sunken with dread.

"What?"

"You just became the most famous archeologist in Egypt."

"Oh that's nothing," she said, teasing him with a dazed half smile, turning back to the tunnel. "When I find what I'm looking for here… I'll be the most famous archeologist in the world."

"Here" Ben said, handing her an oil lantern after lighting a torch for himself and situating more unlit torches in his pack.

They looked at each other once, and shared a brief nod of solidarity, before venturing down the long staircase.

The scuffs of their steps echoed against the walls as they descended into the tomb, their flickering lamps exposing precious little of what lay before them. Once they'd walked down past where sunlight could reach, it was pitch black. The walk in the darkness offered a lull of decompression after their tense exchange moments before. The dank stench of rot and liniment was overpowering.

Edith sniffed, thinking to herself hopefully.

It's not so bad.

Ben lifted his torch to illuminate star-shaped bricks they passed that stood apart from the other enormous slabs of limestone. They were spaced out every few steps.

"Star shafts," Edith said softly. She found herself eager to be reunited with the version of Ben she'd had dinner with the night before. Not to protect herself from his unpredictable wrath, but rather for his sake, to relieve the unease that radiated from every muscle in his body.

She decided to bore him.

"Air vents that were built into tombs, especially subterranean ones, so that the builders within could breathe. They would be sealed up once the tomb was completed because … well, mummies don't need to breathe of course," she smirked, finding his eyes in the darkness.

"Well there you have it," he said, returning his light to the path in front of him. "People who breathe don't belong down here."

They landed on a platform and Ben lit torches and put them into slots on either side of the bottom of the stairwell. The dim light filled the room and illuminated several pieces of ancient furniture along the walls. It was an anterior room and there was a door in the back to pass through to get to the next hallway.

As soon as Edith's eyes landed on the throne in the corner, she was engulfed in golden glittering smoke. Edith panicked and held her breath as the smoke shimmered as it swirled around her, whipping the tendrils of her hair and hems of her clothing as she squeezed her eyes shut from the burning.

She heard the muffled sound of Ben calling her name before it was cut off.

As suddenly as it had come on, the smoke cleared away. When she opened her eyes, she saw two people dressed in ancient Egyptian clothing. There was a woman in a netted dress and gold jewelry, and a man in a waist cloth and headdress. Edith looked around her to try and see where they may have come from. It was beyond her ability to reason how they could have gotten there or what they would be doing, but then they began to speak.

In their ancient Egyptian dialect, Edith recognized that they were professing their love for one another. Edith took a step forward, but she felt like she was under water, the way it felt in dreams. She called out to them, but they behaved as though they hadn't heard a word she said.

She waved her arms to no avail, but then she was struck by something she saw. The woman turned around as her lover placed a golden collar around her neck. Glimmering against her chest was the pendant from Edith's necklace. The crown jewel resting between her breasts at the tip of the golden collar was the lotus.

Then she heard her call him Ramesses. She searched the couple and their surroundings, and realized… She was having a vision of the past. She was seeing what happened on that very throne centuries ago.

She could barely make out their hushed voices, and spotty clarity of the apparition, but she tried to piece together what she could. Ramesses spoke of how the woman would be queen, and the woman inquired of the fate that would befall their son. He responded that though their son was a baby, someday he would grow up to be a great ruler of the land.

The words they spoke revealed her son, Cepos, to be the pharaoh's firstborn son.

Edith's vision tunneled as the information hit her, news that would change history.

Then they vanished into a cyclone of glinting smoke.

From the corner of her eye she saw movement on the opposite side of the room, near a shallow bench situated against the wall. It was the same woman who had been with Ramesses at the throne, and she now sat with a small boy. It was her son Cepos, wearing a headdress with a sapphire scarab. She was doting on him, and her pride shined in her eyes as she told him he would be a king someday. The young boy said that he cannot be king if his mother is not queen, and she assured him that it doesn't matter whether she is a queen. All that matters is the fate of the heir.

Meanwhile, Ben waved his hands in front of Edith's face again, becoming frantic. She was walking around the room inexplicably talking to herself — but, what was really alarming was what had happened to her eyes. An opalescent glaze came over them, rendering them completely opaque. Just as panic was beginning to seep into his veins and course through him like ice, Edith's eyes cleared and she stumbled back.

"Edith!" Ben shouted, half in relief and half to assess her mental state.

"Ben…" she said reaching out.

He took a step forward and steadied her with his hands encircling her waist. She was blinking rapidly, and he ducked down to bring himself to her sightline and search her eyes.

"Can you see?"

"A little… it's coming back…"

"Your vision is coming back? You lost your vision just now?"

"No," she said, becoming more alert. "I could see… I could see the past." Her eyes met his then.

"I saw Ramesses and ... well, it must have been her, it must have been the Weeping Viper. They were dressed just as they would be in 1200 BCE. She was wearing a netted dress, and Ben, she was wearing a collar, a royal collar with gold, beads, and ravens, and it had my lotus as the crown jewel. That's where my lotus is from," she said, her eyes looking a bit wild. Ben gently touched her cheek as he continued to search her all over, his face twisted with concern. "You probably think that sounds crazy."

"I think it's crazy you want to come down here. But..." he said, glancing over his shoulder, ever suspicious of his surroundings "I told you. I've seen what happens in places like these. Your eyes were... they were white," he said shrugging, unable to convey exactly what had happened to them; the milky swirling sheen they had taken on. "You were shouting" he continued.

"I'm sorry, I... I didn't realize," she said, taking a step back, touching her cheek where he had touched it, before hugging her shoulders to herself.

"Hey, don't apologize. Let's get out of here, I think that's about enough for one day. Tomorrow the crew can come in and begin to make sense of what's in here and make some progress on identifying artifacts."

"Wait, there's another door here, this leads to the rest of the tomb," she said, grabbing her lantern and brushing past him, stumbling a bit on her way to examine the door.

"God damn it," he mumbled, holding her by the arm as she wobbled like a newborn colt.

"We can come back tomorrow. I think we should get you some air and see if being down here has any..." he looked around warily, "side effects."

"Okay," she said, still dazed a bit. She was staring at the second door, reading the hieroglyphs.

"Can I help you?" he said, looking her up and down. "Can you walk?" She noted that he didn't have the cunning expression he usually did when he was sizing her up. He was scanning her for injury, running a diagnostic of how her vision had affected her.

"Thank you," she said.

"Edith, I asked if you could walk," he took a swift step toward her and touched her cheek again, tilting her face up to his. "Can you hear me?" he said, examining her eyes back and forth.

She turned her attention to him, and away from the door.

"No, I heard you, I can hear fine. I can walk. I'm not hurt, Ben," she said, grasping at his shirt front. "Thank you for bringing me here. Thank you for coming with me, for doing this."

She thought of how he handled her delicately on the train, and of how he gallantly pulled a favor to get her a luxurious hotel room. She thought of how clearly he hated to be entering a tomb, and what it must be costing him to do it her way. For the first time she realized that she actually never would have gotten this job if he didn't agree to it.

"You don't know what it means to me to be here. You couldn't possibly know what an important day this is."

For the first time that day, she saw him smile. It wasn't mischievous or coy. It was a genuine smile that broke the very troubled look on his face.

"Now I think maybe I'm hearing things," he chuckled, as he brushed his thumb across her dusty cheek, curling his fingers around the nape of her neck. "Which one of the fancy ghosts told you to like me all of a sudden?"

She dropped her grip on his shirt, shrugging his hand from her face. But she was smiling, too.

"Who said I like you?"

"Well, I already knew you liked me. I was just waiting for you to figure it out." He was teasing her, but her eyebrow twitched and she looked down. She didn't want him to be right.

"Anyway, I can thank them later. Let's get the hell out of here."

CHAPTER EIGHT

BY THE TIME they had gotten back to the hotel, bathed and changed, the day was coming to a close. Ben sent her dinner to her room, insisting she rest. She was quietly disappointed that she didn't see him again once they'd gotten back to their rooms.

The next day, the crew toiled over cataloging the tomb and brought back rubbings of the important writings for Edith, including the second door. Over the course of the day, she reviewed all the text pulled from the walls of the tomb, her own memory of the vision, and what happened when she stood before the second door. A theory began to piece itself together in her mind.

A lightning bolt of excitement shot through her when Ben came to her door in the late afternoon. Though she would have normally tried to appear aloof and frosty, it wasn't in her best interest to do so this time.

They sat at a bistro table on the terrace of Edith's room with miniature teacups of Turkish coffee and a tray of fruit and cheese. In retelling the details of her vision to Ben, the way her words rushed out betrayed just how eagerly she'd been bursting to tell him since they left the tomb.

It was truly thrilling for her to unabashedly express her excitement, thoughts, and feelings about everything she'd seen the way she could with Ben. He was uniquely able to understand her because of his own background. Edith had never had a colleague or acquaintance who didn't appear burdened by Edith talking through her discoveries. With him, she was able to be a true version of herself that no one else in her life knew what to do with.

The more she spoke about it, the less shaken she became and was more able to comprehend the reality of what had happened. It helped that Ben didn't question her in the slightest.

Maybe because he had really been there, and whatever he'd seen in her was convincing on its own. Maybe the horrors he'd seen in tombs really was, as he'd suggested, nothing compared to what she experienced. Maybe… there was a remote possibility that he believed her at her word because he took her seriously. An unfamiliar sensation if ever there was one; and from the person she would have least suspected the day they met.

"If Isfetheru bore Ramesses' firstborn son, Cepos would have been the rightful heir to the throne."

"Wouldn't the scandal of fathering a bastard before marriage have disqualified Isfetheru and Cepos from a place in the royal family?" Ben inquired, taking a sip of his coffee.

"Ancient Egypt wasn't like that, actually. There was really no stigma about premarital sex. In fact the ancient Egyptians invented the very first prophylactics in history, using goat intestines—"

She was interrupted by Ben choking on his coffee, and while reaching for water, his sputtering gasps turned into laughter. She glared at him with disgust.

"I'm sorry. Are you, in actuality, just an incredibly large school boy?"

"It's just that this coffee is so hot," he chuckled, wiping a tear from his eye. By the time he leaned back in his chair and took a deep breath in an effort to compose himself, she was smiling too. She would rather see him breaking into uncontrolled laughter at a rude topic than the stone-faced taskmaster he had been yesterday.

"Well, try to remember I am a modern woman, Ben. In the future, I'll refrain from mentioning topics you're not mature enough to discuss yet, like sex."

"We can talk about sex all day," he countered. "I'm sorry I was caught off guard. Who knew goat intestines were so handy." He suppressed laughter again.

She rolled her eyes at him.

"Anyway, as I was saying… where were we…" she asked rhetorically, looking off at the Saharan horizon, trying to pick up her train of thought where it had gotten derailed.

"Condoms," he said, in a low voice.

"Ben!" she snapped, sitting up in her chair with her hands on the armrests.

"Oh, now who's immature?" he scoffed.

"I was discussing the hierarchical structure of family dynamics within royalty of ancient Egypt, not—"

"Oh, now I remember, you were saying you're a modern woman. Tell me more about that," he said, leaning in on his elbows. His closeness, the tone of his voice, and the way he looked at her made her cheeks flush.

He thought he had just been teasing her, but her reaction had caused a shift in the mood at the table. It hadn't been his intention to make her uncomfortable, and he found it incredibly difficult to read her. Erring on the side of caution he thought, at the very least, his teasing had made her… distracted. At the moment he assumed that she very much needed to share what was on her mind regarding the complicated few days she'd had, so he provided her with the easiest route back to neutral territory.

"If there was no stigma around premarital sex, and Cepos was the rightful heir to the throne, then it seems Isfetheru got a raw deal being seen through history as a scheming ambitious viper — when in reality, her claim to the throne on behalf of her son was valid."

"Exactly," she replied.

Edith sat back in her chair, and smoothed a lock of hair back into place. She paused for a moment to let her blood cool. A brief question entered her mind as she attempted to mentally return to her scholarly assessment of the tomb.

Why does he make me feel this way?

She dismissed the thought just as quickly as it had materialized, desperate to avoid confronting a nagging urge that was burrowing deeper each day she spent with Ben. Perhaps each moment, even.

She took a sip of her coffee as her thoughts traveled back in time.

Ben saw that when she looked up at him, she was once again a cool, quick-witted librarian in a singular pursuit, with her kerchief knotted a bit too tight. He was glad to see she had returned to her default mindset, for her sake.

However... he wondered if she would ever willingly show a different side of herself to him without needing it to be teased out of her, and then, having to wonder if he'd done something wrong after the fact. He was unaware of his leg anxiously bouncing under the table as a frustrated ache began to build inside him, growing more insatiable each time she advanced and retreated.

After a long thoughtful moment, she continued.

"It was more than that. It wasn't just lineage by blood. He made her a promise. I saw it. He gave her the collar as a promise. He said she would be queen. So really, she was the one who was betrayed. Her and her son. Their son."

"I guess it depends on his reasoning for throwing her over in favor of Nefertari. Did he break his word for the sake of propriety, or was he lying to her from the beginning to get what he wanted?"

"No," Edith shook her head. "He did love her. If he was just stringing her along for a carnal romp, he wouldn't have built her this resting place of sycophantic splendor. Not only that, but I saw it. He loved her. Ultimately, I suspect he made the choice that was right for his country, as a king should. Isfetheru was the queen of his heart, but Nefertari was the right queen for Egypt."

"Well that makes him a better man than me," he said absently, tossing his napkin on the table.

"Why, what would you do in that situation? Choose love over country?"

"Well, I have no country, so my first order of business would be to find a goat—"

"Stop!" she shrieked, swatting at his shoulder as they both laughed. As their laughter died down, he admired her in the changing golden light of the waning day. She was considering what he meant when he said he had no country when he interrupted her thought.

"So. How do you propose to conquer your next challenge?"

Her response was a puzzled look.

"The second door. Do you have any more jewelry in your shirt? Or maybe a brooch clipped to your garter?"

"Hardly," she said, rolling her eyes.

"But, I do have a bit of a lead. My vision ended just as it had begun. I was engulfed in this… cloud of shimmering smoke. Before the smoke cleared and I saw the vision, I heard her say in ancient Egyptian dialect 'see my true past.' And then again, when I was coming out of my vision, before the smoke cleared, she said 'say my true name.' And then the hieroglyphs on the second set of doors was an incantation… but it was incomplete. It's an incantation I've seen before, but it always includes a name."

"Well, that's easy enough, you already know her name."

"But we don't know her real name. Back then, when someone was put to death and buried in shame for their crimes, it was common to perform a ceremonial curse that changed their name. Then they would be recorded under the new name as an act of erasure to punish them throughout history. I always suspected this was the case with Isfetheru, not only because of her notorious crimes, but because of the etymology of the name itself. The Egyptian word "isfet" means evil doer, and "heru" means far away. So, every indication points to it being a cursed name bestowed upon her as a punishment. There would be no recordings of her life or death under her true name."

Edith was leaning forward in her chair. Ben could see by the fire in her eyes she was setting up a hypothesis of some kind.

"But?" he said, opening his hands for her to continue.

"But… there may be a record of her birth. In my vision, I saw her tattoos and I may be able to match them up with what family line she came from. Then, if I use the approximate dates and cross reference the birth and death records, I might be able to find a birth that was recorded without a corresponding death."

"Where could you find that information?"

Edith's eyes darted around the table as her mind worked, plotting the presentation of her case carefully.

"Well… There are several options but… The information such as these deep obscure records is not open to the public. I know the volumes of the new kingdom era aren't available through my own library in Cairo. If I wanted to get it through the archives in Alexandria, I would have to send a formal request and wait for an appointment."

"Alright, that makes sense," Ben agreed.

"It could be a while until I would get an appointment, potentially weeks."

"Well, this dig itself is expected to take months if not years. You found an extremely rare loophole to get through the first door easily that I doubt can be replicated. Unless you've got another key hidden in your—"

"Hey," she warned, glaring at him.

"—suitcase," he finished with a wicked grin. "It's much more likely that the rest of this dig is going to progress painfully slowly by comparison."

He watched her hands fidget in her lap, and she bit her lip glancing at him coquettishly.

"But?" he groaned.

"There is one place, a private library, I know for a fact has copies of the reference books I would need. And, circumstantially, it makes the most sense and would get me the information the fastest."

He blinked at her expectantly.

She snapped the kisslock on her purse to retrieve an ornate embossed envelope. She opened it and placed the card on the table, sliding it over to him.

Ben mumbled as he skimmed the words in elegant golden calligraphy.

"You are cordially invited to attend a charity gala at the home of…"

His eyes flew to Edith's as he shook his head incredulously.

"Pimsley? You're trying to get into Pimsley's private library?" He glanced back down at the invite "Tomorrow night?"

She smiled and shrugged her shoulders, suggesting he already knew the answer.

"He'd never let you. I've known Pimsley for years, I've been to his house. He is famously paranoid. He doesn't trust anyone in the private wing of his home."

"You see, I think I know someone who might be very skilled at getting me exactly where I want to go," she said, leaning her elbows on the table with a suggestive grin, like he had done moments ago.

When his eyebrows drew together and his jaw set firmly she batted her lashes at him.

"Forget it. You better scoot back into your hotel room and start writing a letter to Alexandria, and figure out how you'd like to kill some time in the desert. If you're suggesting what I think you're suggesting, it's beyond ridiculous. We could never make it back to Cairo in time anyway."

"I thought you were desperate to know what I want?"

"That's right, and you still haven't told me."

"I've told you just now."

"You haven't told me what you're looking for in the tomb. You've just told me a harebrained scheme you cooked up since yesterday. I never should have left you alone in here with your clearly overactive imagination and a fresh stack of mummy comics."

"That's not what did it. It's what you've taught me the past few days."

"What's that?"

"The secret to getting everything you want in life… having a big strong man get it for you."

"Alright, cut the bullshit. It's not happening." He crossed his arms and looked away.

"Why not?"

"Why?" he shouted. "Why are we not racing back to Cairo for a black tie gala, held by the man who is funding this excavation, to break into his library and steal a rare set of reference books out of his private collection?"

She glanced down at her tea cup and pouted dramatically.

"Edith. No," he growled.

"Please, Ben?" she pleaded, and placed her hand on his restless knee, instantly making it still. She could feel his thigh tense underneath her palm. She saw him take a deep breath as he looked at her hand. For a long moment his face was a storm of conflict.

Then, finally, he closed his eyes and released a pained exhale through his teeth, and spoke, his voice thick with resignation.

"We've missed the last train for today," he said, riddled with grief, lifting his dreamy brown eyes to hers again. "But if we hurry, we could make the overnight steamer."

CHAPTER NINE

EDITH TOSSED AND turned under the covers as the breeze drifted from the Nile through the starboard side windows of her cabin. Her mind was racing with so many thoughts that sprung from the past few days. Every night before she'd been so exhausted, she'd fallen asleep before her head hit the pillow. But tonight she was teeming with so many emotions she couldn't sleep.

Primarily, her mind's eye was replaying her vision in the tomb over and over again, and every time it seemed to pick up on more clues. She examined her memories to try and summon the woman's tattoos as accurately as possible. There was a part of her that was afraid once she'd gotten to the reference books, there would be tattoos that looked similar and she wouldn't be able to differentiate them.

Her mind rushed forward to the gala they would attend tomorrow. She worried over the regular female obligations associated with a formal event, and thoughts of what to wear. For the first time, it crossed her mind that she could be arrested for trespassing at Pimsley's home, and then further wondered what type of man he was, and whether he would press charges.

She could ask Ben, he would know. Considering how desperately he protested this plan, he probably didn't consider Pimsley to be all that magnanimous.

In his office, the newspaper mogul had seemed harmless enough, if a bit condescending. But since then, Ben had said many things that alluded Pimsley was more sinister. For example, why would he be so secretive of a home full of acquisitions he was clearly very proud of? Was he just being protective over his belongings… or did he have something to hide?

Every time she tried to quiet the noise inside her head to get some sleep, that's when she thought of Ben.

That corner of her mind had a trove of unanswered questions. What was happening between them? He was prone to teasing her, but she assumed he was the kind of man who would be like that with every woman. That made her think of the gala. Would she see him mingling with other women there, and flashing them that irresistible smile? She'd been to many galas like this before, and she already knew he would be the most coveted dance partner of the evening. He was so handsome. Tall. Charming. Unmarried. Smart. Brilliant, actually.

How would she feel about seeing him flirt with other women? The answer came to her as a feeling, rather than a formed coherent thought.

She seethed deeply.

Then it occurred to her that if he did try finding a date, he would be met with a much warmer reception from any of the ladies there than he'd gotten from her. It was true she'd done little more than hiss at him ever since they'd become acquainted on this strange shared journey. However, as she'd confessed in the tomb the day before, Ben had done right by her on several occasions in the short amount of time they'd spent together.

As of now, she had even more reasons to be grateful. They were headed into what would be his greatest act of kindness yet. A twinge of shame squeezed her chest when she realized the nicest she had been to him was when she manipulated him to take her back to Cairo.

To commit a crime.

Against their boss.

That in itself was a mystery to her. She had *never* used her feminine wiles as a professional strategy. She had never dropped her veil of professionalism with a male colleague before.

It was a dangerous precedent to set, a slippery slope that could quickly ruin a working relationship. Which, as a woman in a male dominated field, was already precarious to begin with. Furthermore, this was the most important assignment of her career. She was partnered with Benjamin Brooks for the length of this project. The stakes had never been higher and there had never been a worse time to play with fire.

In the refuge of her late night ponderance, attempting to blame him was useless. It was true she had suspected from the beginning his calculated charm was a plot to throw her off balance, leaving him the victor of this face off over the widely coveted Cursed Tomb of Argo. But she knew the truth. Whenever Ben saw that he'd successfully spread heat beneath her collar, he retreated just as quickly.

Their interchange over tea this afternoon proved Edith was the instigator.

So the question under all of this was … why?

Why was Edith batting her eyelashes at Ben at a moment in her career when minimizing her femininity was more important than ever?

Why shouldn't he flirt with other more receptive women at the gala?

Why should she care?

Why did he burst through the double doors of her thoughts every time she tried to sleep?

The deeper puzzle she hadn't yet acknowledged was … why did he make her feel a way she'd never felt before?

Now, wide awake in the quiet and gently swaying chamber, shrouded in darkness except for the flickering oil lamp beside her, she considered it. She'd dated and kissed close to a dozen men. She'd been intimate with a few.

But something about Ben was different. It was as if there was an invisible threshold, and every time he was close enough to cross it, he awoke sensations in her body that had been frozen before. Her heart would race, her breath would trip, and she felt flushed all over. And something else, something deeper.

Desire.

That was it, the elusive element she was sure she'd never experienced before. She realized what she'd felt for other men was friendship, and a reciprocation of physical intimacy out of … fondness. They had pursued her, and she decided to acquiesce. Now that she had felt it, she was sure she had never wanted any man the way she wanted Ben. That's why it was so hard to concentrate whenever he was close enough; whenever he gave her that rushing feeling. Because she was drawn to him. She was fighting the urge to kiss him, to touch him, to feel his body on hers the way she had on the train.

That was the thought on which she drifted off to sleep with the soft movement of the barge, imagining a different outcome to landing in Ben's lap.

She had settled into some shallow phase of sleep when she was aroused by an awareness in her subconscious. Fear seized her throat when she opened her eyes to see the blurry outline of a large person hovering over her bed, but then the terror dissipated just as quickly.

Her first breath upon waking filled her lungs with the scent of him, an aroma she'd become familiar with by standing beside him as his skin was warmed by the sun.

"Ben!" she said sitting up in the bed, "What are you doing here?"

He had been leaning over her before with his hands braced on either side of her shoulders, but when she shot up he slowly lowered to sit down beside her. He was shocked too, she could tell, as if he hadn't meant to wake her. Maybe he urgently had to tell her something and was checking to see if she was still awake.

"Is something wrong?" she asked when he remained silent.

"No," he said, and she saw that he was breathing heavily, as if she had startled him, and not the other way around.

Ben couldn't believe the position he'd found himself in. He had been pacing in his cabin until he thought it was late enough for her to be fast asleep, but apparently she had so barely dozed off that just his presence had awoken her. And now whatever luck had always made him quick on his feet had abandoned him.

Her hair was a wild mess of curls he wanted to get lost in. He loved her glasses, but without them her light green almond eyes were not merely beautiful, but totally arresting. The scent of her hair and skin ignited a deep elemental reaction within him, and the small room was filled with it.

Iris and Edith.

He'd found her distractingly gorgeous during the day, buttoned up in her practical boxy uniform. Now that he'd seen her like this, he'd never be able to look at her in the light of day again without thinking of her this way.

Worst of all, when she'd sat up, bringing herself face to face with him, her sheets had fallen around her waist. When he caught sight of the lamp shining straight through her sheer white nightgown, he averted his eyes with a shake of his head, knowing if he looked directly at her he wouldn't be able to stop his eyes from wandering.

He was speechless even though it was critically important that he think of something to say. But the way she was looking at him made the blood drain from his head and go straight to his groin.

Why wasn't she telling him to leave?

"I..." Ben stammered, shaking his head again. Speechless.

When Edith saw Ben turn away, she looked down at herself and realized what she was wearing. Her last thoughts before falling asleep were of Ben's hands on her, his lips. She made no effort to summon the decorum that existed between them in daylight.

She sat up straighter and brushed her hair off her chest. Shadows slipped away as she turned, welcoming the lamplight to reveal her.

Ben turned back to see her staring at him. His breath labored as he saw the suggestive look on her face, the unmistakable inflection of her body language as she angled herself to be seen. His cock swelled as he actually watched the moment her veiled nipples became aroused by his gaze, creating peaks in the fabric.

He looked away again, and finally spoke, hastened by the growing urge to soak her nightgown with his tongue.

"Edith, I should go," he grunted, his voice cracking, responding to the proposition she'd made without speaking.

She threw back the covers and flung herself at him, kneeling beside him and taking his face in her hands, stopping short when her lips were just a breath from his. Then slowly, she tilted his head and timidly pressed her lips to his, as they almost imperceptibly moved in response.

She parted her lips, and kissed him again, his mouth slightly opening for her this time. And she kept kissing him, each kiss becoming bolder, more impatient.

He'd frozen with his arms open wide when she'd pounced on him, unable to move. He had been so caught off guard it seemed his mind failed to take in what was happening, that all of his focus was on feeling her soft mouth open on his, as she planted shy kisses on his lips.

When he regained the ability to take action, he took it.

He curled his arm around her waist, and the other around her neck digging his fingers into her hair, roughly nudging her mouth open with his. When his tongue thrust against hers, a moan escaped that exposed her beyond words. It made him break away to search her face.

Is this you? His eyes seemed to ask hers.

The need he found in them was disarming. His breath was ragged as he kissed her again, urgently, gripping her hair to tilt her head back. She slipped her hands around his rib cage, but when her fingers bumped into his holsters she yanked her hands back.

"Take it off!" she whined, and didn't recognize the strangled desperate voice as her own. He removed it and dropped it to the floor without hesitation. She grabbed fistfuls of his shirt front and yanked his mouth back to hers. Her tongue darted between his lips and then slid back out slowly.

He groaned as his cock strained against his trousers.

Wrapping her arms around his neck she pressed her breasts against his chest, loving how hard his body felt against hers.

"Ah," she sighed into his mouth, like she'd needed it.

She was driving him crazy. The kiss that had started as tentative was becoming frantic. He lunged forward, shoving her back on the bed and hovered over top of her, planting his knee between her thighs, and kissed her again.

She pulled the hem of his shirt from his trousers, and something about that brought sensible thoughts into his mind for the first time since he had entered this room.

"Edith," he grunted, jerking his body away from hers.

"I know," she said urgently, slipping her hands under his shirt, staring into his eyes "Me too."

When he felt her hands against his chest, he shut his eyes tight trying to remember why this was a bad idea. But then, she snuck her arms around his waist and pulled him against her. The full length of his cock pressed against her stomach and her eyes went wide in shock as her mouth fell open.

"Oh!" she said. She looked down at his trousers, and then back up at him again and said, breathless with disbelief.

"You're …"

Fuck it, he thought as his mind let go of everything but this moment, he lost himself in her kiss, and her voice, and her body. In how brazenly wanton she was. He actually shuddered as she spread her legs for him, bending a knee to brush one leg against his side. He gripped her abundant thigh in his hand and heard the muffled sound of her whimpering into his mouth.

"Oh god, Edith," he said as he trailed kisses down to her neck, then her collar bone, as his hand moved up her thigh desperate to touch her; to see if she was wet.

But not yet. First he was going to do what he'd been fantasizing about since she landed in his lap on the train. He caressed the curve of her ass before gripping it in his palm to satisfy a primal ache. She arched against him.

"Finally," he growled, molding the pliant flesh as his cock became rock hard.

Releasing his grip on her, he watched her face as he lifted the hem of her nightgown around her hips. He gave her time to protest.

She didn't.

She involuntarily tilted her hips knowing she was laid bare for him. Hoping he would undo his trousers, she caught her lip between her teeth as she looked down to gaze at the bulge. Was it even possible for it to be as big as it felt?

But he didn't.

He was determined to make her pussy soaking wet before he ever reached it. His eyes stayed locked on hers as he hooked his finger in the neckline of her nightgown.

"I thought you didn't like me," his deep voice rumbled, and he lowered his hand until he'd dragged the fabric low between her breasts.

"I think I…" she managed before her breath hitched as he buried his face between her breasts to kiss her there. She writhed beneath him as the urge to rock her hips surpassed what she could control.

He began to drag the neckline to one side and watched intently for the moment her breast would spill out.

But just when the tightly drawn fabric was about to graze past her nipple, her hand flew to her neck in a panic.

"Ben!" she shouted, yanking them both out of the moment "My necklace!" she patted at her chest hoping to find it there.

"Shit," he said under his breath as his forehead fell to the pillow beside her. He shifted his weight aside as she flew out of bed.

"When was the last time I had it..." she hissed to herself as she rummaged through her suitcase.

He laid on his back reaching one hand to tug at the crotch of his trousers, raking the other hand over his face miserably.

He didn't know if he could recover.

"Check the bed!" she shouted, turning around to face him.

"Quiet down, or someone's going to break in here and arrest me." He sat up in the bed and retrieved his holster from the floor, grumbling.

"Not the worst idea, actually. I should be in handcuffs right now. Safer for everyone."

As soon as he was sitting at the foot of the bed she jumped in and began running her hands under the sheets.

He stood and tucked his shirt back into his trousers as he crossed to the other side of the room. He shoved his hands in his pockets and leaned against the wall to wait for what he knew was coming next.

And sure enough, he saw her stiffen, and she went from frantically searching to rigid and motionless.

When she awoke, he'd been leaning over her in bed. Very close.

"Edith," he sighed.

"Oh my god," she said, staring at the pillow, her hands at her throat. When she turned to look at him his face was hard as stone.

"It was you. That's why you snuck in here," she said standing up next to the bed, staring at him stunned. And then, he saw the next emotion fall over her face. Hurt.

She lifted her hands to her cheeks as the realization landed that he snuck in here to rob her, and she woke up and practically mounted him. She wasn't sure if she was turning bright red from humiliation, or fury, or some potent, acrid mixture of both.

"Give it back," she said. It rushed forth from her voice box as a most commanding and intimidating tone, but ended with a crackle that threatened tears.

"No," he said, his voice low and sharp with finality.

"Give it back now!" she shouted.

"You're not going back down there." He pushed away from the wall and suddenly he was shouting too. "It's dangerous. You didn't see what happened to you in that tomb, Edith. You got lucky this time. Try it again and you could fall into a trance and not come back. I've seen worse happen."

"So you were planning to just dump me in Cairo? Is that what we're doing?"

"No," he scoffed, "I'm getting you into that library," he said, tossing his hand toward the horizon, as if it was understood and settled.

"What's the point, Ben? If I'm not going back to the tomb this is over. For both of us. You can't get through without me."

"Oh, yes I can. Just tell me what needs to be done. You can translate via correspondence from the hotel, like every other translator who doesn't work on site, like I said from the beginning. And if that doesn't work, hell, I can shoot the door down, and be done with it. I'm going to get you that book. I'll use a cannon if that's what it takes —"

"You can't!"

She threw herself at him in a hysterical rage, beating her fists on his chest, and the force of it knocked him back against the wall again, and her with him.

"You can't do that, you'll destroy it! You'll destroy everything!"

She was screaming nonsense and thrashing at him until he wrapped his arms around her, pinning her hands at her sides. She jerked as hard as she could to free herself, but it was no use. His arms locked her against him like steel.

When she attempted to land a kick, he bit off an expletive before lifting her in the air effortlessly. Vicious howling rage gave way to an impotent murmur when her protest sputtered out on a ragged sob. Then, only when she quieted could she could hear what he'd been saying close to her ear.

"...hey, hey, calm down, shh. Okay. It's okay."

And she did calm down, if only to try and breathe, resting her head against his chest in spite of herself.

He returned her to standing, and loosened an arm to stroke her hair for a moment before releasing a terse sigh.

"Okay," he said, and she looked up at his face. "We'll do it your way."

She shut her eyes tight and exhaled at length, her head lolling to one side in relief, before shoving his hands away from her.

"Can I have my necklace back, please?"

Her brows furrowed at him, and when she saw him glance down, her hand flew to her chest. She looked down to see she was wearing her necklace. She closed her hand around the pendant, shut her eyes and took a deep breath. She wanted to hug him. She wanted to punch him. And just a few minutes ago, she'd wanted to—

"Go to bed," he said, maybe a little too firmly. She was so disoriented with emotional whiplash, she just did what he said without an argument.

She crawled into bed, burrowed in the covers, and saw him place a chair at the foot of the bed against the door of the cabin, and sat in it.

"What are you doing?" she asked.

"Going to sleep," he said, slouching in the chair a bit.

"You can go back to your own room."

"No. We got the tickets so late I wasn't able to get the cabin next to yours. I'm all the way on the other end of the steamer, and I don't know who's on board. That's why I came here in the first place, not to…"

"Kiss me?" she interjected.

"You kissed me."

"You kissed me in a few places—"

"Good night, Edith."

"You really should go back to your cabin. Pimsley would never know. He doesn't even know we're coming."

He looked puzzled for a moment. She thought he was acting as her bodyguard because he'd been hired to. The reason he'd come to her room had nothing to do with Pimsley. He realized that while pacing in his cabin.

But she didn't need to know that.

"Well, he'd find out if something happened to you."

Edith laid in bed. She didn't know what to think. She was mad at him. She was grateful to him. She wanted to slap him. She wanted to see what he'd do, right now, if she dropped her nightgown. She wanted him to know how damp she was between her thighs.

And suddenly she remembered something he'd said in the heat of the moment.

She reached over to turn up the oil lamp a bit, and sat up slowly, this time drawing her knees to her chest.

"How did you know?"

He looked over at her, and she saw the recognition on his face before he turned away again.

"Know what?" he said flatly, clearly not in the mood for another quarrel.

"I'm going to get you that book," she repeated his own words back to him.

He gnawed on his cheek for a moment.

"That's right. That's what we're going into Pimsley's library for, isn't it?"

She crossed her arms over her knees and stared at him.

When he glanced at her again and saw the set of her jaw, he turned to face her, casually leaning his elbow at the foot of her bed. The ruse had been dropped.

"You didn't think I'd figure it out? I guess that makes sense considering you have such a low opinion of me. Well... most of the time, anyway," he said, cocking his brow suggestively.

His teasing had become bitter, and she was acutely aware that something had shifted. When the sun came up, and they were back to their normal places, they'd both know she'd been desperate for him in a weak moment.

It reconfigured the dynamic considerably.

"When?" she asked. "How long have you known?"

"I suspected from the beginning. That is, I suspected there had to be a reason you'd signed on for this dig under such specific conditions. Being so eager to take a job that would make your entire career doesn't exactly put you in a position to drive a hard bargain. And yet you had odd stipulations with no explanation for them. But I knew as soon as I met you... you don't do anything without a reason."

"When we met, you thought I was a typist."

"Oh, is that how we got off on the wrong foot?" he chuckled, amused. "I wouldn't have meant that as an insult, though you make it sound like one. Who's the chauvinist now?"

She huffed.

"Are you suggesting I should have assumed you were the foremost Egyptologist in your field the first time I set eyes on you? You're passing judgment on men with an unrealistic set of criteria, don't you think? For someone who demands to be taken seriously, you're jumping to some rather unfair conclusions."

"You're changing the subject."

He was silent for a long moment.

"It was what you said when we encountered the Medjai."

Her eyes dropped to the blanket beside her as she considered for a moment. Then remembered.

Maybe this time they'll be right.

Edith touched her hand to her lips lightly. He really never missed anything, did he. It was as if he hung on her every word.

"So… The Book of Light. The counterpart to the famous Book of Death," he recounted, his voice low and colored with disdain. He'd openly resented them going into a tomb well known to be cursed in the first place. Bidding her to acknowledge just how deeply cursed this mission was exacerbated his dread considerably.

"The book to break all curses cast from the Book of Death," she added.

He nodded slowly, as the final piece of the Edith Taylor puzzle shifted into place.

"So, as I suspected, that's what this is really all about. A librarian's quest for a book. How poetic."

She straightened against the brass rails of her cot, ready to share the whole story with him, at last.

"It's no secret that the Tomb of the Weeping Viper was never meant to be discovered. The location alone was chosen for the express purpose of keeping her whereabouts forever obscured. It's no stretch of reason to consider the possibility that a book that was never meant to be found, a book as powerful as The Book of Light, could have been buried with her," she reasoned.

"The Medjai obviously arrived at the same conclusion."

"As did you," she said.

"You want to break the curse."

"Yes. I'm just a librarian on a quest for a book, and I want to break the strongest known curse of ancient Egypt," she said, keeping her usual resolve, but shifting her shoulders in a way that belied her self doubt.

"You're not just anything."

Her eyes narrowed at him before continuing.

"Just like the Book of Death, the Book of Light must be guarded by a curse. Think about it. Why else would the grave of a criminal be protected by a curse so powerful no one has ever been able to get inside?" she looked down for a moment, shrugging almost imperceptibly again. "If disrupting the Book of Light does unleash a curse, the book itself will also hold the answers to breaking the curse. And it will also hold the incantation that will free the Weeping Viper."

"So, that's your plan."

"Yes," she said, still looking down at her linked hands.

"And you don't want it on your conscience that anyone else could get caught in the crossfire. That's why you forbid the crew members down into the tomb until you've cleared it yourself."

"It's true that if I go down for this book, I don't want to drag anyone down with me. But I also didn't want anyone to get to the book before I did… someone who might disrupt the curse and then not know how to stop it." She paused for a moment. "For the record, when the time came I didn't want you caught in the crossfire either. I would figure out a way to go down there by myself. I'll admit, I hadn't figured out how to achieve it. But I would have tried."

The notion that she thought she could get away with chasing a curse through the catacombs without him made a smile spread across his face.

"How noble," he grunted.

She had no trouble admitting to herself she was relieved to see his half-smile again, even if underestimating her was the source of his amusement at this particular moment.

"Oh? Don't think I didn't notice your convenient timing the other day. You made sure you were the first to pass through the three arches of the tomb. Just in case the rumors are true, and the first to trespass is the first victim of the curse?"

"I was also the first to attempt to open the doors."

"How early did you have to get up to achieve it?"

"You kept me waiting a while."

They shared a look that was honest, for once. How they saw each other. How the care was creeping into their hearts. Neither of them was alone. They both knew they were falling.

A sigh slowly deflated her chest, and her shoulders slumped in relief. Hearing herself say it all out loud for the first time made her feel unburdened, and fragile. Finally facing it made her acknowledge how preposterous it actually sounded. Still, there was something freeing about sharing it with him. And in that moment she saw just how right it was for him to be the person she shared it with.

"So," she tested.

"So," he responded, his tone softening considerably.

"What do you think?"

"You care what I think, Miss Taylor?"

"Well… I'm interested in hearing another perspective," she said, tipping her chin up a bit.

"I think it sounds like you've got it all figured out," he said noncommittally.

"Do you think it will work?" she whispered.

He looked her in the eye, his smile widening more. "I think we're about to have a hell of a time finding out. Because there's no way you're doing it without me."

A tingle rippled over her as she absorbed his response. She bit her lip to avoid rewarding him with a fully dazzling smile. She was still angry about the necklace.

And, yes damn it, a bit frustrated that he hadn't come to her room for a different reason.

She laid back down in her bed then, truly exhausted on every level. And yet, her stubborn brain, which had been particularly troublesome tonight, snagged on another thing he'd said… in the heat of a different moment.

Finally.

"Ben," she said, wincing, hoping he wouldn't get impatient with her chatter.

"Yes," he said softly, invitingly, swelling warmth in her chest.

"I'm sorry about … before. When you first came in here."

"I'm not."

"What do you mean?" she said, trying not to sound too eager, but also desperate to hear him say he wanted it too.

In profile, he took a deep breath and exhaled slowly. He stood up, and came to the bed, his broad frame towering over her. She felt her heart throw itself against her ribs.

"Because now I know how bad you want it."

When her jaw dropped he laughed, then blew out the oil lamp.

CHAPTER TEN

"I DIDN'T KNOW you lived on the east bank. Very posh," he said, emphasizing the British word in his American accent. They had disembarked from the steamer at a point along the corniche, a promenade along the Nile crowded with tourists. Once they'd taken a turn away from the waterfront, they continued to walk until the metropolitan bustle gave way to a greener, quieter suburban neighborhood popular with British expat families.

"It's my parents' winter home, but they never winter here. So I mostly live on my own. If I can't come back for Christmas on the continent, Elliot will come out to be with me." She tried to imbue her voice with its usual pert and erudite quality in hopes he wouldn't be able to tell something had flattened in her today.

When she woke that morning, Ben was gone. The first thought on her mind before she had even opened her eyes was of him, of all that had happened in the wee hours between night and day. Emerging from her cabin, she saw that he was standing close by on deck, but when she joined him, he behaved no differently than the day before, as if it had all been a dream. As if romantic, or perhaps merely physical, entanglements that happened to take place in the dark of night were to be kept compartmentalized from their courteous professional arrangement.

He was making bright small talk and cracking jokes to make her laugh, teasing like always. But now it left her hollow. Not the banter that hinted at the possibility of something more, that every innuendo was an opportunity to fall back or push it further. Now the playful volley was a retreat, a few steps back from the line they'd already crossed. She tried to recall how much of last night was initiated by her.

Edith, I should go.

Well. Maybe there was a limit to how strongly a man will protest a woman in a see-through nightgown. He could have been just humoring her. Perhaps she'd made more out of it than it really was as she'd fitfully fallen to sleep. Maybe he considered every woman kissable to some degree, as a rule. Maybe that's just how tall handsome men's brains worked.

I thought you didn't like me.

He had flirted with her, certainly. It always seemed like a light hearted joke, an effort to get her out of her shell, or perhaps distract her from a more pressing conversation. But she was unsure if there had been any indication he was interested. But then there was that one word.

Finally.

"A winter home, you say. I didn't realize you were …" he trailed off when he realized she was no longer walking beside him, and turned to see her standing before the gate of a massive mansion they had just passed. He had to tilt his head back to see the entirety of the place.

"… Lady Edith?" He had been about to tease her about being rich, thinking it would be an exaggeration. But when he saw the size and style of the house, he realized that she wasn't only rich, her family was a member of the aristocracy.

"I suppose, technically," she shrugged, swinging open the gate to stroll up the walkway. "Who cares about all of that, anyway?"

"I would think you'd care enough to mention it."

"Why? Now you'll only want me for my money," she said, smirking as she rang the doorbell. Something about catching him off guard had lightened her mood.

"No self respecting man would take a woman for her money," he scoffed, jogging up the steps behind her. "No one would ever take me seriously," he whined in a high pitched voice.

She realized he was mocking her and punched him in the arm, feigning shocked offense. He flinched with a yelp, and rubbed his arm as if she'd wounded him.

A petite, rotund maid opened the front door to see Edith still beaming up at Ben with laughter in her eyes. Her first reaction was perplexed at catching the tail end of their interchange. Her true reaction, a split second later, was a warm greeting.

"Edie! Back so soon?"

"Hello, Myrna. This is—"

"Let me fetch Gregson to receive your guest." Myrna waved her hands to interrupt Edith, and scurried off through a doorway beneath the grand staircase.

"She wouldn't have wanted anyone to see a maid opening the door. She's probably expecting a delivery," Edith explained, but as she turned to look up at Ben, his face radiated delight.

"Edie?" he said, as his eyebrows tipped apart in endearment. "Can I call you that?"

"No, ugh." She rolled her eyes at him, stifling another smile.

Ben tore his gaze from the curve of Edith's bemused lips to peer around the foyer of her grand house. The double doorway was directly opposite a wide staircase that split at the landing into two separate flights leading to the hallway above. It was a magnificent open room with shining tiled floors flanked by a dining room to one side, and a parlor to the other, both furnished and decorated with heirlooms typical of an old English family. A far cry from his apartment in downtown Cairo, and yet he found himself unsettled to consider Edith living here alone.

Moments later, Myrna reemerged with Gregson, a tall elderly butler, who approached to relieve Ben of his duffle bag and Edith's suitcase.

Edith began to untie her kerchief as she and Myrna ascended the stairs. Edith rushed to catch Myrna up on the party they'd be getting ready for.

"We don't have much time. We'll just have to see what's back from mending and go from there. You can dress Ben in one of Elliot's tuxes." She stopped at the landing when she heard Ben speaking to Gregson behind her.

"May I show you to your guest room, sir?" Gregson inquired.

"No, thank you, not directly. I'll just be going out."

"Where are you going?" she said, instantly cursing herself for prying and how eager it would seem. Just because they'd been together all waking (and precious few sleeping) moments of the past few days didn't mean she had any right to keep track of his whereabouts.

"I need to run a few errands. I won't need as much time getting ready, since you'll be the one using your feminine wiles to get me out of jail tonight."

Gregson and Myrna instantly shared a wide eyed glance, and then looked to Edith. Edith's eyes darted between them.

"I was only joking," Ben said, rocking back on his heels and pulling an awkward apologetic face in Edith's direction.

"He's American," Edith whispered to them with a knowing look. Gregson and Myrna eased instantly in a collective sigh of relief.

"Very good, sir. Shall I arrange the car?"

"No, thank you. I won't be back for lunch," Ben said with his eyes on Edith as she ran up the stairs. He waited until she was out of sight before turning to walk out the door.

Ben turned the corner to get back to his own part of town. He'd put such an effort into acting natural for Edith, his face crumpled into a scowl the moment he'd left her street.

He had noticed something was off with her this morning. He assumed part of it must have been that she was tired. She had barely fallen asleep when he came into her room in the dead of night, and then… well the rest was history.

It was just as he knew it would be. When he saw her this morning, not only did he see the straight-laced librarian who was too adorable for words, but he also saw her sleepy eyes and her creamy nightgown. He saw the lips swollen from his rough kisses, he saw her shapeless top and knew it concealed the buxom chest she'd pressed against him, and sighed. He saw the face of the girl who believed he had come to her room to take her to bed, and she had wanted him to.

He sucked a breath into his tightening lungs as he remembered it now. Part of him was pained to know how close he'd come to having her. But the bigger part of him, the part that mattered, wouldn't have wanted it to happen that way, after he'd come into her room uninvited.

He was relieved that it came to a stop when it did, even though the interruption was a source of pain and humiliation for her. She'd felt foolish for having thrown herself at him after learning he'd lifted her necklace. But it came nowhere near how rotten it made him feel for nearly ravaging her directly after stealing her most prized possession, knowing that she wouldn't be so willing if she had known.

Worse yet, if she hadn't realized the pendant was no longer around her neck, things would have gone much further.

Rehashing his plans from the night before made him feel like such a fool. Did he actually believe she'd willingly relinquish her place on the expedition? He wasn't thinking. All he knew was that he couldn't bear the idea of her going back down there.

He thought he'd held his breath the entire time she was under the spell of that tomb.

In his time robbing the graves of the ancient and cursed, he'd seen men's souls sucked from their bodies. A bright young archeologist on his first dig had been eaten alive by a swarm of scarabs that somehow survived in a sealed tomb for three thousand years. A statue that managed to stand the test of time suddenly crumbled and crushed another excavator for no reason supported by the laws of physics…and then there was the curse of King Tut. Over the years, almost every person on that dig had died, all in mysterious ways.

All he was thinking last night was that the necklace was her only way back into the tomb, and if he took it, she couldn't go back. She'd be safe. He was already planning on spending the night outside her room, unable to be sure she was safe in her cabin alone. He'd waited until she was asleep because, for some reason, she resented the notion that she needed protecting. That made him smile, a little.

As it turns out, he was doing a terrible job as her bodyguard. All she had to do was bat her pretty eyelashes and he folded like a house of cards. There's no telling what he would agree to when she was standing in front of him wearing nothing but a wisp of fabric so sheer it was almost nonexistent.

He had concluded, as she slept, to not make any assumptions about how she had behaved last night, and to refrain from assigning meaning to it. He'd just caught her in a vulnerable moment. In the light of day, she might be embarrassed, and wouldn't necessarily stand by an impulse she acted on while half asleep. Erring on the side of caution, he wouldn't mention what happened last night unless she did.

It was the gentlemanly thing to do, he thought, as he turned to enter the barber shop.

By the time Edith had bathed, eaten lunch, told Myrna absolutely everything that had happened since they'd packed her suitcase together, and gone through the excruciating process of getting ready for a formal gala, including brushing out and styling her unruly curls, there was only time to eat dinner standing up in the kitchen. Her father would likely blow a gasket if he saw the way she ran the house when they weren't there, but she couldn't be bothered with a full dinner service. Especially when she found out Ben hadn't come back.

She finished her meal and folded a dainty napkin to dab at the corners of her mouth primly before hiking her dress up around her thighs and scrambling up the stairs. Upon reaching the landing, she righted her dress and walked the hallway to the front foyer of the house where they'd arrived this morning. She hoped she wouldn't have to wait too long for Ben once she'd gotten her overcoat on.

But when she rounded the corner beside the grand staircase, he was already there, looking up the stairs to the exact spot he'd last seen her. He withdrew his pocket watch but when he looked down to glance at it, she caught his eye and he did a double take.

It was funny, she thought to herself. She was jealous thinking about him schmoozing with other girls at this party. Now she realized, dumbfounded, she'd imagined him going in his khaki work uniform, covered in dust. It's true, that's the only way she knew him to look since they'd met, but still there was no logic to her assuming he'd go to a ball looking like that. It struck her as comical that she had been green with envy before she even knew he would look this good.

He was absolutely gorgeous.

His hair was neatly combed, and seemed shorter and more tidy than it had been when last she saw him. He was clean shaven and it emphasized his jaw showing his face to be almost impossibly handsome. His tux was sharp and fit him perfectly, which was inexplicable for, as far as she knew, he had been gone all day. She knew that because she'd wondered where he was with more frequency than she cared to admit. But since he'd arrived just now, there would have been no time for him to be fitted for a tux from Elliot's wardrobe.

It dawned on her, as she appraised him now, how strange it was that they'd never met before. Of course, Ben wouldn't have moved in the same social circles as she did. But they both lived in Cairo, and if he'd been working for Pimsley for years, they were bound to have other mutual acquaintances. She'd never been to one of Pimsley's balls before, but she was certain she'd know most of the attendees there.

Wherever he'd been, one thing was for certain. If she'd ever seen Ben before, she never would have forgotten it. They'd met in a strange, contrived ambush in Pimsley's office, where they were almost inevitably positioned to be set against each other. But if she met Ben at a party, like this, she would have fallen for him in a heartbeat.

But then… heaven help her… he smiled. She thought her knees might give out. Suddenly she was desperate to see him covered in dirt and stubble and wearing beat up cargo pants. It was the only reason she stood a chance at maintaining her opinion of him as an adversary in the first place. How would she concentrate on their top secret mission with him looking like this? Especially after last night.

Ben put his pocket watch back in his waistcoat, having forgotten to check the time. Edith looked like a movie star. Her hair fell dramatically to one side in big, soft waves. She wore a golden satin gown that made her olive skin glow and glided luxuriously over her generous curves. The way it hugged her body seemed even more revealing than what she barely wore to bed. Never was the drastic contrast between her chest, waist, and hips on display like this. Her face was accentuated with shadows and light, and her lips were the deep color of wine.

When he was able to tear his eyes away from her dress, it was the look on her face that destroyed him most of all. She was happy to see him. She seemed smug to be responsible for the look on his face.

Edith's smile widened when she saw Ben's mouth working to form a greeting of some kind, opening to speak, and stopping short. Finally surrendering to simply clear his throat.

When Edith heard Gregson approach from behind her, she realized she and Ben had just been standing there staring at each other.

"Lady Edith, the car is ready. You must be going if you're to be received on time. I have your overcoat."

When Edith turned to shrug on her jacket, Ben saw that her dress was backless and looked to the ceiling for mercy while his jaw tightened until he thought it might crack. When Gregson opened the door for them, she turned to face him again, closer this time.

"Ready?" she said, fluttering her lashes.

"You're gorgeous," he said, almost stern, when he was finally able to form words. He was as serious as she'd ever seen him. Not a trace of teasing in sight.

He gestured out the door, waiting for her to proceed before following behind her. He nodded at Gregson before following her out. As soon as they were in the car, Gregson's face softened from his professional grimace.

"What a nice sort of chap for Edie," he said wistfully, before shutting the door.

The car ride was short, as the stately home of Ronald Pimsley was in a nearby neighborhood. But Myrna and Gregson would have detested the idea of letting Edith walk in these shoes.

In the close quarters, in the darkness of the back seat with street lights whizzing past, she wished she could be even closer to Ben. She wanted to scoot over in her seat. It was the kind of tiny gesture that speaks for you without words; but more importantly, his reaction would inform her of what she was dying to know.

"Do you remember the plan?" Ben asked her. He'd been looking out the window unable to stop thinking of reaching out for her hand but unsure if he should. He was determined to make himself wait until she indicated what she wanted. As of now, she was sitting as far as she possibly could on the other side of the car. He had decided the only way to distract himself from thoughts of touching her was to talk to her. But then she turned to look at him and he remembered why he had thought it was a good idea to stare out the window in the first place.

"It's not that hard to remember. Mingle until everyone gets drunk, then slip into the library."

"You'll have to follow my lead on this one. I didn't like this idea from the beginning, but I'll get you where you need to go… if you do exactly as I say."

He saw her squirm in her seat slightly before agreeing. It was against her nature, and he knew it. Considering what he'd gleaned about her past as a woman in academia and archaeology, he could certainly see why she was so reluctant to surrender any small measure of control or autonomy. But he was the only person who could get her what she wanted in every step of this pursuit, so she would have to let him help her.

He dropped his voice so the driver might not hear.

"I know, technically, we just met…" he stammered uncharacteristically, "but I hope you've seen enough to know you can trust me."

It was at that moment that they pulled up to Pimsley's house and the car came to a stop. Once the driver had gotten out of the car, Edith leaned in to Ben, closing the short yet agonizing distance that had been between them for the length of the car ride.

"I do trust you," the words themselves hit Ben like a ton of bricks. But the way she was looking at him, the way she said it, changed the mood of the conversation and engaged a magnetism between them.

Maybe she was emboldened by the moment of privacy. Maybe she wanted him more than she cared about her pride. Maybe she blurted it out because the driver would be opening her door in a second.

"... but I don't believe I have seen enough of you. Yet."

It was a confession. It was permission. It was a plea. She wasn't half asleep, or half naked, or half drunk. Ben felt the final barrier of his restraint drop in the moment he knew for sure the feelings were mutual.

Tension crackled between them as they leaned into each other with a shared understanding of where they were headed, of what was between them. Just as he reached for her, the driver opened the door. Ben looked on, awestruck, as Edith rose from the car and sailed through the gates on the night air before he followed after her.

The clicking of her heels on the sidewalk was always a sound that ushered in an exciting evening ahead. But the unspoken promise she'd just made with Ben was an anticipation like nothing she'd ever felt. She was giddy with the knowledge that she'd be getting back into that car with him tonight. Her body was humming with expectancy. The current surged when she felt his hand rest low on the back of her coat as he took his place walking beside her. The conversation she'd initiated was far from over. It was only beginning.

A footman was ready to help Edith out of her coat, but Ben stepped in his way. His arms came around her slowly to clutch the lapels of her overcoat. She didn't know if she'd imagined it, or if his knuckles really brushed against her breasts as he parted the coat and slipped it off her shoulders.

He handed the coat to the footman without taking his eyes off her, and when she turned around he didn't even try to hide that his eyes had been fixed on her ass before he looked up at her. He smiled, but his gaze was deadly.

Regret creeped in over this game she had instigated.

She'd been excited knowing that her words would be sizzling between them throughout this formal gala, that in a room full of stuffy statesmen and socialites, there would be something underneath. Something only they knew.

She should have known he would take it as a challenge, and of course, he was going to tease her. He was going to make tonight just as hard to get through for her as it would be for him.

Now as he put his hand on her back it was against her bare skin, and she was so shamelessly eager for his touch it sent goose-bumps up her spine. Breathless and blushing, she looked up at him. He watched her mouth as she wet her lips. At his height, he could easily see down the front of her dress and watched as her breasts rose and fell with her quickened breath. His eyes lingered there so deliberately that it felt like a caress. His hand slid lower on her back—

"Edie!"

The fire in her veins turned to ice in an instant.

The jovial voice was unmistakable and she turned to see that, as she suspected, George Fletcher was coming toward them with a group of his friends. He was wearing the tux she'd seen so many times before, not a thread out of place. Pomade coiffed his hair, a blonde that matched his porcelain complexion, blotched from a few fingers of brandy. It wasn't the drink that made his large mouth grin amiably; he was bred to thrive in social settings. George was handsome in a British way, and slight among men of average height, but still taller than Edith. Convenient in every way.

She took a strategic step forward, in an effort to look like she was coming toward George, but really attempting to establish a more appropriate distance between herself and Ben.

Ben silently dropped his hand from her back.

"George, hello," she said, trying to sound bright, but her throat felt squeezed. He gave her a brief, smacking kiss on the mouth and Edith could feel a wave of scarlet shame rising from her neckline to her hairline.

"Darling, I had no idea you'd be here or I would have sent the car. How naughty of you to come alone, and looking absolutely delicious too," he said as he drew her hand out to let his eyes rove over her performatively.

Oh dear lord, Edith thought.

She was so assaulted by embarrassment and shock her mind had gone totally blank. All she knew was that she couldn't see Ben. He was the whole step she'd taken behind her now, and it would be unseemly for her to whirl around to gauge his reaction, and anyway, she didn't need to. He was probably livid. And rightfully so.

"Miss Taylor!" Robert Pimsley was now hurrying over, alerted by George's booming greeting. "Ben," he continued, shaking Ben's hand. "What are you two doing in town, you've only just left? And Ben never comes to my parties!"

"Edith had to consult with a colleague in town regarding her findings and it couldn't wait. While we're here, she didn't want to miss an opportunity to spend time with friends."

His words were direct as an arrow and made her squirm. She was in the wrong somehow, but couldn't quite figure out why. All she knew was that Ben wouldn't have been expecting... whatever was happening right now.

"Yes," Pimsley said excitedly, making a broad gesture with his hand. "I've just been telling George about Miss Taylor's great success on her first day at the site in Argo. You'd better hurry back tomorrow or you'll be so bogged down with reporters you won't make another lick of progress for a month!"

"Yes, darling. Very well done, indeed. You must be so delighted with your little adventure. Such good fun." George was slurring his words already. "Imagine our girl surpassing what dozens of men have tried to do, and on her very first try." He turned back to his friends and they all guffawed in genuine amusement. It would never occur to George that his words were incredibly condescending. He'd meant it as a compliment.

"And who's this very tall fellow?" George said with a bleary eyed smile.

"I'm Edith's bodyguard," Ben said, stepping forward into Edith's view and giving George a handshake that seemed a bit too firm, clapping him on the shoulder with his other hand.

"This is Benjamin Brooks, one of my best men. He's supervising the crew on Miss Taylor's expedition. Seeing that she doesn't get into too much trouble."

Edith fumed so deeply she wondered if you could get a third degree burn from inside your own body. The embers of contempt she felt for constantly being surrounded by men who belittled her was now accompanied by an even more wretched feeling… she couldn't bring herself to look at Ben.

"Ben, this is George Fletcher," Pimsley continued.

"Edith's fiance," George said, beaming up at Ben. His face was aglow with the pleasantries of a good party and a stiff drink, and he had no idea the impact of what he'd just said.

She couldn't help it now, and actually cringed, squeezing her eyes shut.

"Benjamin Brooks, I'm sure I've heard of you," George said, squinting.

"Yes, Ben was at Oxford," Pimsley offered.

Her eyes went wide and her mouth hung agape as she dropped propriety and now whirled to see Ben's face. Caught in a wince, the muscles of his jaw bunched with tension around a belabored exhale, before lifting his gaze to search her face.

CHAPTER ELEVEN

THEY WERE FINALLY released from the disastrous exchange when a friend of George's announced it was time for billiards and cigars, and Pimsley spotted another guest he hadn't yet greeted. Ben stalked away from Edith toward a table of champagne next to the bar. The satin column of her dress confined her legs to tiny steps as she shuffled hastily behind him.

Ben. The petty thief. The charming scoundrel. The Oxford graduate. She'd been such a fool, on so many levels, she didn't know how she'd ever recover her signature pomp.

"I'll take a suffering bastard, neat," he growled to the bartender. He downed a glass of champagne while he waited. He was looking out over the crowd of people dancing to the music of the live band. Edith wasn't sure if he knew she was standing there. She wondered if he'd ever acknowledge her existence again.

"I… I had no idea he'd be here."

"Your fiance?" Ben answered sharply, still not looking at her.

"George? Don't be silly, he isn't my fiance..." she laughed it off, but she didn't sound casual, she sounded nervous. "He was just joking... because he's asked me a few times."

Ben's eyes flashed hotter than a solar flare. He leaned down with one elbow on the bar bringing him closer to eye level with her. He looked directly into her eyes now.

"Your lover, then," he said. He wasn't asking. She began to flush again, and she felt her cheeks burn.

"Why are you so angry," she shrugged, and even as she said it she knew it was a pitiful attempt to turn the tables. But her own anger and frustration was a natural side effect of how humiliated she felt. Not only for the position she was suddenly thrust into, (she would figure out how exactly it was her own fault later) but also for the way that Pimsley and George had talked about her in front of Ben. Patronizing her like a little girl playing in the dirt with a gardening spade.

It was painfully ordinary, it happened every day... why did it seem like such a blow for it to happen in front of Ben? Probably because Ben was the only man she'd ever met that didn't treat her that way.

"Why should I be mad?" he said, retrieving his drink from the bartender and taking it like a shot. "Let's dance," he said, slipping his hand around her waist and ushering her onto the dance floor.

Ben's great strides wove through the couples gliding around the dance floor, as Edith's heels rushed madly to keep up. He slid his hand up her side and along her arm to hold her hand out, and pressed her fully against him with his other hand against her back. Her wide almond eyes looked deeply into his, an apology brimming within them, as her free hand traveled very deliberately.

She pressed her palm against his chest as he swung her around the dance floor in a waltz, let it drift up to his cheek and rest there for a moment before curling her fingers around the back of his neck. She'd seen him soften slightly, his eyes closing for a moment, as if distracted by her touch, but it hadn't been as effective as she hoped.

She could caress his cheek or run her fingers through his hair as he towered over her, but he was commanding every move they made. Pressing her firmly against him but standing at his full height, there was still a distance between them. Desperately she wished for him to lean down closer, but it would all be on his terms. Tonight was actually supposed to be on his terms, as she'd already agreed to. Maybe the best way to bring him back to her was to give him the satisfaction of her surrender.

"Why didn't you tell me about Oxford?" her hushed tone was calm, and there was no challenge or her signature smug attitude within it. Vulnerable, she stared up at him deliberately with a pliant, hopeful expression. Though she already knew the answer.

"Well, between you biting my head off or ripping my shirt off, I've hardly had the chance."

She exhaled curtly and looked away. Truly, she'd earned every jab he'd ever doled out, and she never felt it more keenly than in this moment.

"I guess I deserved that," she said, making an earnest effort to remain repentant.

His chuckle was sinister.

"Oh, I can't wait to give you what you deserve."

She went to respond, but was cut off before she got a word out.

"The thing is, I'm single," he continued, "I actually don't have to explain myself to anyone. You on the other hand…" Now he was finally pulling her in closer, moving his lips a degree closer to her ear, dropping his voice to a lower volume she'd come to anticipate. For some reason now, though, she was sure she wouldn't like what he'd have to say.

"You are in a tricky position. You'll either have to tell old George you asked me into your bed last night… Or lie."

Asked was a charitable way to describe it, she thought.

She had never made a habit out of apologies. Being defensive was her default; too loath to lose any ground, on any front. Even to Ben. Even on this.

"You sound jealous, Ben," she said coolly, setting her jaw.

"Jealous of what?" he said, and he was close to her ear now, a position that could only be achieved due to her high heels. He began to move his hand lower on her back.

"Jealous of hearing him call you Edie?" It squeezed her heart to hear that's what bothered him.

"Jealous that he's probably seen you in this dress before I did? Jealous of what else he knows about you that I don't, because I'm jealous he's had more of your time than I ever will?"

His hand was still inching lower down her back, his palm against the bare skin there, as he guided her effortlessly in time with the music, as skilled and smooth at dancing a waltz as he was with everything else. She was becoming intoxicated by him. His body was so close. His words were so candid. It made her eyes prickle to think of what this dance could have been if they hadn't run into George.

"Are you?" she said on a shaky breath.

"Yes," he said softly, and she shut her eyes tight at the effect it had on her to hear it.

He held her close, and his cheek was pressed to hers now. The very tips of his fingers slipping beneath the fabric of her dress. Suddenly all she could think about was kissing his neck and working to undo his tie. She wished they were alone.

"Do you let him fuck you?" His voice was hard and cold as the limestone of the tomb. She gasped and pulled away as a reaction to his words flared inside of her. Shame and also… something else. Something deep that riled within her when she heard nasty words come out of his mouth. And it was familiar. She'd felt it last night.

She pulled away from him, but he held her tighter.

"Honestly Ben, that's none of your…" pulling away and seeing his face had stopped her from finishing that lie. His eyes were dangerous. She had wanted to sound just as hard and cold as he had, but even to herself she sounded like a brat throwing a fit. But more than that, she knew if she told him it was none of his business, Ben would make it true. It would be none of his business. And she couldn't bear it.

"We've been seeing each other casually for years," she said, averting her gaze. It turned out she couldn't bring herself to look him in the eye.

And suddenly he was loosening his grip on her, on her hand, on her back, and everywhere.

"Really, a guy like that, huh?" he scoffed, straightening, pulling away from her cheek.

His voice was suddenly calm. A breath could fit between their bodies for the first time since he'd yanked her onto the dance floor.

"Why, because he doesn't make a living as a petty thief? Are you under the impression that it's more masculine?" It was such a low blow she couldn't believe she'd said it, but she was lashing out viciously. Really, she felt she might start to cry, which would be an English crisis.

But it didn't phase him. He took it in stride, as if she hadn't said it at all.

"I just wouldn't think he's your type."

"Oh, what do you care, Ben. It's not like I'm your type."

"No?" he said, one side of his mouth curving slightly.

"You're type is more like Ingrid, wouldn't you say?"

He paused looking genuinely confused for a moment, then a light of recognition washed over his face.

"Who, Toots? Oh, she's a hell of a good time. She'll take your shirt in poker." He looked her up and down that way he did, with a lascivious look on his face. "I'd pay to see that. We should set it up next time we're all in town."

Her heart shattered. It was the first time he'd ever suggested they'd go their separate ways when it was all over.

She pushed away from him, but just then he used the protest to his advantage and spun her in a dramatic twirl. And he was smiling again, showing no trace of anger or resentment. She thought it was what she wanted, to see him back to his usual self. Unfortunately, she realized it was an indicator that all of this meant nothing to him. At least when he was furious it was proof he felt something for her. Maybe he'd already decided to make it none of his business.

"She's just a friend, Edith," he said, pulling her back into his arms casually.

She didn't bother to hope it might be a good sign that he was trying to reassure her. Rather, she assumed he was making it known how little he attached himself to women.

"Well, maybe you don't have a type. Maybe you just flirt with every woman… the way you flirt with me."

"And your type appears to be… George." He very clearly had trouble bringing himself to say it.

"And that shocks you because he's upper crust rather than … a rugged gun toting brute? You can't imagine me dating someone from my own limited social circle abroad who shares a common background."

She was still dragging out her regular insults ignoring that the longer she knew him, the more it seemed like Ben actually was from her social circle sharing a common background. He just didn't look like it, or act like it.

"I didn't think you'd be in a relationship with a man who didn't take you seriously. I thought you had more self respect."

She felt the wind knocked out of her lungs like he'd struck her across the face. For all the time they'd spent shooting barbs at each other, this one cut deep. Stopped dead in her tracks, she was frozen, unable to take another step. Stunned. He released her and stepped back. He bowed slightly at the waist, with a lock of hair falling against his forehead.

The music had stopped.

Ben grimaced when he saw the hurt on her face. He hadn't wanted to be so harsh, but he couldn't stop himself. He desperately wanted to come across as aloof as possible. She didn't owe him anything, after all. Why should she? Because he forced himself into her room last night, and groped the fiance of another man?

Edith was right. He had no right to care. He had no business touching her in the first place, no matter how bad he wanted to. When this was all over, she'd go back to her glittering balls and noble palaces, and he'd move forward with the reason he was doing this dig at all. Or, all of the reasons he'd forgotten once he met her.

He needed to get out of here for any hope of recovering from the whiplash he'd suffered.

From last night alone, he couldn't be certain. It might have been a fluke. And he wouldn't take Edith unless he was absolutely sure.

But in the car, she'd said it.

One moment he was staring at her ass beneath a painfully flimsy swatch of satin, knowing later this evening it would be his.

In his hands. The next thing he knew he was being introduced to her fiance of several years, seeing a look on her face like she couldn't believe she'd been caught walking in with Ben. Maybe the moment he went blind with rage was the moment he realized she was just as likely to walk out of here with George tonight.

It had been the shock of his life last night when the haughty librarian threw herself at him. Until then, he'd wondered if she'd ever come out of her shell, but boy when she did, she came all the way out.

Then, while the tension between them grew too dizzying to keep up with, there it was, another curveball, hurtling at him. Now he wasn't so sure he really knew anything about her. Hell, she could go home with someone else entirely. She certainly seemed to be keeping her options wide open.

For some reason she'd stopped herself from saying it, but it truly was none of his business. She was a modern woman. He'd been warned. Yet, here he was berating her for it.

All nuance aside, he knew one thing for sure. She wanted him to fuck her tonight. She wanted it bad enough to get on her knees and beg for it, and he knew it. She knew that he knew it.

Taking that into consideration, she did owe him answers about her relationship status. He should know if being with him meant she was betraying someone else. Suddenly he wondered why it hadn't occurred to him before. Of course Edith Taylor was engaged. She was magnificent.

Desperate to escape, he looked around the room to see it was sufficiently sloshed.

"Come on boss, let's get back to work." He tucked his hand into her elbow and discreetly drew her out of the ballroom. Once they were passing through the foyer, Ben had dropped her arm but he was still leading her as if by an invisible leash.

It wasn't just because she'd agreed to do things his way this night, but it also felt very natural. His body language, his commanding presence, and air of his nature exuded confidence. All of those reasons were observable only because of the true reason she was sure Ben knew exactly what he was doing. What she'd said in the car just before they got here. She did trust him. What was too heartbreaking to face in this moment of precarity was that she'd just watched him realize he couldn't trust her.

As they wove out of the foyer and turned down a dark hallway, Edith chided herself once again for getting embroiled in emotions when she should actually be focused on the very consequential moment she was currently navigating. Her thoughts took a welcome reprieve and turned to the task at hand: breaking into Pimsley's library.

She tried to focus on her determination, as Ben certainly was. It was clear that he knew the layout of Pimsley's house, though Pimsley had just mentioned earlier that Ben never came to his parties. She'd lost count of how many turns they'd made.

Pimsley's house was more robustly decorated with replicas of ancient Egyptian artifacts than any house she'd ever seen, and certainly breaking with the norms of great British houses. Every space and surface and wall was adorned, not quite cluttered, but certainly not leaving many places for the eye to rest. Now that they were in the dimly lit hallway there were so many treasures whizzing by her she scarcely had time to react to the rarity of all of them. She stopped short when one such treasure caught her eye.

"Is this a replica of the Oxyrhynchus Papyri?" She rose to her tiptoes to examine it.

"Edith!" he barked in a stage whisper, which sent her racing after him once more.

Finally, they reached a side door to the exterior, and silently slipped out. They stood outside in the heat and darkness of the evening, pausing to take a breath having achieved their first objective of sneaking out. Ben grabbed her hand and turned to leave.

Edith grabbed Ben's arm before they continued into the landscaping.

"Wait!" she whispered, and gripped his bicep as she removed her heels. He was resisting the urge to find it endearing, but couldn't help but smirk when she shrank a few inches.

Once she was standing in her stocking feet, her shoes dangling from her hand at her side, he carried on leading the way around the perimeter of the house. Out of the corner of his eye, he saw that she was sauntering as she usually did, like she had to mail an urgent letter.

"Damn it, Edith. Come here, get down close to the wall. It's not a parade."

She huffed and fell into step behind him, trying to be more inconspicuous. Or at least as inconspicuous as one could be in a floor length metallic satin evening gown.

"Where are we going?"

"We have to take a way that won't be watched. All of the routes to the library from inside the house will be guarded, assuming everyone is in the ballroom."

They took an exterior stairway that would have been for maintenance workers and Ben withdrew a switchblade from his pocket. He flicked it open and knelt down to pick at the lock on the door.

As she laid her back flat against the wall, she thought wonders may never cease, there was no limit to the volume of weaponry he could have stowed on his person at any moment. Waiting, she heard the sounds of lightly scraping metal, and her own deep breaths in the still of the night. Then she heard a click. Ben opened the door until it was just ajar, and entered partially to see the coast was clear before motioning for Edith to follow him.

Once they were inside the servants' quarters, they had access to the house with no further barriers. The staff would be occupied by tending to the party, and the rest of Pimsley's private quarters would be locked to the outside, off limits to everyone.

The tiled, echoing hallway of the servants' quarters ended with double doors, where the lush carpeted hallway of Pimsley's private wing of the house began. They crossed the long carpeted gallery, passing the Pimsley crest, and centuries old family portraits, finally ending at another set of large intricately carved double doors.

He opened one of them just enough to push Edith in, but just as she reached for the light switch, his hand covered hers intercepting it. He flattened his back against the door that remained closed and lifted the lapel of his tuxedo to reveal his gun holster. But in the sheath for one of his ever present pistols was a flashlight he withdrew and handed to her.

"You left one of your guns at home? For me?" she whispered coyly.

"Yeah, yeah, just get to it," he snapped gruffly.

"Wait, where are you going?"

"I'm just going to stand watch," he said before closing the door behind her.

"Wait!" she said, but he was already gone. She felt unsettled that everything had become an awkward mess so quickly, and seemingly without time to clear anything up.

By the time she drew her first breath inside the library, everything that transpired between her and Ben got dropped at the door. When the aroma of old books hit her, she looked around with her mouth agape.

Moonlight from the wall of windows opposite her gleamed off of rows and rows of two story bookcases. The dark intricately carved woodwork ran up the walls, past the second floor balcony, to frame the coffered ceiling. She set the flashlight on a desk near the entrance, and opened her evening bag to withdraw and don her glasses. As she tied her hair with the scarf she continued to marvel in awe at the dreamy masterpiece of a library.

She stalked long rows of shelves, back and forth, taking in the volumes that constituted Pimsley's private library, different thoughts whizzing through her brain triggered by the titles she saw. Surely she could be locked in this room for a year and not mind it.

A long while later when she'd found several reference books from the time period she needed on the second floor, she used the rolling ladder to pull them out and began searching the table of contents for the right information. In the lull of the mundane activity, her mind wandered far enough that waves of guilt were able to penetrate her concentration.

It was hard for her to own up to the notion that she'd been deceitful when this situation had never occurred to her before. Warning Ben that at some point today they might run into George probably would have been a good idea. There was no way around the fact that George being at this party was extremely predictable. But that's assuming that she thought of him at all… the truth was she hadn't.

It sounded horrible, but it was true. Since she'd met Ben, he'd taken up all the space her brain had for men, and then spilled over into all the other areas as well. She couldn't think of what she wanted for breakfast without being bombarded with thoughts of what Ben looked like popping a date into his mouth.

Anyway, how could she bring it up without presuming something that she wasn't sure of until… well, she still wasn't sure, if she was being honest. It would have been presumptuous to tell Ben about George when as recently as yesterday they could be described as contentious professional rivals.

But then there was that one word. That word that passed through his lips as he bit her neck, and slipped his hand up her skirt.

Finally.

It suggested he must have wanted more so badly that it made the brief span of a few days feel like an agonizing wait. In that case, if she knew they both wanted the same thing… what should she have said about George?

As an extremely intelligent and capable woman she was disturbed by how much trouble she was having making heads or tails of what amounted to some sort of ambiguous social misstep. If she removed her bias of wanting to be right, she had to admit it was true that if she had never gotten the opportunity to work on the Argo project, she probably would have gone to this party with George. How could she explain that she'd forgotten he existed to either of them.

That's it! She thought as she found the volumes she needed while flipping through the pages of the reference book, and everything else faded to the background again.

CHAPTER TWELVE

SHE HADN'T THE foggiest idea how long she had been searching the reference books by the time she heard the door lightly click, and the sound of Ben's footfall come up the stairs to the second level of the library. She was sprawled on the floor surrounded by books, her hair tied up haphazardly with a scarf and her glasses perched precariously low on the bridge of her nose. She was just finishing a page when he stood before her. He was so tall, especially with her sitting on the floor, she had to practically look to the ceiling to meet his eye.

"How's it going?" he said. There was something light and mischievous in his eyes, but his face was still stoney as before. Maybe he was softened by the way the neckline of her gown fell when she was leaning over a pile of books.

"I found the volumes I need, now it's just a matter of study until I can find the answers and reach a conclusion." She switched off the flashlight she'd been using to search the two open log books side by side, leaving them in the darkness bathed in the glow of the moon.

He turned silently and stalked away to look out a window at the other end of the balcony.

"Ben," she said as he seemed to search for something outside on the street below them.

He turned back to her, the tightness in his face replaced with curiosity. She glanced down to the double doors, where she'd seen he barricaded them in with a fire iron.

"I don't know if I'll be able to find it before we're caught," she whispered.

"We won't get caught, you know these things run into the wee hours of the morning. And all of the servants will be tending to the party."

"Still, it could take hours more, and I don't even know how long I've searched already. Not to mention, we'll have to make an appearance back before too long."

"You found the reference books you need?"

"Yes."

"How many are there?"

"Just these two. Births and deaths from the right time period."

Edith gathered the discarded log books she wouldn't be needing as Ben spoke, only leaving out the two that held the key to the next door.

"Okay," he said, rubbing his jaw, the rough shadow already growing in there. "We'll take these two, and you can bring them back to your house. We can hide them there until I can return them to the collection."

"What if he notices they're missing?" She stood, propelled by her distaste for wrongdoing, and soothed herself by replacing the books she didn't need back on their place on the shelf.

"Pimsley is a collector, not a student of Egyptology. For him the thrill is in possession, not appreciation."

Edith glanced at the place left where the two reference books she needed ought to be, their brethren slumped in their absence. When she began to gnaw on her lip, Ben read her expression. As he closed the gap by pushing the book ends until they all stood straight as soldiers, his voice broke into her worried thoughts.

"I will return these books before Pimsley knows they're missing. It won't be traced back to you, I promise."

Edith remembered the oath she'd made in the car before the night had taken a turn for the worse. She would trust him.

"Well, alright I suppose."

He nodded curtly and looked back out the window.

"You are an excellent second in command, after all."

When he ignored her attempt at humor, she realized he hadn't said anything sarcastic since he walked in. Rather than checking if he had a fever, she decided to meet the tension head on.

"I suppose charity galas make you terribly grumpy?" she said.

"I never wanted to come," he reminded her as he shrugged.

"Aren't you pleased I found what I'm looking for?"

"A jackhammer would have done the trick, and with no threat of jail time."

She made a strangled noise of disbelief in protest and whipped off her glasses.

"Why do you always resort to destruction of historical sites rather than the utilization of historical knowledge?" she quipped.

He turned around to look at her blandly with his hands in his pockets. Leaning back against the bookshelf he crossed one leg over the other lazily. She narrowed her eyes and affirmed her statement.

"I don't care if it's faster, or easier. Preservation is more important than efficiency."

"Okay," he shrugged, lifting his eyebrows.

"Yes… well," she trailed off.

She turned away with a huff. Then she swung back around and went to speak again when he stopped her.

"You just can't stand that I won't let you draw me into a spat, can you?" he said, pushing off of the bookshelf and moving toward her, a chilling calm in his voice.

"Don't be absurd, I'm simply stating the fact that—"

"Why?" he said, moving closer.

"Because artifacts are to be—"

"Why didn't you say something?" he said, stopping a step away from her.

She opened her mouth and then when she realized what they were actually talking about she closed it again. Then came back at him with a slightly different angle that discreetly evaded his question.

"Say what exactly? Nice to meet you Mr. Brooks, if at any point in this expedition I try to mount you while half naked, you should know that there's a man I've gone to parties with?"

Ben blew out a breath and smoothed his tie, looking away thoughtfully.

"Well, I was thinking something more like, Ben," he said, his eyes sharpening. "Since I've managed to find the time to tell you all about my hopes and dreams, my brother's career, my parents' winter home, and the contraception methods of the ancient Egyptians…"

Edith closed her eyes and drew in a deep breath.

Ben advanced a step closer.

"…and despite what happened last night," he said in a lower voice, as his gaze traveled down her body suggestively, "…I should mention that you'll be seeing me kiss my fiance later this evening."

"I didn't kiss him, he kissed me."

He barked a dry laugh, and she knew how petty that sounded. She dropped her haughtiness and decided to try coming clean.

"I want to tell you, but… it sounds bad."

"It can't possibly sound worse than it did in the ballroom," he scoffed.

"I don't owe George anything, it's casual."

"George," he spat the name, "the man you've been sleeping with for years who just introduced himself as your fiance?"

"Well, if you must know, George is handy for parties like this, and when people ask me if I'm seeing anyone. And to be perfectly honest, men in general. I'm passionate about my career, about academia, about discovery. If I were to just say that I'm not interested in getting married, I would have to beat men off with a stick. Not that I'd be any prize as a wife, spending my days and nights at the library as I do — but that's just how dreadfully persistent men are, especially once they've been rejected. As it happens, when you say no to a man, they don't care to take the word of a woman. They'll only leave me be when they hear I'm the possession of another man."

Ben shook his head and looked away, as his jaw tensed.

"That's a bit cold for old George, don't you think?"

"Of course not, George and I have an understanding."

"George's understanding of your relationship is that you're getting married," Ben said, the dangerous look resurfacing in his eyes.

"George doesn't want to get married anymore than I do. His parents want him to get married, that's the only reason why he'd ever even asked me. He loves the idea of having a wife for practical purposes and otherwise leading separate lives. Did you notice he's playing billiards with his good old boys, and not the least bit interested in you twirling me around the dance floor with your hand halfway down my dress?"

Ben's face twisted in something she thought might be contempt, and she continued, willing him to understand.

"I need to socialize and have a presence at society events like this to keep my parents happy. I'm living in their house and they don't care for my lifestyle," she said, as if it was the most logical thing in the world.

"You were right," he said, turning away from her again, "Your side of the story does sound worse."

"Why do you care?" she whispered harshly now that his back was to her again, and he rounded on her.

"Why are you sleeping with a man who doesn't respect you, Edith? Someone who would talk to you like that?" he was shouting, and even in the darkness she saw a shade of crimson begin to creep up his neck.

Is this what he was actually mad about? She wondered, taken aback.

The anger drained from her as she realized the answer to his actual question was more complicated. Her eyes searched the carpet as she wished she could be anywhere but in the midst of this conversation, attempting to justify her compromises out loud.

"Men..." she began, and could hardly look him in the eye. It was so embarrassing. "... have certain expectations of an arrangement like ours."

She fell silent, and wouldn't look at him now, and it made something inside him feel wild and caged.

"Oh Jesus," he said, tugging his collar like he might overheat. He raked his hand through his hair, and decided.

"I'll kill him," he said whirling around again and making for the stairs.

"Ben, stop!" she said as he shrugged out of his jacket and draped it over the banister, revealing his gun holster with only one pistol.

She threw herself at him before he could reach the stairs, slamming his back into the bookshelf with her landing against his chest. The wood of the structure groaned as the impact rattled the rows of books above them. Ben hunched to shield her as they both flinched waiting for the impact of any falling objects. When the books stilled they looked up at the shelves that extended all the way to the ceiling.

When they were in the clear that the history of Egypt wasn't falling down around them, she rapped her fists on his chest again.

"You idiot." She straightened, smoothing the front of her dress, continuing in the hopes they could remain level headed. "If I only went out with men who took me seriously I'd never leave the house."

"Do you hear yourself, Edie?" he said, softer now, his hands still encircling her waist. The position she was in, and the options in front of her, were beginning to sink in for him. "The only reasons you've given for being with George are other people's expectations. His expectations, your parents' expectations, societal expectations."

"Damn it, Ben, I am not with him," she turned and stomped back toward the pair of books.

"Okay, since you're so caught up on semantics, you've given him your time, and your body."

"I'm sorry to be so disappointing," she said, feeling her eyes well, being at a loss for any more words, as the longer she spoke them out loud, the less there seemed to be any justification for it.

"Edie, forget about me," he said, following after her. "This is about what you want, and what you deserve." He was tender now, his anger swept away by his admiration for her.

"Well, why would you be so jealous over a woman with no self respect, anyway. I don't know why you're lecturing me on the type of guy I should be with… you're not the type of guy who should be with me. A handsome, charming, adventurous Oxford graduate certainly doesn't have to chase after uptight dowdy librarians." She turned around now, looking up at him.

He looked at her incredulously. Why did she keep saying that, he wondered.

And then he knew. She didn't know. She needed to hear it.

He took another step toward her, so close they were almost touching. She felt her back come up against the rolling ladder she'd used to retrieve the reference books. Staring into her eyes, he let the silence hang in the air. He wanted to make his next words perfectly clear.

"Uptight, ambitious, gorgeous librarians who don't like me became my type the day I met you."

He leaned over bracing his hand on the bookshelf behind her, with the half smile that made her stomach flutter.

"I do like you," she said leaning back against the ladder as he moved in, letting her head fall back against a step to look up at him.

"I started to suspect that last night," he said, pulling her hips against his.

Her heart began to hammer in her chest.

"No. Before last night," she said, rising as high as she could on her tiptoes. His smile dimmed as her hands ran up his shirt feeling the solid muscles of his chest underneath.

"You asked why I never mentioned George," she said, weaving one hand into his hair, as the other drifted back down over his chest again. "I forgot he existed"

He hung his head and closed his eyes on a sigh, as she continued. The way she was running her hands over him clouded his mind.

"All I could think about all day was what I wish happened last night."

She stepped up onto the bottom step of the ladder to lift herself up into his arms and press her lips against his.

The moment she did, he unleashed on her just as he'd done the night before, as if once the invitation had been granted, he couldn't hold back. When his tongue brushed against hers it sent a shiver down her spine.

"Edith…" Her name escaped his lips.

She yelped when he abruptly lifted her higher up on the ladder so they were nearly face to face. The height in comparison to her usual stature would have been dizzying if she wasn't already lightheaded.

"All I think about is what I wanted to do to you last night," he said.

Summoning the memory of the night before heightened their desperation for each other. His mouth possessed hers. Every time their lips parted, he was impatient to taste her again.

She'd found a rhythm with Ben that was like nothing in life. It required no practice, and bore no apprehension. His body sought to know hers, and she responded with a welcome that was innate. His kiss was searching her and she wanted to be found.

Here, whenever they crossed an invisible threshold of proximity to each other, her oppositional nature vanished. Anything he desired, she surrendered. Suspended where time stopped and minds quieted her only ambition was to be his possession.

It was a freedom she hadn't known she craved. His kiss, his touch, was an escape more full than any other. She was well aware that her default state was defensive, and she made no apologies for it. She'd never known that being defenseless could be so intoxicating.

The mutual assault of kisses seemed endless. Each retreat was chased. Each sprint was followed by a languid reprieve. Each thrust was met with a swallowed moan. Until they came up for air and found disbelief in each other's eyes.

Their lips met again as his hands slid up her rib cage to cover her breasts. She moaned into his mouth as the pressure of his hands closed around them. When he brushed his thumbs over her nipples through the satin fabric she thought her body would melt through the rungs of the ladder into a puddle on the floor.

"I love when they do that for me," he said, his mouth breaking away from hers. "I could see them through your dress tonight." He plucked them, feeling the hard buds between his thumb and finger and her breath hitched.

He thought of seeing through her nightgown, and felt the blood drain from his head and fill his cock. He trailed kisses down her neck across her collarbone, nudging one of the straps until it slipped off her shoulder. His mouth moved lower, planting wet kisses over the soft mound that swelled over the drooping neckline.

He tore his lips from where she was spilling out of her dress to look in her eyes. He'd realized they were right here last night when everything came to a screeching halt. He was about to see if she'd let him peel off that nightgown, so close he could taste it.

The only sound in the cavernous library was their labored breathing as he stared at her, frozen in anticipation of the moment they'd nearly shared. Last night felt like moments he'd stolen, and yet, it was also his stupidity that robbed them of any satisfaction.

His fingers were still digging into her breasts, holding her dress up now that the strap had fallen off one shoulder. He let go, and one side of her dress sagged leaving her breast bare. She resisted the urge to cover herself, and her back arched slightly as she gripped the ladder behind her. He raised his hand to sweep the other strap off her shoulder, and the top fell around her waist.

When she gasped he exhaled a raspy chuckle just before he took her wrists and raised her hands to grip the ladder above her. Her ribcage felt tiny bracketed between his hands as his mouth closed over her breast, flicking his tongue over the peak. His hand slid up her ribs to clasp her other breast firmly, molding it between his fingers. On one side the sensation was wet and gliding, and the other was his rough palm against her bare skin. It took her breath away.

She felt a throbbing begin between her legs. Last night she'd felt damp, but tonight she was soaked. Edith had done some heavy petting with men before, but something about Ben was awakening dormant feelings in her. As though she was an instrument only he knew how to play.

"I was dying to do this last night," he said, scraping his teeth against her skin, as his worship of them became rougher.

"What if someone comes in?" she whispered.

He straightened to see she was flushed, and glanced down at the doors he'd obstructed.

"They'd need a battering ram to get in," he said, slipping his hands beneath her skirt as he brought his lips close to her ear to whisper, "… and I promise you'd finish before they did."

Her hand flew to her mouth, as his words made heat spread within her.

He continued to tease her breasts with his mouth as he lifted her knee and hiked her leg over his hip. His hand drifted up past where her stocking ended and the soft skin of her thigh began, and underneath her garter belt, he groaned between her breasts when he discovered she wore nothing underneath. His fingers spread across her ass before grasping it, like he had last night, but harder.

Then he watched her face again as his other hand slipped between her thighs — before she shifted her hips to dodge him.

"Wait!" she shouted, covering her mouth with both hands this time, her arms pressing against her breasts.

Startled, he jerked away from her, dropping her skirt.

"Okay, yeah," he said, panting himself. "Let's…" he cleared his throat, scratching the back of his neck absently. "I'm sorry. Tell me what you want. Or… what you don't want." He was stammering, hating himself for pushing her too far.

"I want to! I just feel very… damp," she blurted out.

He nodded, but the look on his face showed he was clearly struggling to understand her.

"Perhaps I should freshen up. This has never happened to me before." She shook her head, but when she went to step down, his hand flew to her waist to pin her where she stood.

"Wait… what?"

"I'll just be a minute—"

"Edith—"

"—I promise"

"Wait, listen to me," he said, he flattened her against the ladder with his body again, face to face, eyes clear. For a moment, he only brushed back a lock of her hair. "I know I was judgmental about your boyfriend," he waved off the face she made, unwilling to continue fighting about the other man she'd kissed tonight. "And I'm sorry about that. I was an ass. But if you're a virgin, you have to tell me that."

"I'm not a virgin, Ben."

"What's never happened to you before?"

"I'm just so… wet," she whispered.

Ben groaned and adjusted himself in his trousers, and her eyes went wide over the graphic detail she saw when she looked down.

"I'll just run to the powder room," she said, as he was pulling her against him again.

"Don't you dare," he said, the corner of his mouth quirking as his hips shifted against hers. She felt the hard bulge she'd just seen him grip in his hand and it didn't help the rapidly escalating predicament between her legs. He kissed her again, taking her forearms from where they covered her chest and linking them around his neck.

"I don't want to be untidy for you," she whispered, tilting her hips attempting to fit herself to him. Then his bewildered smirk became a wicked grin against her lips.

His hand went to the scarf in her hair, uniting it and letting it drift to the floor before he dug his fingers between the locks at her nape.

"Miss Taylor," he said, lifting the hem of her dress with his other hand. "You're going to be very untidy… for me," he whispered against her neck. Her lips parted as his hand fisted in her hair. "Filthy."

Slowly, holding her head back, he slipped his other hand between her thighs, and she gasped when his fingers rested against the dewy hollow there.

She was so ready for him, he just barely dipped his fingers within her, so shallow it felt like torture, then swept them over her clit once, and her entire body bowed. Then he did it again, and again, establishing a pace, feeling her become slick as she murmured, bending one knee to a higher place on the ladder to satisfy the urge she had to spread her legs as wide as they would go.

Tension built where his fingers were sliding over her, and her body began to respond beyond what she could control. He reveled in dominance as he looked down and watched her quickly becoming delirious with need. Whimpering as she gripped the ladder behind her, her exposed breasts tilted by the arch of her back were on display for him, she rocked her hips against his hand.

"Oh my god, Ben," she moaned.

"Should I stop?" he said, looking down at her face.

"No!"

He changed the rhythm, this time in lazy circles.

"No one's ever touched you here before?"

His voice took on a darker tone as he said it. A wave of goosebumps rushed over her.

"It didn't feel like this," she panted, unable to stop her rolling hips.

This conversation was turning him on to such an extreme, almost painful degree, he feared he might finish before they really started.

"You've never felt this wet before?"

"Mm-mm," she said, nodding as she gripped the ladder, then correcting herself.

"I mean, n-no... I haven't."

He hummed in approval.

He'd never been as hard as he was right now listening to Edith repeat, over and over, that she had never, in her life, been this wet for another man. And yet, the subtext of what she was saying was somehow able to supersede his own sick satisfaction. As she was slowly approaching a climax, he was growing angry.

"And when you fuck English gentlemen, do they not make you come?" he said, his hand becoming rough between her legs.

"What?" she snapped, becoming impatient.

“Never mind,” he said, pulling his hand away from her, the hem of her dress once again fluttering to her ankles. His hand released her hair and she straightened to gape at him.

Breathless, she crossed her arms over her chest and panic closed her throat at the hard look on his face.

What had she done?

CHAPTER THIRTEEN

"DO YOU REALLY want me to relay my experiences with other men? Right now?" she stammered frantically.

"Don't bother," he said, turning away and removing his gun holster.

"It's all very swift and polite if you must know."

He cursed under his breath as he faced the banister.

"You didn't let me freshen up. Please don't stop, there's a bathroom down the hall, I can be back—"

The words vanished in her throat as she watched him lean in bracing his arm on the ladder above her, and lift his hand, wet from pleasuring her, to his mouth and drew them slowly between his lips, tasting her like she was dessert.

"I hope that puts to rest the idea that I would ever be put off by how untidy I've made you."

He stood up straight again.

"Take off your dress," he said, turning back to face her.

Hope fluttered in her chest.

"What?"

"Take off your dress and get on the floor," he said, working at his cufflinks and dropping them in his pocket before moving onto his tie.

"Now," he barked.

"Ben… why are you upset?" she said, still unsure how she'd messed this up.

"I'm not upset with you. But you should know, everyone you've been with has been doing it wrong."

The look on her face made him even more angry; she was clearly humiliated by what she was hearing. His hands moved to his belt buckle, and she squeezed her thighs together.

She was already disoriented, but now watching him undress was mesmerizing to her. His hands stilled when she dropped her arms to grip the ladder behind her again. He was only distracted for a moment, letting his eyes roam over body, her bare chest and torso heaving, her dress slung low on her round hips. His gaze returned to her face as he whipped his belt out.

"You should also know," he said, briefly kissing her twice as he unbuttoned his shirt, "telling me that I make you so wet that you're confused is the sexiest thing I've ever heard in my life." Once he removed his shirt he laid it open on the floor.

Then he stood before her in his undershirt with his pants unbuttoned. She stared at his arms, enamored, as each subsequent state of undress revealed something about his body she felt she could spend an entire day admiring.

He took her hand to guide her down from the ladder and turned her around to remove her dress himself. As the zipper descended down her backside she heard a rumble in his chest. The dress slipped over her hips and he groaned. Left only in her garter belt and stockings she stepped out of her dress and he draped it over the ladder.

"Lay down," he said, gesturing to his shirt laid on the floor.

She laid down on her back, propped up on her elbows and he shook his head as he stared down at her. Her skin was flushed, her wet lips were parted and swollen from his. Her round, full breasts were glistening from his mouth. Her wide hips curved dramatically, sloping to where her knees pressed together.

"God, Edie. You're so beautiful," he said, kneeling down in front of her.

"Remember what you said," he whispered as he lowered himself over her. "You'd do exactly what I say tonight."

"I thought you meant for our mission in the library." Her hips began to tilt as she arched her back, her body aching for his touch.

"Well," he said with his half smile that made her stomach flip, "we are in the library, and I am on a mission." They both laughed breathlessly with fire in their eyes.

His mouth took hers again, forcefully. His tongue roamed in her mouth and over her lips. She laid flat on her back as she tugged his undershirt out from his waistband and he felt his cock swell as she snuck her hands around his waist underneath. He reached behind him and whisked off his undershirt and he heard her purr beneath him like she'd unwrapped an indulgent gift.

Her hands were running over his back, his shoulders, his chest, his arms, as his lips possessed hers over and over. His hand was drifting up her thigh, up her waist, to her breast.

She arched her back, and her legs fell apart. He raised up on his elbow and placed his hand on her knee to gently press them open wider. When she spread her legs for him he watched her thighs part to reveal she was swollen and soaked in her own arousal. His cock strained against his trousers at the sight of her; his mind flashed with thoughts of watching that pliant threshold stretch to receive him.

He covered her with the flat length of his fingers and stroked her slowly as his mouth returned to her breasts, alternating between each of them with his lips, tongue, and teeth.

The sensation of his entire hand making a lazy mess of her caused her blood to go molten all over again. Tiny shockwaves rippled through her from the element of surprise in him sucking softly at her nipple, or snagging it lightly between his teeth.

Then her building arousal escalated sharply when he switched to swirling two finger tips around her clit while he sucked hard on her breast. His breath became muffled when she dug her hands in his hair pressing his face into her breasts as she writhed beneath him.

Her eyes opened when his hand stopped, and his mouth left her skin. He eased back to watch his fingers sink inside her. Once she felt two fingers of his huge hand, her head fell back to the floor, unable to think through the mind-numbing fullness.

"Ooh," he moaned, "so tight."

He was panting as she was thrusting her hips against his hand, delirious with pleasure and heat and a thousand other feelings there weren't words for. She felt something building, and all of her muscles were tensing and curling up.

Ben watched his fingers moving, sinking deeper each time. When she grabbed his wrist his erection raged. He curled his fingers against the soft spot within her to bring her to the edge. He looked up to see her eyes closed tight.

"Tell me I'm the only one who makes it feel like this."

"Oh Ben," she bit her lip, feeling self conscious, but wanting the wicked rush of giving him what he wanted.

"Say it," he growled.

"Only you," she panted.

"Do you want to know why I make you so wet? I'll tell you," he rasped.

She nodded deliriously as sweat beaded on her brow.

"Because you want to take my thick cock deep inside you."

"Oh Ben, please—" she didn't know what she was begging him for. But she was sure he knew.

"One more question, Miss Taylor," he said, slowing his fingers.

"Don't stop," she said, raising onto her elbows to protest.

There was only one thing that could tempt him from watching her face as he delivered what he now knew would be her first orgasm.

His hand paused within her as he lowered himself to kneel between her knees, and her eyes widened in disbelief.

"Has anyone ever tasted your pussy before?" he said.

"What?!"

Holding her gaze as he lowered his face between her legs. She saw his tongue glide over her clit, before his lips closed around her in a reverent kiss.

"I'm going to kiss you right here until you come."

Then as he coaxed her with his tongue, caressed a spot inside her with his fingers that made the world stop. He fell back into a deliberate rhythm, as he'd done before, but it felt different; smoother, and softer, and liquid. Her entire brain evaporated, and her body became restless. Inside she felt a brewing storm.

The far away babbling nonsense she heard didn't register as her own voice, shrill and undignified as she begged him don't stop — keep going, just like that, right there.

She was pulling his hair, and grinding herself against his face, and he was thrusting his fingers in and out of her faster, and harder. When she squeezed his head between her thighs neither of them were concerned with whether or not he could breathe.

"Mmm…" she felt his lips vibrate against her core, and her moans gradually escalated.

Feeling all things at once, she floated on what was rising inside of her until suddenly her climax came as a snap. She called his name as a wave of pleasure broke over her entire body, rippling over her, and through her, ceaselessly as she throbbed against Ben's lips. She was flooded with sustained ecstasy as the waves kept coming, and her body's restless stirring began to subside.

Her consciousness slowly seemed to return to her body to find she was breathing heavily, shimmering with sweat. His touch had held, but slipped away before it could become uncomfortable.

But she wanted more. Ben rose to lean over her again, bracing with his elbow as he feasted on her neck.

"I want you," she gasped, "now."

"We don't have to," he assured her, his voice thick and ragged "I could come all over your luscious tits right now." By the time he'd finished the sentence he was gripping his cock through his trousers.

"Maybe later," she said, reaching to stroke his crotch.

He dodged her touch, and the amusement drained from his face as he bid her to tear her eyes from his raging erection.

"I'm serious, Edie. This isn't a transactional gentleman's arrangement. I have no expectations."

"No," she said, shaking her head slowly, lips pouted, brow furrowed, as she spread her hands across his chest, itching to touch him somehow. She was drunk on him.

"From now on, there's only one reason you're going to let anyone fuck you. Certainly only one reason I will."

"What's that?" she said facetiously, biting her lip.

"Not because you owe me something."

"Yes."

"Only because you want to."

She took a deep breath and looked him in the eye.

"I want to feel that again. But this time, I want to see..." She felt awkward working up the nerve to say nasty things the way he did. "If you are as big as I think you are. I can already tell," she said, not looking down this time, but pulling his hips down to grind against hers, sucking in air when the ridge in his pants fit against her still sensitive apex.

"You know how bad I want it," she teased, summoning both of their memories of what he said in her steamer cabin.

A sound that probably originated as a chuckle came out of him as a pained growl, and he thrust against her.

Nodding curtly on a deep breath he sat up to kneel between her trembling thighs as she clasped her hands at her waist, pleased with her powers of persuasion.

Once unzipped, his trousers fell a degree exposing the architecture of his hip bones, and a thatch of dark hair that turned the dial in her brain to radio silence. With one hand pressed to her inner thigh, he lowered the waistband until it freed his gorgeous, heavy cock, extended to its shocking full length. She saw a glimpse of its entirety, broad and rigid and perfect, before he gripped it in his fist with long slow strokes as she watched.

"Ben," she whispered, mesmerized.

"Yes?" he said with his signature lazy half smile even as he heaved jagged breaths.

"You're huge."

"Mmhmm," he said, lowering himself over her.

In a swift move that disarmed him, she hooked her leg around his waist and he fell forward, his forearms landing on either side of her, and she reached down between her legs to wrap her hands around his cock and began to stroke it the way she'd seen him do, every inch, slowly, in her tight, little fists.

"Fuck" he said, drawing the word out in a groan.

"Mmm," she purred against his ear, arching her back to press her breasts against his bare chest.

"You're so… hard," she said, speeding up the rhythm she coaxed him with.

"Sweet Jesus, Edie," he said shuddering, "You really are a fast learner."

His eyes drifted shut and she felt his cock swell as he thrust into her grip.

"I don't have any protection… you could make me come just like this… ah, yeah, just like that," he groaned.

"No need, I keep a calendar," she said, lifting her eyes to meet his "I'm sure."

He pulled back slightly to look her in the eye.

"Edie, are you really sure? We… we've only just met." He thought it sounded feeble and awkward, but with her hands working his cock, he couldn't think of any other way to say what was a genuine concern to him at the moment.

"You don't strike me as the kind of man who puts this much thought into a quick…"

His eyes darkened under his furrowing brow, as he pulled away from her. Clearly upset, lips parted ready to speak, but not saying a word. For a moment they were silent and still, hearing only their heartbeats in the dark quiet space around them.

"Mmm," he grunted, his voice deep and gravely, "but do you?"

"I didn't mean it like that—"

"How long did you date George before you let him—"

Knowing what was coming, she clasped her hand over his mouth before he could say the bitter words.

Her other hand drifted down between them until it found him again. The hand over his mouth relaxed until it was just her fingertips against his lips, as the fingertips of her other hand gently traced the rock hard length of his shaft.

"Three years," she said, her hand closing around him again.

His face went blank.

"Not because I wanted a proper courtship; because I wasn't interested." Her grip around him tightened again.

Ben kissed the fingertips resting on his lips, then took her hand and pressed another kiss to her palm before it covered his cheek. His other hand went to her thigh, and as he spread her legs, his mind was a mess with conflicting thoughts.

How livid he'd felt when she suggested this was just a fling, what an egregious mistake it had been to let her see. That battling with the knowledge that she was begging him to fuck her after a few days, when she made other men wait years.

"Ben, as of this moment, you know me more intimately than any other man on earth."

"Yeah?" he said, and he took his cock from her and nestled it between her folds. She was still feeling the quakes of her climax, and his touch made her spasm.

"Yes," she sighed, feeling the head of his cock pressed against her threshold.

He dragged the head up over her clit once, and then back down between her lips to slide into her. When he nudged the head of his cock inside, and a tiny squeal rang in her throat. He watched her face as he pushed deeper, and she was so tight he forgot to breathe. Her hot, slick sheath welcomed him in one long slow plunge. He sank all the way to the bottom as she moaned beneath him. He paused there for a moment, and then felt her squeeze herself around him. He couldn't believe the fit of her.

He withdrew slowly, then drove in again with a swift thrust that made her cry out. And then again.

"Like that?"

"Yes," she whimpered.

He tortured her first, delivering fast, rough strokes that were separated by a beat, enough of a pause for her to contract around him like a vice. Then, gradually his hips moved faster, until finally, they were steady, plunging into her, giving her what they both wanted. He pushed her legs back so she could take him deeper.

There was no more talking, or teasing. There was only a feeling. There was no thought, just action. The noise was nonsense and gasps and the sound of him drilling into her and the sound of her taking it.

She felt the heat of pleasure rising within her again, the tension that she now understood building torturously toward a transcendent release, but this time it felt different. Better. Bigger. Bolder. Deeper. Ben was tapping into a well of euphoria hidden at a depth that had never been reached before.

When she'd seen him, it was enormous and thick, and when he drove himself into her clenched fists, she'd felt he was hard as an iron beam yet soft as silk. Now as he drilled into her hard and fast, she felt what they became together. He filled her and she was insatiable, never wanting it to end.

Feverishly spiraling toward another orgasm, she had no sense of how distant the release might be. Each time she felt his shaft slam against the wall inside her, she wanted it deeper. Each time she felt his steely hips slap against the cushion of her thighs, she wanted it harder.

"Yeah baby, give me another one," he said as he brought her close to her climax. He rose up on his knees, lifting her hips from the floor, gripping handfuls of her thighs to shuttle her up and down his length.

It was as if each thrust was aimed at a bullseye only he knew about, and he never missed his target. She heard herself cry out, unable to bear the sensation. The change in angle was a match to the powder keg. In a few swift strokes, she was catapulted to her climax, pins and needles stabbed across her scalp and her chest, and she came so hard that she felt herself bathing his cock.

"Fuck, that's tight," he growled as he felt her sheath wring him.

"Do you want my cum?" he said with his jaw tense; he wanted to make her cum forever, but he couldn't delay any longer. He had to feel himself fill her with it, and every second longer was agony.

"Yes!" she shrieked before she could stop herself from sounding hysterical and desperate to take it.

He groaned while she soaked his cock, as her orgasm clenched around him. He intensified her orgasm with long deep strokes until finally, with a roar, he pushed her legs against her chest and planted himself as deep as she could take it, and collapsed into his own white-hot climax exploding deep inside her. He rocked his hips into her soft flesh, emptying every drop of his triumph without withdrawing an inch.

Awash in an unspeakable pleasure she'd never felt before, Edith trembled as her other senses crept back by way of periphery. From far away, the aroma of aged pages inched closer. Still air encountered the perspiration of her skin, the cooling a contrast to the patches of her that were warmed by heavy arms, and broad drifting hands. Muffled at first, the sound of Ben's heart beating in his chest began to ring clearer. His deep shuddering gusts of breath rustled the wild locks of hair stuck to her temple.

Then, after a long while, she was just breathing. At some point she had gone from being sprawled on the floor to being all curled up against him. Lightly brushing his fingertips over her back, and legs and arms, transmitting tiny sparks of delight all along her body as he held her through her climax subsiding.

She raised up on her elbow to observe his unseemly state of dress. She was still in her garter belt and stockings, though at some point the barbaric nature of the act snapped one of her ribbons. He was shirtless, but still wearing the unfastened bottom of a tux that once again concealed his groin.

"Oh, Ben. Where were you when I was in university?"

His eyes were still shut as he laughed, and the sound caged a butterfly in her heart.

"Baby, if we met in college you never would have made it to Egypt," he smiled, and now she had seen that smile from between her thighs. If it was magnetic before, it melted her now.

"Oh yes I would," she smiled brilliantly, her complexion splotchy and sheening with sweat. "I could have used a body guard a long time ago."

He looked at her then, as he swept her hair back from her face and cradled her cheek, then his eyes dropped to her lips. The look on his face was full of adoration, but his brow furrowed.

He stood and began to do up the button and zipper on his pants. When he put on his undershirt, Edith stood up. He bent to pick up his rumpled shirt from the floor and as he began to button it up, he turned and walked toward the other end of the balcony.

She worried for the briefest moment that he was just leaving. Every step he took further away made her feel colder.

A tiny wisp of relief puffed out the breath she'd been holding when she saw he was just looking out the window again as he refastened his cufflinks. The same window he'd been looking out of when he came in.

He was walking back over as she turned to the ladder to get dressed herself.

But just as she reached for her dress, he came up behind her while donning his worn leather holster. He swept her hair from her shoulder, and kissed her neck as he placed his hands on her waist.

"Bend over," he said as his knee went between her legs, spreading them.

In a lifetime of fighting, something about doing everything Ben told her to do was thrilling. When ordinarily she would question, and doubt, and push back. Tonight, she spread her legs and bent over.

She bent slightly, but he grasped her neck and pushed her down further. The quiet, confident dominance in the gesture sent a shiver up her spine. She heard a murmur of approval rumble in his chest as his hand gripped the backs of her thighs and spread her open. She felt something trickle down her skin while Ben watched, and she thought he must have seen because his fingers dug in to grip her harder. Her eyes squeezed shut and she smiled with the absolutely despicable knowledge that he'd bent her over to shamelessly watch the evidence of his release pour out of her.

He withdrew a handkerchief from his shirt pocket and began to mop up the mess he'd made that dripped out of her as he watched. She whimpered as the soft cotton swept over the fully exhausted erogenous zone. Then he put the handkerchief in his pocket, and as she stood back up he kissed her neck again, and then her shoulders.

"You can get dressed now," he whispered and she could hear the wicked smile in his voice.

She stepped into her dress, and after she pulled on the straps, he zipped it. Then he turned her around and held her face with both hands as he kissed her.

Suddenly, she felt nervous and awkward and hated herself for it. When moments ago, almost completely naked, she would have done anything Ben told her to. Now, standing here, with him kissing her tenderly against a bookshelf, she was unsure. Maybe because they were right back where they started …

however long ago, however long she had been in the sex trance he'd put her in. Maybe because now she didn't know where they stood, or how to act, in the midst of what just happened.

She was relieved, at least, since a moment ago she was terrified he was about to just get up and walk away after one of the most memorable hours of her life. But instead, he'd caressed her, and cleaned her, and helped her into her dress, and was holding her in his arms kissing her now.

He leaned back to look in her eyes and it reminded her that she didn't have to worry about it, for the same reason it happened in the first place. It was Ben, and... She really trusted Ben. She trusted him with this memory, and with the knowledge of her body. And furthermore, she trusted that everything would be okay in the aftermath. And as their eyes met, she realized that he was at a loss for words too.

"Thank you, Mr. Brooks. I think that's the most fascinating thing I've ever learned in a library... as a librarian, I hope you can appreciate the gravity of that confession."

He laughed and leaned in slightly, and he was just about to kiss her again, but stopped himself. With a little shake of his head he finally said. "Anytime," with a grin, "Let's go."

CHAPTER FOURTEEN

HE KNELT DOWN to gather the two books she needed, tucking two spare dance cards between the pages to keep her place in them.

"What are you doing?"

"Come on, we've got to get going," he said, returning the flashlight to his holster.

"We can't go Ben, I haven't finished yet!"

Puzzled by his haste, she grabbed her shoes, put her glasses and scarf back in her bag, and traversed the spiral staircase on weak knees as she raced after him. Hadn't he just said the party wouldn't be over for hours?

Feeling pulled in so many directions, she worried something may have snapped within her. Ever since she met Ben, he began to permeate all of her thoughts, and she felt her career focus slipping at the worst possible time. It would be even worse now than it was before. They were sneaking off the scene of a crime and she couldn't help but wonder whether he'd be sneaking into her room tonight.

At the double doors of the library, Ben retrieved a briefcase she didn't know he had stowed there. When he popped the brief-case open she saw there were folders and documents inside. He placed the stolen books on top and snapped the case shut again.

Ben removed the fire iron he had slid through the door handles, and they exited the way they'd come in, through double doors of the library. They walked briskly down the gallery hallway to the servants' quarters hallway they took to the exit. When they got back to the same side door they'd left from, she went up a few steps and Ben was still standing on the landing. She turned to see that he wasn't coming up the stairs with her.

"Put your shoes back on," he said, holding his arm out to steady her. She did so, but when he saw the question in her face he continued.

"You go on ahead, I'll be a few minutes."

The library haze must have evaporated in the dry desert air, because for the first time in what seemed like an eternity now, she wanted to argue with him. Protest. Ask questions. Make demands. But due to the urgent nature of their circumstances, she silently slipped into the party.

At the table of champagne and took a flute, sipping on it delicately as she wondered if what she'd just been doing was obvious. It felt like a cloak she was wearing, as if it weren't only written all over her face, but emblazoned across her entire body. Logically, she reminded herself that she'd never looked at anyone else and thought it was obvious they'd just been surprised with multiple orgasms.

Just then a familiar female face caught her eye and began to approach. She was moving at a rather elevated pace, she noted.

"Edith! How lovely to see you. You're looking so well." Margaret was an acquaintance in the small society of English abroad in Cairo for the winter season. They had always been friendly at parties.

"Hello, Margaret, you're looking wonderful yourself."

Ordinarily, she knew Margaret to be skilled in polite small talk. But it became apparent quickly that Margaret would be getting straight to the point this evening.

"Edith dear, tell me who you came in with this instant! He was the talk of the evening among all the ladies, as I'm sure you can imagine. You'll have to introduce us…"

Edith nodded blandly, thinking to herself she had been spot on. Benjamin Brooks couldn't come to a party like this and end the evening as anything but the most eligible bachelor in Cairo. That was before she knew he went to Oxford, and whatever else that suggested about his background that remained unknown to her.

Yet, the cunning side of her thought that the other single ladies didn't have to know that. Or any other hidden talents she'd recently learned about him. Furthermore, she knew that anything she told Margaret would spread like wildfire.

"He's just a hired hand from the Tomb in Argo. I'm the Archaeological Director, in fact. Did you know?" Edith asked rhetorically before continuing. "Pimsley hired him to escort me on site, and when traveling, considering how high profile the project is. I believe he has some sort of military background, you know, that sort of thing." She leaned in, adding for good measure, "He's possibly a felon, unfortunately, but you know how hard it is to find bilingual laborers. I had to let him borrow one of Elliot's tuxes for the evening."

"Miss Taylor," she heard Ben say from behind her.

Shit.

How long had he been standing there? What had he heard? Would she ever stop saying the worst thing at the worst time when under pressure?

Margaret saw her moment, and she took it. She shoved past Edith.

"Any port in a storm," she whispered over Edith's shoulder before stepping into Ben's personal space.

"Hello, Mr. Brooks. I'm Margaret Dawson. I'm a close friend of Edith's."

"Hello Miss Dawson, it's a pleasure to meet you." He took the limp hand she offered, but didn't take his eyes off of Edith.

"Edith was just describing you rather humbly, but I heard you were at Oxford. It just so happens I have several friends who were there you might know. It's possible we've been in the same circles for years and haven't met."

"Yes, I'm sure that's true. We really must be going. Again, it was lovely to meet you." Ben turned to Edith. "Miss Taylor, as I was saying, your car is ready. Right this way."

He lightly touched Edith's elbow to guide her from the ballroom to the foyer. Onlookers be damned, she wasted no time in clearing up anything that was about to get miscommunicated.

"Ben, she was asking about you, I was just —"

"Edie, darling!" George, with splendid timing as usual, just so happened to be in the foyer. He leaned in to attempt a sloppy kiss and lost his balance. Ben caught him with a handshake, clapping his free hand on George's shoulder.

"Great to meet you, pal. Edie has to go."

"Well, alright you two, have fun," he slurred, stumbling back into the ballroom with a grin still plastered on his face.

Edith continued to stammer as Ben helped her into her jacket and whisked her down the stairs weaving through the crowd.

"Ben, Margaret was just saying that... well, there were interested parties —"

"Edie, I have to go."

"What?"

"I'm going to miss the steamer if I don't leave right now."

"You're... what? What are you talking about? We don't have to go back tonight."

"We don't. I can't miss another day on site; they're categorizing and cataloging the first hall of the tomb. You go home and get some sleep, and finish your research. Find the key, then come back... to Argo."

"Well... I don't need to pack, I can come with you right now."

"You shouldn't risk traveling with those books," he reasoned.

He saw the nerves creep back into her features, and instantly felt the need to soothe her.

"If I told you I know how to get the books back to the collection safely, and there would be no repercussions, would you trust me?"

"Yes, I trust you," she said, taking a step toward him.

The logic of what was best for their shared objective wasn't matching up with how wrong it felt for them to be separated.

"What did you take?" she asked him, knowing he was rushing her, needing to know before he disappeared.

"What?" he said impatiently.

"I saw you do that thing on George. That thing you do, the handshake. What did you take?"

He looked down, with his lips curving on one side. He reached behind his lapel and pulled out the photo of Edith that George had kept in his wallet.

Her lips parted as she blinked at the photo, then up into his eyes. The smirk on Ben's face fell as he stared back at her, and then his gaze dropped to her mouth. He inclined slightly as if he would kiss her, but then glanced up at the large crowd scattered over the staircase, and stopped himself.

Edith followed where his eyes fell and saw the steps teeming with guests spilling out of the ballroom in need of fresh air. Socialites, business men, politicians, high society wives. Margaret had even followed them outside and was standing on the balcony clearly on a fact-finding mission regarding the relationship status of one Benjamin Brooks.

An opening to do one thing right tonight presented itself, and she took it.

She pivoted Ben until they were both standing in full view of the crowd. She snuck her hands inside his jacket to wrap around his waist and lifted her face to his.

"Edith, what are you —"

The kiss she planted on his lips was overtly sensual. He was only caught off guard for a moment before the taste of her engulfed him. Pleased to sense him getting lost in the moment, she felt his hands spread across her back. Deepening the kiss, he leaned in bending her backward as she wrapped both arms around his neck to steady herself.

It wasn't merely performative. It was genuine. The ardent kiss they would have shared if they were a real couple reluctantly parting ways after a glamorous event, wishing they were off for a private nightcap instead.

When she pulled away his eyes were still closed and she watched them blink open in a blank stare as he straightened. She looked back at the crowd to see many onlookers, including a very pouty Margaret.

"Give that a week. It will be the talk of Cairo."

He laughed with a half smile as his forehead dropped to hers and he lifted his hand to her cheek. Then, he cleared his throat, releasing her. "I'll see you in Argo," he said, and ushered her into the car.

The car door slammed and Ben stood with his hands in his pockets watching the car pull into the street.

At first Edith basked in the warm tingle the kiss had left on her skin, enjoying smug satisfaction at successfully landing the point she was trying to make. Maybe she couldn't always say the right thing when push came to shove, but she hoped she could dispel any doubt in Ben's mind that she had qualms about being seen with him.

The car rumbled down the street, expanding the distance between them. Time lapsed from the gala to the aftermath. Party lights faded into the rear view mirror and she was enveloped by the darkness of the night ahead. A pang stabbed at her when she remembered how much she'd been looking forward to the ride home when she assumed Ben would be with her. Longingly, she cast a glance across the backseat where he would have been. All she saw there was the mysterious return of the briefcase.

When Edith looked up from the reference books the next afternoon she was startled to see a steamy cup of tea and a stack of petit biscuits. Her favorite kind. That meant that Myrna or Gregson must have come and gone within the last few minutes, replacing her last set of dishes with a piping hot refreshment. She hadn't even noticed. It had to have been Gregson, she amended on second thought, because she saw a few stacks of books had been tidied.

It was his usual effort in the futile attempt to keep her study clutter free and organized. Edith was certainly a fan of order and calm, especially at her job. When it came to tidying her study, however, she didn't see the point when there were discoveries to be made. Putting references back in their place if they were only to be used again tomorrow seemed an awful waste of time. And anyway, how was she supposed to predict which references she'd be using again tomorrow? It was best to just leave them all where they lay.

She craned her neck one way, and then the other, attempting to work out the creaky sensation of spending too long in one spot. As she did so she surveyed the room, indeed littered with stacks of books, but otherwise, it was neat. It wasn't spacious, but the windows were large, keeping it bright and lending an airy and open feel. She delighted in her rose colored velvet curtains, which added an elegant feminine touch to the space against the rich wood shelves that displayed countless leather bound books with gold lettering.

Lifting her arms overhead in a back bending stretch, she glanced at the clock to see it had been hours since she settled into her study this morning.

She hadn't been the least bit surprised this morning when she sat down to a breakfast laid for many more than one. But then, it never was. Edith had barely cracked the top of her soft boiled egg when she noticed Myrna had snuck in, loitering around the credenza with a feather duster in hand. Before long Myrna had kicked off her shoes and taken her place at the head of the table as Edith spilled the details of her evening.

Many years ago when Edith informed her parents she'd secured a position at the Cairo library, there was never any question as to whether Myrna, one of the family's maids, would join her. The family discussion that resulted opened with father saying "Edith and Myrna must stay in the house on the East Bank."

The siblings Edith knew from her upbringing in British society suggested that she and Myrna were not like sisters, but closer. None of the animosity or competitive nature she saw in other families existed between the two of them.

Myrna had met her match years ago, when she'd kept bumping into the tall, dark and handsome Naeem at the market. After they'd become lovers, it was revealed that their rendezvous were no coincidence. For Naeem, it had been love at first sight, and Myrna followed suit not long after.

Edith remembered fondly their long ago late night giggling confessionals where Myrna would relay the details of her relationship. And it was Myrna who ultimately urged Edie to take George up on his offer of a mutually beneficial public affair. But this morning Myrna munched on toast as Edie made confessions of her own, that she hadn't known what she was missing when she'd been sleeping with George.

"I didn't know I could feel that way. I guess I assumed that my evenings with George were the same as what you had always described with Naeem. I thought that maybe it fell short of the rapture you always talked about because I was never really infatuated the way you two are. But now I think it's actually more… in the technique."

Edith had been staring off and rambling when she noticed Myrna's suspiciously averted eyes, restlessly wiping her buttery fingers on a napkin, before a guilty twitch snagged at her lips. Edith's eyes narrowed at her.

"Myrna!" she gasped, "You knew!" Edith's fists rapped on the table, causing the silver to clatter.

They were interrupted by Gregson, who just so happened to be passing through the dining room on his way to post letters.

When he seemed to notice Edith having breakfast, he casually inquired about her evening. Soon he was enjoying Edie's relaying the highlights of the party over his soft boiled eggs with soldiers. His eyes sparkled with rapt wonder as they chattered about the centerpieces, what the band was playing, and the best looks of the night. Edith didn't have a chance to revisit her quarrel with Myrna before they had all finished their breakfast and went on to their respective chores for the day.

Edith sipped her tea in her study pondering her own objective as she stared down at the two open books before her. It was late in the day and her eyes were beginning to cross. Checking every birth and death between the two reference books was tedious work, but it simply couldn't be helped. The answer to the riddle, the key to the second door, would be in one single name. Just a few letters strung together in a line amongst the birth records that didn't have a corresponding spot in death records. One family at a time.

She crouched down in her chair, bringing her eyes level with the desk, to see the thin section of pages that she'd spent the majority of the day going through, dismayed when her eyes shifted to the still hefty stack of pages she had yet to examine.

Her elbows plunked on the table as she cradled her face in her hands. Ben had been right. Even hopping on a late night steamer, and pulling a secret heist in the library during a glamorous ball, gaining access to the rest of the tomb really would feel painfully long compared to having a convenient key hiding in your cleavage. Oddly she wished he was there, even if just to say he'd told her so.

"Oh, just give me the answer," she groaned absently.

Suddenly she heard a murmur in her ear a split second before the rustle of the book pages alarmed her. She opened her eyes to see the pages of both books flipping wildly. A shrill yelp burst from her lungs as she leapt up to shut the window at the opposite end of the room.

When she turned around she lamented that the errant winds had disrupted more than half of the pages of the book. Stalking back to her desk to see the ratio she'd just mourned had been inverted. Now both books were open to pages near the end.

"Oh I've lost my place!" she shouted, stomping her foot with her hands balled into fists. She hadn't yet devised a system to mark which pages she'd searched and which she hadn't.

Then she froze. Her eyes had been trained so diligently in this task, that she spotted it right away. The book's pages had opened to the same family. The birth of one family line in one book, with the corresponding deaths from the same family in the other. Before she could speculate what the odds of that were, she was already processing the discrepancy she instantly spotted.

There it was. The name. The name that was recorded at birth, but not at death. Two names, in fact. Mother and son.

"Oh, my word," Edith hissed in disbelief as she raised her hands to her face. She sat at her desk, pointing to the name on the page.

"I know this family!"

She flew to a bookshelf, stepping up on a chair to reach a book whose location she knew by heart. It came down hard as she opened it on the desk and rifled through the pages.

"The Didia family," she said to herself. "That's it, that's the tattoo. This is her family line." Then she began to read aloud from the book. "The Didia family were guardians of heka, ancient Egyptian magic." Looking up from her book momentarily, she was stunned.

"Oh, you were more than a belly dancer, weren't you, Viper. All this time."

Then a thought came to her, and she searched the page again, landing on a section that stopped her.

"The Didia were high priests and priestesses who were master artisans. They perfected traditions of musical instruments to drive away evil, engraved ivory wands to cast spells, and… forged amulets for protection."

She reached toward the corner of the book, but her hand froze. She shook her head to dislodge the apprehension, drawing a fortifying breath, and pressed on to turn the page. There she saw examples of the Didia family's craftsmanship in tools of magic. All over the page she saw gleaming green peridot stones.

There was a long, elegant engraved wand with gem stones encircling the handle. There were modest collars strung with copper beads and gemstones in between. There were dainty jars with gemstone stoppers, that were intended for holding elixirs and potions. There were rings, bracelets, and pendants.

With shaky fingers she pulled the chain around her neck until the lotus emerged from its hiding spot. As she'd done countless times, she traced the pale green peridot stone in the center with her fingertip.

When she looked from one page to the next, she saw more instruments that weren't jewelry. Stamped copper globes for dispersing smoke, and crackled clay trays for gathering ash, and a bronze stylized hand sculpture with two fingers pinched to hold a thin stick of incense.

Flipping back to the previous page once more, she searched for what she'd missed. The words were mumbled at first, but then became louder as the meaning took hold of her.

"The Didia tribe additionally specialized in their own blend mystical of incense; they used it in their heka practice as a way to bind incantations, strengthen spells, and granted visions for guidance. The recipe of the bouquet was passed down in verbal tradition via apprenticeship, and all traces of it were lost to history when the Didia tribe went into hiding after Egypt ceded to the conquest of Rome."

Edith could smell the shimmering smoke as she read the passage, she could feel it in her lungs, and the burn in her eyes as if the room were filled with it.

Slumping back in her chair, Edith stared out the window she'd just slammed shut, wondering where that gust of wind had really come from… though somewhere deep down, she already knew.

That evening Myrna came to Edith's bedroom to find her sitting perfectly still in front of the mirror at her vanity. Her eyes were glazed and staring blankly and she held her brush suspended midway through a section of her hair. When Edith heard Myrna's cheerful greeting she snapped back to the present and saw her reflected in the mirror, pulling the brush the rest of the way through her locks and setting it on the vanity.

"Penny for your thoughts, Edie. You were miles away."

Edith's eyes cleared, as she pulled herself away from pharaonic Egypt, and back to the present.

"Well, it will cost you more than that. I'm still not speaking to you," Edith said, smirking as she put her hairbrush back in her drawer and slid it shut.

"Hmph," Myrna huffed, planting her fists on her hips. "You're not being fair. When it comes to matters of the bedroom, there's a lot I didn't tell you because… well, I just figured what you don't know can't hurt you. That is, if you end up with someone like George Fletcher."

"Maybe if you told me the truth I would have known what I was missing and found someone other than George Fletcher," Edith said, a little brusquely. In truth, she was still a bit miffed.

"Well you got there in the end, didn't you?" Myrna smirked as she folded some underthings near an open dresser drawer. "Or, I guess Benjamin Brooks got you there, heh heh…" Myrna barked out an exaggerated, saucy laugh, a rare sign of her northern British accent escaping through her professional dialect.

"You know I never would have married him, Myrna. You could have told me he didn't know what he was doing."

"Why are you acting like this is news? You knew many of George's shortcomings, and you still didn't cut him loose."

"Giving George a chance was your idea." Edith glared at her friend with a playful smirk.

"I only suggested that because you were never interested in finding anyone. If I'd told you, 'Lady Edith, is there anything you desire from the market, and also, it sounds like George is terrible in bed,' we can't be sure what you would have done. And if you'd broken it off, I feared you would remain alone."

And then she was staring off again.

Myrna felt disquieted by how Edie had behaved since she'd been home. She'd never been knocked off balance by a man before. But here she was. Every time she saw Edie today she'd lost her head in the clouds. Granted, it was just as likely her mind was occupied by other matters. After all, she was on a quest within the tomb her lady had been talking about for as long as she could remember. Yet, it was still alarming that Edie had so much on her mind during a very inconvenient time in her career.

Considering that she was set to return to the tomb the very next day, Myrna wouldn't think there was a man on earth who could distract her from her work.

Then again, Myrna had seen Ben with her own eyes, so it was no mystery as to why. To put it plainly, the man was a five-course meal, and that was before Edie had told her about … the library. She wasn't about to reminisce on that while she was folding laundry or she'd get hot under the collar right where she stood.

Myrna sat on the edge of the bed to be nearer to her, so that nothing would be left unsaid this time. "I'll tell you one thing, Edie. I'll admit, perhaps I was misguided in nudging you toward George. But I just wanted to see you happy. Besides, if you kept staying in every night, who would keep Gregson abreast of the latest society fashions?"

"In hindsight I don't know that it was worth the gossip," Edith grumbled.

"Really, Edie. You should hang on to this one," Myrna said softly.

Edith met her eyes in the mirror.

"That might be easier said than done. He's…" Her hands came together to fidget absently. "… unconventional. Who says he'd want to be hung on to?"

"It sounds like once you got a hold of him, he liked it quite a bit."

"Myrna!" she threw a powder puff at her, and they burst into a fit of laughter in the dissipating plume of talcum.

Edith turned to face Myrna then, leaning on the back of her chair with eager eyes.

"There is something you can do to get back in my good graces."

"What's that?"

"Explain the mechanics of male intimacy."

"I thought you already knew that."

"Well, yes, in theory. But I could use some tips."

"Oh, I see." Myrna thought for a moment. Edie had it bad. Then a grin spread wide on her plump cheeks.

"What?" Edith asked.

"I just love to discover there's something you don't know. It's such a rare event."

Edith rolled her eyes and turned back to smile at the mirror.

"Well, enjoy it while it lasts," she said, retrieving some lotion from another drawer. "I've never wanted to do anything for a man before. I may never revisit the peculiar urge again."

That night, Edith lay wide awake. She had packed her train case for the next day, and gotten into bed an hour earlier than usual. Her suitcase was next to the door. She couldn't wait to sleep so that she could wake up and get back to Argo.

Her mind had been tripping over the discovery of the Didia family ever since this afternoon. The discovery had unlocked so many other connections. What it had meant of the true history of the Weeping Viper; what it uncovered from the past that previously remained shrouded in secrecy.

It made her question whether the lotus was more than just a key, and if perhaps, she was more than just a librarian. It never occurred to her to wonder whether her family's connection to the lotus had any deeper meaning than any other jewelry acquired one way or another.

Were any of her ancient ancestors close to the Didia family? If so, who were they, and what role did they play in this story?

As questions lead to more questions, yet never any answers, it was ultimately something Myrna had said that broke through the cycle of conjecture.

The past few days had been such a whirlwind, such an onslaught of information, and thoughts, and feelings. It was such a feat to take in the current events, that Myrna had brought up something Edith hadn't considered at all.

The future.

You should hang onto this one.

He often surmised that the dig could take months, or years. She always disagreed on the basis that his estimations assumed they would remove the doors without damaging them, rather than using the ancient magic for the doors to open themselves.

Weeks, months, or years… what would be next? It was also the first time she'd considered what was next for her. She had always hoped for an opportunity to propel her career, but had never dreamed it would be on this scale. She'd merely hoped to get enough jobs to be a working archaeologist. Just having the official title would have satisfied her beyond her wildest dreams.

When news broke that they'd gained entry to the tomb, there were bound to be opportunities that presented themselves to Edith. She might get a position back in England, or be hired to head a dig somewhere else. Though, she specialized in Egypt, so she would probably get preferential placement on any upcoming digs there.

Where would Ben be then? Should she be asking that? When it came time to make decisions about what was next in her career would she factor him in? Would he factor her in? What would he do? Where would he go?

As her head was a flurry with the new information, and how exactly she'd been lead to that information, and now the additional overwhelm of envisioning her future. Ordinarily thinking of Ben brought on a great deal of tension, but as of this moment the angst of a workplace flirtation paled in comparison to the gravity of the thoughts that had plagued her all day. She felt a wave of relief when her brain found thinking of Ben to be a comfortable resting place.

When her mind wandered down those paths, she caught herself with disgust. How pathetic and clingy could she possibly be. There was probably nothing less attractive than that.

CHAPTER FIFTEEN

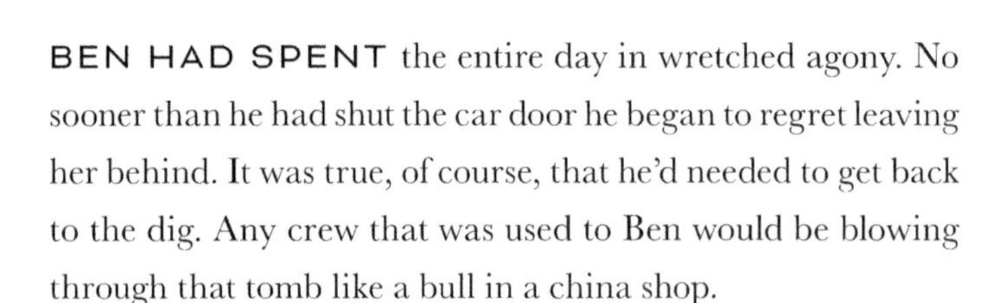

BEN HAD SPENT the entire day in wretched agony. No sooner than he had shut the car door he began to regret leaving her behind. It was true, of course, that he'd needed to get back to the dig. Any crew that was used to Ben would be blowing through that tomb like a bull in a china shop.

He had to get back and oversee every grain of sand that was disturbed, for any disregard for preservation could alter history. Even that thought in itself made him wonder what the hell was really happening to him.

She's the head of the dig, he thought. That's why you're suddenly worried about protecting every inch of the tomb. It has nothing to do with you and her.

It was also true that she'd needed to stay behind. Traveling with the reference volumes was risky in itself, but storing them in their hotel rooms where they could easily be found was worse.

Yet, he'd still spent that night on the steamer thinking that it was riskier to leave her. News of the dig was bound to break, and she could be back there on her own. She could be en route when it happened.

If he hadn't tucked her into that car that delivered her to the safety of her mansion, she could have been right there, in his cabin on the steamer. The unwelcome thought of Edith disembarking from the steamer to be swarmed by a crowd of unruly photographers with flash bulbs crackling all around her like fireworks was enough to keep him up all night.

After all, he was hired to be her bodyguard. That was likely the main source of his concern, he assured himself.

He couldn't believe how badly the day had gone. His entire crew had already picked up on it. He was either lost in thought, or snapping someone's head off for dropping a chisel. It wasn't like him at all to lose sight of the big picture by getting bogged down in all the tiny details. But once the shift had taken place in his mind, he couldn't shake it. He had become meticulous about keeping the artifacts intact.

He had even started referring to dusty old pharaoh trash as "artifacts."

Early the next morning, Benjamin was waiting at the site of the tomb, as was the rest of the crew. It was always important to get an early start, and he had heard that Edith had gotten in the night before. He was aggravated that she hadn't come during the day when it was safer, and he could see for himself that she was well. Though somewhere in his brain he recognized his anger was unfounded.

It had only been a few days, but as he saw her approaching the tomb, he thought she might be a mirage. The closer she got, the edgier he felt, and his restlessness crowded out his ability to be self aware.

She was in her uniform. Glasses too big for her petite face, hair in a knot, crisp shirt, the hem of a pleated skirt brushing at her calves. Her tiny soft leather loafers that, it dawned on him, he preferred now even to the heels she wore to the gala.

He glanced back to shore to see the crew busying themselves in the tents. They had been debriefed exhaustively that they wouldn't be unearthing treasures today because Edith would be attempting to advance to the next door.

He'd forgotten to correct his intense stare by the time they were standing face to face. Once again, just like their first day in front of the tomb. He thought of it now, that Ben on the first day would be shocked to know how the days before him would unfold. They had opened many doors since then.

The tight expectant features of her face made him think she was nervous. Of course she would be. It hit him in the gut at that moment that their personal entanglements were muddying the waters of a consequential day in her career.

For the first time, he had misgivings about his pursuit of her. Had he rushed her? Would he have better honored her life's work by setting aside his wild attraction? She had been very clear about her determination not to be side tracked… before flinging her half-naked body at him in the steamer, at least.

Ben realized that his thoughts were playing against a long pause between them just staring at each other.

"I found her real name," Edith said, her speech seeming a bit rushed.

I knew you would.

"Did you finally look in the phone book like I told you?"

She rolled her eyes, but a faint smile ghosted across her lips. He swept his arm toward the tomb, ushering her to go before him.

Edith got a flutter in her chest approaching the tomb. The double doors were no less formidable now that they looked slightly less dusty and the seams were visible. Edith smothered the urge to look back for a reassuring glance from Ben before taking the chain from around her neck. If she had, she would have seen him studying her, rather than the doors.

She stepped forward and after one fortifying deep breath, pressed the lotus into place. Her heart leapt when, just as before, the lotus sunk into the door until it was flush with the rest of the engraving.

Cursing under his breath, Ben yanked Edith back, rough in his haste, just as the doors swung open. For a moment she scrambled to stand upright as her arm was held tight in Ben's fierce grip.

"You've done this before," he barked in a whisper, as if the tomb had ears.

"Oh, don't you start," she said, yanking her arm free of him, and brushing the dust off her skirt.

Ben lit a lantern and they headed down the massive stone stairwell. They descended in silence for what felt like ages. Edith figured she must have been riding high on adrenaline the last time she'd been down there, because she didn't remember it taking so long. Or maybe it just felt long now that she and Ben were cautiously observing stiff formality.

"So, what is it anyhow? It sure can't get any worse than Isfetheru."

"Oh? Right… well," she said looking around her "You know, I think I'd prefer not to say it out loud until the right moment." The lantern light flickered across her face, revealing she was spooked.

"You give these mummies more credit for decorum than I do. Who's to say they won't pop out of these star holes just to get back at us for being here in the first place?"

"Star shafts."

"You're such a know-it-all."

"I just know more about it than you, which is not saying much."

"Since when are you ever not saying much?"

She went to swat at his shoulder, which by now was a comfortable way to end a conversation between them.

He caught the strike midair before she could land it. They stopped on the same step and looked at their hands as her fingers slipped away from his. When their eyes met, with a jolt of electricity, she went skipping down the stairs rushing, as usual, to fill the silent stairwell with words.

Ben followed after her, amused by the practically humming nervous energy radiating from her.

"If the door has been locked for three thousand years, I doubt that any old turn of phrase will do the trick. You think the mummies are unpredictable, but I don't think they carved specific instructions in stone for nothing. I had to dig in the, ah —" she stammered over the word library, but tried to recover just as instantly, "— records… I had to dig in the records to find the magic word, I'm not about to go blurting it out inconsequentially."

"Right," Ben smirked, shaking his head as he plodded down the stairs behind her. Maybe she'd never let her guard down, but at least it was plain for him to see what it cost her to keep it up.

She got to the platform at the base of the stairs and whirled on him.

"What's that supposed to mean?"

"I believe it means I agree with you, but I'm sure you're armed and ready to correct me," he said arriving at the bottom of the stairs.

"Ah, so you think I'm too uptight to recognize sarcasm when I hear it, so you can mock me without being questioned on the validity of your argument. What are you laughing at?" she fumed, more outraged the further his signature half smile tilted.

He paused as his eyes traveled over her face, from her irate crumpled eyebrows, to her scowling lips; yet under his stare all of her features began to soften. He leaned down bringing his face nearer to hers.

"Stop flirting with me, we're at work," he said in a low voice that stirred her blood like a cocktail straw.

"How dare —"

"What the hell…"

Her combative nature dropped like a hammer when his eyes were drawn past her and she watched the levity drain from his face. She spun around to see the second set of doors at the back of the ante room.

They were glowing.

She broke out in a sprint.

"Edie, wait!"

Now it was Ben's face rife with fury as he raced after her and Edie's alight with anticipation as every step vaulted her closer to the pale golden glow of the next entryway.

They got to the second set of doors to see the radiance was coming from within the grooves of the carved symbols and scenes, as if it was backlit by candle light. . The surface of this set of doors was crowded with more words as the weight of this curse was in the engraved spell that guarded this door.

But the scene depicted in the center was the same stylized illustrated character from the front door, the Weeping Viper in profile, but this time, her arm was raised in the air brandishing a dagger and she was surrounded by snakes. As the door was lit with a pale flicker, the eyes of the snakes were glowing red.

She traced her fingers over the illuminated tableau, pressing her lips together to keep from even mouthing the wrong words. Ben crossed his arms over his chest and withdrew his pistols from their holster. A disturbing scowl set his jaw as he battled the unwelcome thoughts of what could happen to her.

This time, she did glance back at Ben briefly and though the look on his face was hard as the limestone beneath her fingertips, the sharp nod he gave was imbued with all that was between them. Against every screaming cell in his body, he was right beside her and that's where he would stay.

His confidence erased her apprehension. Arms dropped to her sides, she stepped back and took in the full view of the inscription, and began to speak.

Reciting the incantation in the language of her ancestors, the gorgeous lyrical dialect sweeping off her tongue effortlessly. The light continued to flutter, but with each word she spoke, the corresponding hieratic engraving activated, glowing furiously as a fiery ember.

Once Edith arrived at the final verse to recite the Weeping Viper's true name.

"...Amnara!"

When the last syllable sealed the spell, the door shifted forward and then swung open, and Edith leapt clear of its path and bumped into Ben's chest.

He wanted to encircle her in his arms, but his hands were occupied with pistols, and in a heartbeat she had stepped away.

Though the room was dark, she approached with sure steps. Just as she had expected, and Ben had feared, the moment she crossed the threshold, Edith was taken under by the vision.

The last thing he saw was her levitating body go slack and become enveloped within darkness.

A cyclone of shimmering golden smoke engulfed her, and when it cleared, she was back in time. The whispering door and whooshing winds that carried the smoke subsided, leaving her surroundings silent. Unlike before, she was no longer in the tomb seeing apparitions play against the furniture displayed, but standing in the palace she recognized from depictions of the reign of Ramesses the Great. The dank and musty smell of the underground had been replaced by the heavy scent of incense filtered through hot, sweet desert air. Warmth from a long-ago sun spread over her skin, smoothing the goosebumps the cool, still subterranean atmosphere had raised there.

Beyond the row of massive columns, the city was an uproar of laughter and song for what must have been a Feast Day. Edith could identify the celebration for the God Amun, as the dense crowd of townsfolk far below made a joyous parade through the streets toward the flotilla of sailboats. They carried baskets piled high with offerings of fruit and flowers, and led goats and sheep to be sacrificed for the God Amun.

Between two columns before her stood the woman from the first vision.

The Weeping Viper.

Amnara.

She was even more resplendent now, many years later. Her robe and sash woven of the finest linen draped over her golden bronze skin and lovely curves. Her wig of glossy black locks was of the highest quality, fit for a queen, yet absent a crown.

A modestly dressed servant entered from an adjoining room carrying a collar necklace, arms raised high to drape it on her lady's neck. Amnara held up a hand to dismiss the adornment.

"He requested that I bare my neck and shoulders this day. He will finally reveal the surprise he's been preparing for so long," Amnara said.

The servant gasped, clutching the forgotten beads to her chest in anticipation.

"Will you be Queen?"

A smile spread across her face reaching to crease the corners of her eyes.

"That is never to be," Amnara replied. "Neither is it what I desire. I am content to live as his companion."

She cast her eyes out over the crowd once more.

"To love and be loved by a great man is too consuming to share in the duties of rearing a kingdom." She glanced back at her friend with a look of earnest reassurance. "To be a queen is to shoulder the responsibility of all your subjects. I want only to care for him, and for our son."

The hum of a gong sounded and echoed against the polished stone walls.

"Well, run along to care for him, then," the servant teased, patting her arm affectionately before hurrying along to her other duties.

Amnara swept out of the room with a skip in her step. The giddy anticipation to see her partner was plain on her face, even after so many years.

At the threshold of a grand room, Amnara stopped short. As if she had hit a concrete wall of apprehension, her demeanor changed instantly. Her shoulders shifted slightly as she took a stance that was more alert. Concern fell over her face like a shadow and her lips parted. The gong that had rung moments ago from the room before her was still humming; an almost imperceptibly low frequency that felt like a tickle in her ear drum as her spine began to stiffen.

"Ramesses?"

There was silence.

Then the apprehension was whisked away just as quickly as it had come, replaced by urgency and dread. Amnara sprinted the short distance to enter the room.

Edith's hands shot to her ears as Amnara shrieked so sharply she thought the walls might crack. When she opened her eyes again, her hands slipped from her ears and covered her mouth to muffle her own screams.

Ramesses' lifeless body was a heap in a pool of blood on the stone floor, one arm outstretched toward the balcony inches away from a discarded purple cloth and a crumpled length of papyrus.

Edith looked on as Amnara's hands roamed over him, clutching at his body desperate for signs of life. By the time she found the stab wound in his back, she was in shock.

"My love?" she sobbed, in disbelief, staring down at her palms, now covered in blood.

When the nearby guards rushed in at the sound of her screams, that's how they found her. With blood on her hands. They looked on, momentarily frozen to assess the scene in front of them, as she gathered the purple cloth to apply pressure to his wound. As she balled it up a small strip of papyrus on a string of twine fluttered to the floor, landing open afloat in the pool of blood.

Amnara was able to read the note before the red stain seeped from the edges to the center.

"A gift fit for the queen of my heart."

Amnara howled, taken under by unimaginable grief, just as the words of her partner's last love note vanished, swallowed by crimson.

A tear rolled down Edith's cheek as she watched the tragic scene burst into shimmering ashes floating on a mild desert breeze, disappearing before the air around her stilled, and cooled, and darkness descended once again.

She would have fallen to the ground if she hadn't already been wrapped tightly in Ben's arms.

"God damn it," he shouted "Edie, are you okay?"

Edith's eyes began to flutter and the moment she regained consciousness she began coughing. Ben noticed golden shimmering soot from her nostrils. He undid his bandana and wiped her face trying to clear it away.

"She didn't do it, Ben," Edith croaked, gasping for air.

"Okay," he said, nodding. He was distracted by witnessing that Edie's second vision had taken a more drastic effect on her than the first.

"Amnara… She didn't plot to kill Ramesses. She was framed. The attempt on his life happened while she wasn't even there," she said, before hunching in a mad fit of hacking again.

"Let's get you out of here. Everything else can wait for tomorrow."

He helped her rise up and she let him. Her exhaustion was so encompassing it didn't occur to her to argue.

While she'd been in the past, Ben had lit the torches around the room to show she was surrounded by breathtaking painted walls, rich with color and detail. Life-sized painted figures stood all around them in brilliant shades of ancient mineral pigments. Filled with awe, she turned in a slow circle to take in the splendor. However, by the time she'd completed the rotation her delight met its demise as horror clutched at her chest.

Each of the portraits' subjects were standing with Anubis, the God of Death. Each one was the plaque of a sarcophagus, sealing a mummified body inside. The bodies of Amnara's closest loved ones.

"These are the catacombs."

Edith looked to one side to see a woman in plain dress, and thought of the servant from her vision. But when her eyes shifted to side, she caught a sight that made her eyes burn with the threat of tears. It was a teenage boy bravely facing Anubis. A boy with a headdress adorned by a sapphire scarab.

A sigh shuddered from Edith as she felt a surprising pang of grief at the knowledge that she stood before the grave of Cepos. The first heir of the Ramesses the Great, prince of the Golden Age of Egypt. The murdered son of Amnara.

"The burial chamber of Cepos. Son of a king. And the most scorned woman in history."

Ben glanced at the painting, and his eyes seemed to drift beyond it before he cast them to the ground. His face was grim, and his distaste for the injustice of pharaonic Egyptian law was plain to see there.

She glanced over her shoulder to see the final door. Flanked by two statues of Anubis guarding the treasure room. One hand held the staff's upright, with their other hand outstretched toward the entry. From the staff's dangled orbs of stamped copper that held incense. In the dim light, she couldn't make out the scene carved in the door, and she knew Ben wouldn't allow her to linger and examine it. Unfortunately, she also knew he was right.

CHAPTER SIXTEEN

ONCE THEY REACHED the platform at the base of the stairs leading to the exit, they knew something was wrong right away. Even from that far away, they could see that the doors were shut.

"Ben..."

"I know."

Panic sizzled like static in the glance that passed between them before they bolted. Edith could only manage a few strides at a running pace before she needed to sit down and catch her breath.

Once at the top, Ben immediately started pushing the doors, and gradually applying more force. Then, he was ramming his shoulder into the door with all his might.

"Someone must have taken the lotus," Edith said, sprawled across the steps once she'd made it to the top of the stairwell.

Suddenly registering that if the door was shut, the lotus must be gone.

Ben lit two torches and put them on either side of the landing.

"If anyone from the crew sees the doors closed, they'll know we're in here. I don't know why the doors would be closed in the first place. But it's a busy work site. Someone will come close enough to the tomb soon." His brows furrowed as his eyes darted between her bedraggled face and the doors that imprisoned them. "I wanted to get you back to your hotel room to rest, but why don't you sit down here for now."

"If the lotus was in the doors, they'd be opening, which means someone must have taken it. How will the crew be able to get us out of here when they do find out that we're missing? Furthermore, how can you be sure they'll know we are still in here at all? They could just as easily assume that we left and took the lotus with us."

While Edith spoke, Ben was trying to calculate in the back of his mind just how much oxygen was in this tomb, and how long it would last them.

"We'll cross that road when we come to it. We don't know the lotus was taken, and even if it was, we don't know that it wasn't a simple error of someone from the dig site."

While puzzling out the circumstances in her mind, Edith had caught her breath and made it to the top step to sit up right, marginally more composed. Ben sat on the other side of the steps, resting his back against the door. Long moments passed as he offered her water and crackers from his duffle, and they used his bandana and her scarf to freshen up the thin layer of soot they had both been bathed in.

After sitting a while in companionable silence, he noticed the worry drawing deep lines on Edith's face.

"No one's going to demolish the door," he said, reading her thoughts. "They're afraid to even use a letter opener on this site after the day we had yesterday."

"What do you mean?" she said.

"Nevermind."

"I thought you were a man who fired explosives first and asked questions later?"

"Yeah, well…" he grumbled rubbing the stubble on his chin.

Her face brightened.

"Ben, are you being gentle on site for me?"

"Yes, Edith, you're the head of this dig. As you have told anyone who will listen."

"Even though you could have destroyed plenty of precious timeless artifacts while I was gone!"

"Listen, don't read too much into it," he said, and she saw the hint of a smile tugging at his lips in the flickering torch light.

"That's sweet…" she said, trailing off.

"What?"

"I'm just wondering, the more I get to know about you. I just can't seem to make heads or tails of why you'd be in this position, working for me, like you said. You studied at Oxford."

"It's a lot easier for a man to get into Oxford than a woman."

"Yes, I've gathered as much. You didn't tell me to spare my feelings."

"I wouldn't say all that, it just didn't come up."

"Right, you would have had to bend over backwards to work it into conversation one of the six or seven times a day I mention Oxford."

"Well, anyway, you were saying..."

"Yes, your compassion for my failures aside, you did study at Oxford. But you also have quite the reputation and length of digs on your resume. You could be doing less harsh work for better pay, and ... well I would otherwise assume you do it for the love of archaeology, but you very clearly hate being in this tomb, or near a burial ground. It makes me wonder how you'd even get into something like this. How does the kind of man who ends up at Oxford also have the cunning street smarts that you do?"

"The way that you talk about me going to Oxford makes it sound like you're completely shocked."

"Well, it's true that at first you come across as rather rough around the edges, but you shouldn't take offense to the fact that you simply seem too capable an adventurer to also be an academic. I've met many in my life and they don't have the roughened hands of an explorer. I thought you had an upbringing that was more—"

"What, you saw a grizzly American thief and you thought I must be an orphan with a troubled past? You read too many books, lady."

"Well, yes, distinctly."

He laughed, undeniably charmed by her.

"My father was a diplomat. I know how to make my way around a new city, and I guess running around the streets getting into trouble just comes naturally to me. I think usually I would have been in a boarding school but… my mother wanted to keep me close. To answer your question… she's why I'm on this dig."

"Really, how so?"

"You said I could probably make more money doing less dangerous work and stay clear of tombs. That's all true. You know I'm not in it out of respect for history, unfortunately for you. But I'm actually not in it for money. I need something more valuable than money."

"What's more valuable than money, but not history?"

"Treasure."

"I don't follow. Treasure hunters do it for money."

"I'm doing it for a bargaining chip."

"Oh?"

Ben leaned forward bracing his elbows on his knees, staring down the depths of the pitch black stairwell, and released a long exhale.

"I did study at Oxford. Like I said, I've always been comfortable with travel, and taking risks, so naturally I was drawn toward archaeological sites. Not the kind here in Egypt, but of history that is more… well, square, to be perfectly honest."

"I don't follow. What did you study?"

"Geology."

"That's not square — it's fascinating!"

"We're talking about rocks, but okay. You're one in a million, kid."

“Hmm.” She made a sound of disapproval.

“I’m not saying I was well behaved, or anything. I’d done plenty of odd jobs on the side that weren’t strictly on the up and up. But one dig that I was on with a team in France uncovered some pretty astonishing artifacts relating to Bonaparte. I was unaware at the time, but the public figure funding the dig wanted the goods delivered to America. I guess I was naive to not know that it was illegal.”

Edith imagined a fresh-faced, lanky Benjamin Brooks getting caught up in a scheme and worried about what his mother would think — it made her chest feel tight.

“So, when we got busted, I was drafted into the French Foreign Legion to avoid incarceration by the French federal government. To this day, I can’t step foot in America without being arrested for my involvement. It was all the plot of a politician and some old money, so they had to make a big deal about someone taking the fall, and unfortunately, it was me.”

Edith realized she preferred thinking of Ben as a carefree street tough who flies by the seat of his pants. Learning he was a geology nut who’d been taken advantage of while he was young and naive drew deep lines in her face.

“Out of everyone involved, I was the most green. The others had strings they could pull to get out of trouble. I came into this hoping that I could discover a rare treasure significant enough to negotiate the terms of me settling that dispute. I know that my mom would feel a whole lot better if the issue was finally settled, and I was allowed back in the states.”

In the dark, she heard him shifting to sit back against the door of the tomb with a sigh.

"Oh Ben..."

"I'm sure you're pleased to hear it. I know how you love to be right."

She felt a pang for every unkind thing she'd ever said to him. A few days ago she wouldn't even let herself smile at his joke. But now her pride couldn't compete with her heart. Unable to walk, she just began crawling on her hands and knees to make her way from her side of the stairwell to his.

"Ben, I don't —"

"You always knew. You thought I was a filthy scoundrel from the beginning and had no problem telling me so."

"Ben, I'm —"

"I'm sure you've come to your senses by now."

"I have," she said.

He leaned toward the sound of her voice getting near.

"Ready to run back to old George, then?"

"No. I've come to my senses... and seen that I was wrong about you, and I'm sorry."

"Oh. I thought you must have ran into him after I left town."

"Why would you think that?"

"You just seem... a bit distant since you got back."

When she thought she was close enough she reached out to find him and felt her hand land on his chest. She believed she'd know the feel of that chest anywhere.

"Is this better?" she said, settling to sit behind him.

"No," he said, pulling her into his lap.

"Why do you keep bringing up George?" she asked, her breath catching as his arms came around her.

"George… your sweetheart?"

"Ben," she said with her hands cupping his face. "George is nothing to me, and I'm nothing to him. He was my date to parties before I met you."

"What's that supposed to mean? As if he won't be your date to parties now that we've met."

"He wasn't my date to the gala."

"You made it very clear I also wasn't your date."

Edith burned with shame at the memory of her putting distance between them, and introducing him as an employee. Twice.

"Ben, I don't know what you are!" She threw up her hands, exasperated.

He looked her in the eye and all of his teasing was gone.

"Don't lie, Edith. It isn't ladylike. We both know what I am."

"A scholar?"

"A criminal."

"The only man who's ever truly satisfied me?"

"The only man who ever will," he said, his voice deepening, as he reached his hand up to her cheek in the dim torchlight, and pulled her in to kiss him. His lips brushed against hers, as his hand went to her hair.

A kiss that began as a sweet reunion gained a momentum that hurtled toward greed. His mouth was possessive and impatient, and seemed to punish her for the intense need she ignited within him.

He broke away to trail kisses down her neck before he reached her scarf, tied up high tight. He began to tug until it loosened.

As her collar loosened, he kissed her throat, and worked at the buttons of her shirt, clearing the way for his mouth to go lower.

She shifted to straddle his lap and he groaned when she pressed herself against the bulge in his trousers. With her shirt undone by a few buttons, he placed his lips between her breasts where her collar fell open and slipped his hands up her skirt. Digging his fingers beneath where her slip stretched over her thighs, he felt her hips roll. He planted his kisses across her breasts above the satin and lace.

"I can't stop thinking about you," he said as he moved his hands to the button of one of her garters. Her fingers dug in his hair with the anticipation of his hands working under her skirt.

"Well, we're together practically every waking moment," she said breathlessly.

"You were gone for almost three days," he said, stopping to glare at her, pressing himself where she began to ache between her thighs. Her heart fluttered at the acknowledgement that he'd suffered in her absence.

"It was your idea," she panted.

He couldn't wait until she was undressed and his tongue soaked the satin of her bra, the flick of his tongue flooded her system with need.

"You're right" he said as she whimpered, "I'll make it up to you… let me —"

She braced her palms flat against the stone door behind him.

Just then, the wall gave and rumbled open swiftly. As the door swung away behind him, Ben fell backwards. Edith fell forward.

She looked up to see a large gathering of crew members, and another group of people who weren't on the crew. They were all men in suits holding cameras with the crackle of flashing bulbs breaking out across the crowd.

Press.

It would appear that the news had spread.

Edith's first encounter with the realities of fame, and the recognition she had so desperately craved, came at the moment she was straddling Ben with shirt gaping open, and he lay flat on his back with his hands gripping her thighs.

Ben sat up, cradling Edith to his chest as he shouted back a phrase in Egyptian that made everyone scatter, including the crew. Edith dismounted Ben and sat on her heels making an attempt to button her shirt, but she was blindsided with humiliation.

"So much for making a big splash in the world of archaeology. I wonder what the odds are of me ever being taken seriously now."

The door groaned, and Ben hoisted Edith over his shoulder just in time to dive out of the way before it swung shut behind them again closing with a loud gritty thud. Ben set a dazed Edith on her feet and went straight to examine the door.

The lotus was gone. Without it, they would have no way back into the tomb. Their eyes snapped to each other simultaneously.

"How will we get it back?" Edith said, just as Ben was saying, "We'll get it back."

"Oh, no," Edith said, looking pale as her hands raised to her cheeks.

"Don't panic yet, someone on the crew might have the key," he said, trying to ease her worry. "Either way, Edie, there are ways to remove this door while keeping it intact."

"No one's ever been able to do that before; this is a famed tomb — people have tried."

"That was before it had ever been opened. It just opened by itself a minute ago."

"No, it had to be open already, it wasn't locked like it is now."

"I tried to open the door, I pushed as hard as I could, and it wouldn't budge. It can open again, even if it's locked right now."

"Maybe the key was in there, and someone unlocked it and ran away just as it opened."

Ben grabbed his pack, suddenly impatient.

"You need to get back to the hotel."

"We?"

"You."

He grabbed her hand and began walking briskly down the quay, knowing the walk back to the hotel would feel a lot longer than it looked.

The moment Ben had gotten Edith to her room, he told her to lock the door, and left. She had taken a bath, after being covered in the strange shimmering soot that billowed around her both times she'd had visions in the tomb. Afterward, she laid down in bed and spent the rest of the afternoon between her crisp cotton sheets and linen covers. Exhausted, she pondered whether it must have been some sort of adrenaline that got her all the way back out of the tomb after passing out. She spent hours thinking about her vision, and what it meant.

It meant that Isfetheru, or really, Amnara, was put to death wrongfully for a crime that she didn't commit. It was bad enough that her legitimate claims to the throne on behalf of her son were technically valid all of this time. She had been painted as a scheming gold digger, when in reality, she hadn't even committed the crime to begin with.

She tried to stop herself from wondering where Ben had gone with a look of stone cold determination on his face. He had tried, and failed, to assure her that she would find her necklace, that it wasn't the result of any sort of foul play.

But how could that be? No one on the site, even the young men, would have crossed Ben. She had heard them ribbing him about how they wouldn't dare to use anything more aggressive than a toothpick in their excavation within the tomb. Everyone would have known not to touch the lotus.

Then she remembered something that Ben had said that hadn't made any sense. Ben had pushed the doors as hard as he could when they got to the top of the stairs to exit the tomb, and it wouldn't budge. But then, they opened when they barely leaned on them. They hadn't just opened, they swung open, just like they did when they had been activated by the lotus. But how could someone have closed the doors and removed the lotus, and then opened the doors with the lotus again, and then retrieved it from the door and run away in time so that no one would see them?

Luckily, she realized the answer to the question was easy to get a hold of. The crew and all of the reporters were standing there just as she'd tumbled out of the tomb on top of Ben. It was mortifying that they'd all seen her in a compromising position in a state of undress, but the silver lining, and more important than her pride at this point, was the realization that someone must have seen what happened to the door, and who made off with her lotus.

It was possible that there might even be photos of the culprit, before all the photographs of her underwear were taken.

Just then, she heard a knock at the door. When she answered it, Ben was standing there holding a burlap sack. He was still filthy from the golden soot from inside the tomb, and she realized that he hadn't been back since he left her here hours earlier.

She could see he was caught off guard to see her wearing a nightgown. It took him a moment to proceed. Knowing that she had such an effect on him made her feel an uneasy pride.

"I just wanted to check on you and see how you're doing after… what happened in the tomb."

"You mean being photographed on top of you with my blouse hanging open?"

"I was thinking about passing out from smoke inhalation. But, you'll be happy to know that you won't need to worry about the incident with the press."

"Oh?"

He tossed the burlap sack within the doorway of her room, and she heard a crunch. She was startled at the discordant sound, but she looked inside and realized that it was filled with cameras. Many of the light bulbs had been shattered, and the sack still made the sound of broken glass settling.

She beamed at him.

"That's where you've been all day?"

"I need to get cleaned up. I'll be back in an hour to take you to dinner."

She hoped she wasn't blushing, as it would likely come across as immature. And yet, it was thrilling to her that Ben was asking her to dinner. The brief thought passed through her mind that it would be lovely to be asked to join him for dinner under more normal circumstances.

She was dismayed to realize her initial reaction to that thought was that, under normal circumstances, she probably would never have given Ben a chance. On paper, he wasn't quite courtship material for Edith. But in person, she'd never wanted anyone more in her life.

The more she got to know about him, the more she admired him. Even though she had already known he was a thief. Even in spite of the fact that he'd just admitted he was a wanted felon. Maybe she admired him even more for having admitted it.

"I can meet you down there, you don't have to come all the way back to my room."

His lips spread in half a smile.

"I've been in the room next to yours this whole time. You didn't know that? There's an adjoining door connecting our rooms right there."

"Oh," she said, glancing back. Then she smirked. "Well, you never mentioned. How was I supposed to know?"

"I'll be back in an hour," he said laughing to himself.

He turned to leave, then with a shake of his head turned back and lunged back into her room and captured her face in his hands to kiss her. It was meant to be a peck but when she moaned, and he tasted her, they both sank into it, until he finally tore himself away, and shut the door.

Later, Edith paused with her glass of wine halfway to her lips and said, "Thank you so much for getting all of that film from the photographers."

"Don't mention it," he said, downplaying the kindness considerably.

"I wanted to tell you…" he said, visibly uncomfortable to bring up whatever he was about to mention. "I was also trying to get information about the lotus. It seems that… no one on the crew has it. And they didn't see anything either."

"You mean they didn't see who took it?"

"They didn't see anyone take it. They didn't see it happen."

"It doesn't make any sense. If the lotus wasn't in the door when we leaned against it, then how did the door swing open?"

"Even if that was the case, it still doesn't add up. They couldn't have gotten down the quay and through the crowd without being seen by a crowd of people."

Edith's eyes were darting around as if the way to solve the puzzle was somewhere on the tablecloth.

It was unfortunate, he thought, that she was so new to this. Her background was in a realm of meticulously kept records. She was used to having a question, searching for the answer, and finding it. There was something she had yet to learn about this strange and often bleak landscape of cursed and haunted burial grounds. You often find yourself trying to apply logic to a subject ruled by magic. You may have a question whose answer lies with the dead.

"How are you feeling?"

"I'm fine, I laid down all afternoon."

"I told you this might happen."

"Oh, don't start."

"I'm not kidding, Edie. This isn't about me. It isn't bravado. This is Ben Brooks informing Edith Taylor, if you keep going into that tomb, it could get worse. I told you, the curse in that tomb could put you into a trance you can't come out of. Or worse."

"I am well aware that Mr. Brooks advises against it professionally. But I know that Ben understands why I need to go back. There's still another door."

"Mr. Brooks will continue to share his experience, and assist you as long as it takes, as he was hired to do. But Ben..." he lowered his voice and mumbled the rest, "is terrified of what could happen to you."

"We'll both be fine," she tried to assure him. She wasn't being dismissive or brusque as she may have been a few days ago. She was genuinely trying to ease his mind.

"You can't say that. You can't know what will happen. And you can't deny that what happened to you in there today was much worse than the first time."

"But Ben, she was framed! All this time, that's been the real story of the Weeping Viper, the real story of Amnara!"

"Edith," he ground out her name, dragging his hand over his face.

"But, Ben, there's more. I didn't just find her name, I discovered that she's from a significant tribe. I'm shocked I didn't recognize her tattoos from the beginning, but I suppose..." she shrugged sheepishly, "there was quite a bit going on, and it slipped through the cracks."

"What do you mean?" he said, leaning in.

"Amnara was from the Didia bloodline, a lineage of High Priests and Priestesses. A tribe that practiced magic. That's the significance of the lotus; they were artisans of protective amulets and they used peridot as their signature gem stone. Ben, the integrity of her birth, the pride of her name, has been wiped from history for a crime she didn't commit."

"So you're saying you'd die to bring her truth to light?"

"I'm saying that..." she took a deep breath, grateful to have someone she could trust without hesitation. "I believe that because I'm bringing the truth to light, I won't be harmed. I know you've seen some evil magic, but I think this magic is protective. We're both down there, but I'm the only one seeing the visions. Maybe she knows I'm there to free her. And I don't think I'll be killed in that tomb. I think I am the one who's safe from the curse... and I'm the one that needs to break the curse."

"Well. I guess we don't have to squabble about the consequences of you going back into the tomb too soon anyway."

"How refreshing," she said, lifting a glass to her lips, but stopping right before she could take a sip. "Wait a minute, why?"

"Because you can't get back in without the lotus." It wasn't a dig at her about losing her necklace, he wouldn't have teased her about that. He was simply lightening the mood by gloating about getting his own way after all.

"Oh, just stop it," she said. She swatted at him with a napkin. In retaliation, he slipped his hand under the table cloth and plucked at her skirt to snap her garter. She gasped, and faked an offended expression.

"Well, two can play at that game," she whispered, reaching for his lap beneath the tablecloth.

She yanked her hand back when she heard the clink of her glass and realized the waiter was standing there filling their waters. Startled by his presence they both said in unison, "We'll take the check!"

CHAPTER SEVENTEEN

MOMENTS LATER THEY were at her door again. She'd opened it with the key and stepped inside, but Ben remained on the other side of the threshold. She turned to see him standing, leaning with his arm raised against the door jam.

When she tilted her chin up to look at him, she was close enough that she had to tilt her head back.

"You should get some rest," he said.

"I feel rested," she said, leaning against the door jam, bringing herself even closer. "I don't think it was all that bad as you say it was. I must have only been out for a moment. And I was tired once we got back, but I laid down all day." She had to stop herself from batting her eyelashes at him.

If he was about to cut their evening short, she could still maintain some modicum of respect. She'd hardly run after him.

"I guess I'll just always think it's that bad when you faint." He looked down before meeting her eyes again. He was attempting to tease, but finding himself unable to shake the gravity of what he felt. "You can't be too careful, as far as I'm concerned."

Okay, hell, maybe she would end up running after him.

"You could always come in. It'd be easy to keep an eye on me from… right over there," she said, nodding her head toward the bed.

She saw something dark flash in his eyes that was familiar, as he did whenever she made a lewd suggestion that was a departure from her office hours demeanor. He leaned into her room, slightly. She leaned a bit too, thinking, if she just went onto the tips of her toes now her lips would be halfway to his lips. She cursed herself for wearing her flat worn leather loafers rather than the heeled satin slippers she'd packed.

He smiled down at her. They both knew he could close the distance between them with very little effort. They both knew she wanted him, too. But there was that mischievous look in his eye.

"You really should just relax for the night. I wouldn't want to …" he looked behind her around her room "…keep you," he said, meeting her eyes again.

"Well. Good night, Edith," he said, pushing away from the door jam, letting the door begin to close.

"Good night, Ben," she said just before the door knob clicked.

Edith stood and stared at the door for what felt like an eternity. Then she kicked off her loafers and flopped back on the bed.

He hadn't wanted to come in, she thought. And then, like a schoolgirl, she began to rack her brain for what may have changed her mind about … them… over the past few days. Since the night of the ball, in the library, where it seemed like there's nothing he wouldn't do to get an invitation into her hotel room. When it seemed like he felt an evening with her was like giving a dying man a cold glass of water. But then there was a knock at the door on the far side of her room.

The door Ben had said was a door between her room and his. Pride dashed aside and she ran to the door to open it.

"I thought you didn't want to keep me?" she said with a smile.

"That was a lie," he said, bending to sweep her up in a kiss and pull her into his room. "I do want to keep you."

He sat on the sofa along the wall, drawing her into his lap. He made quick work of her tidy kerchief and the top buttons of her blouse, and she realized they were picking up right where they left off.

"Yes, let's start over…" she whispered, thinking of the tomb.

"Sure," he chuckled, smiling wickedly against her neck. "Miss Taylor, you must be more careful on these bumpy train rides. It appears you've fallen right into my lap," he said, thrusting his hips as he pulled her ass tighter against his groin, exactly as he wanted to do the day they met.

Giggling, she raked her hands through his hair as his hips lifted her before settling back into the cushions.

"Oh Mr. Brooks, I really should be getting back to my seat."

"Alright," he said, undoing the next button on her shirt and burying his face there to scatter kisses across her chest.

"But before you go, I have to say when I first met you, I thought you were the most beautiful woman I'd ever seen."

"Oh..." she said breathlessly.

She squeezed her eyes shut as his hand went to her knee, and just his fingertips snuck beneath the hem of her skirt.

"I was wondering if you might like to..."

He kissed her as his hands slid underneath her skirt, but this time he didn't bother with her garters.

"... let me fuck you hard in a library." He swept his thumb over the crotch of her panties as he said it, and she felt a rush of wet heat, just like every time he said something filthy.

He slipped his fingers inside her panties and rubbed her naked clit as she whimpered. All of the tenderness he'd had in the darkness of the tomb had been left behind. Rather than showering her with soft romantic kisses, he ripped her bra down exposing her breasts as he teased her just to the edge of a climax, but offered her no release.

His hand came out from under her skirt and he hooked his hands behind her knees, spreading her legs apart until she was straddling him, then dragged her closer until her wet panties were fit to the bulge in his trousers.

When they made contact there they both moaned as if they'd been lovers separated for years, rather than barely acquainted colleagues who'd only been separated for 42 hours.

She thought to herself, why does it feel like that? It was as though she'd known Ben for years. His body felt right with hers like no other man ever had.

She unbuttoned and removed his shirt, wanting to feel herself against him, wanting to see his broad, muscular chest, wanting to feel her breasts pressed against it again.

Once both her garters were freed, one hand slid underneath her slip to grab her ass and guide her hips where he wanted them.

She placed her hands behind her, on his knees, and leaned back to grind against the long steel shaft she felt there. Arching her back as he removed her shirt, and then finished the job of removing her torn bra.

For a moment, he leaned back as she pleasured herself on his cock through their clothes, watching as she arched her back and rode him.

"Make yourself come while I watch," he panted.

Then she leaned forward with her hand behind him on the couch, continuing to ride him with her chest hovering over his face.

"Not yet…" she said.

His hands came from under her skirt to grab her breasts, as he buried his face in them, sinking his teeth into one of them. She felt the two day growth of his beard scratch the soft skin and it gave her goosebumps.

She stopped the movement of her hips, and slid off his lap to stand up in front of him.

"Take it out," she said.

Their eyes were locked as he unbuckled his belt and unbuttoned his pants. She unbuttoned her waistband and let her skirt fall to the floor. Ben slid lower in his seat to reach into his trousers and withdraw his cock, gripping it as his eyes roamed over her body. They watched each other as she undressed and he stroked himself. When she dropped her panties, Ben groaned to see her slick and ready.

Seeing her get down on her knees before him brought his hand to an abrupt stop.

"Hey —"

"Hi," she said, replacing the hand he used to touch himself with her own.

"What are you doing?"

"Oh, nothing."

"Don't tell me you've done this before?"

"Why?"

"If the men you've been with have never gotten you off properly, your pretty little mouth should be nowhere near their pants. That's just … ah… ungentlemanly," he said, stumbling a bit as her fingertips began to loosely travel up and down the long, thick length of him.

"I've never done it before."

"Edie… who have you been talking to?" he teased.

"Hush now."

As Edith stroked him faster, a pearly bead of cum emerged. Ben saw the pink tip of her tongue tentatively lick it from the head of his cock, and his eyes rolled as his head fell to the back of the couch.

The taste was unfamiliar, and it was thrilling that she'd never done it before. It felt right for it to be happening with Ben. He watched as she parted her lips and took him, slowly, deep into her throat, her mouth sliding down around him in one drawn out motion. She pressed her tongue against him experimentally and felt him swell.

"Oh, fuck." He closed his eyes as she drew back, suctioning with her mouth until he felt her lips slide over the tip again. Then she repeated, going faster, stroking him with her hand as her mouth followed. His control began to splinter as he threaded his fingers through her hair, and began to thrust himself into her throat.

"Mmm," She murmured in approval.

He felt the hum of her lips against his skin, and knowing she wanted him in her mouth made him feel like he might explode. He wanted to fall to the floor and hammer her into the ground.

"Edie, I'm about to come."

Her swollen red lips came off of him with a smacking sound.

"In my mouth?" she said, still working him in her fist.

"No," he panted. "I need to have you in my bed."

She slipped beneath his covers as he removed the rest of his clothes, and then he joined her. He kissed her with his tongue, and his lips, and his teeth as his hands moved to her breasts. Pressing them together, he lathed his tongue across her nipples, one then the other, rubbing them with his thumbs as his fingers dug into the soft pillowy flesh. When she was whimpering, he drew one of her breasts into his mouth and sucked hard as he slipped his hand between her legs. He slid two fingers between her lips to find her slick with anticipation.

"Mmm," he murmured against her breast as he felt how wet she was. He heard her breath quicken.

Then his hand was moving in rhythmic circles over her clit, driving her nearly to the edge before he plunged his fingers inside her to rub against her soft spot. She laid flat on her back with her legs spread wide and when she felt herself near what she desperately wanted, she tilted her hips when his hand slipped out to caress her again. He brought her to a fast, intense climax efficiently as a maestro, and she felt her orgasm snap, feverish and fluid as sweat broke across her brow.

Just as she had last time, the molten liquid pulse of her climax made her crave the fullness of him inside her, and she reached for him.

He rolled on top of her and slid the head of his cock against her wet lips, teasing her with it as she came.

"Do you want this?"

"Yes," As she said it, he nestled his cock at her entrance and felt the snug fit of her constricting around him. Once his head was in, he pressed deeper and a groan escaped his lips at the incredible friction.

Edith moaned and thrust her hips to take him deeper, and he pulsed inside her as her sheath gripped his cock. Suddenly he thrust into her, sinking the entire thick length with one stroke that made her cry out. Then he continued, and was pounding into her harder and faster.

"Is that how you want it?"

"Yes," she said, as she quivered beneath him, being driven over another peak as he penetrated her.

"Do you want it deeper?" he said, his lips curving.

"Oh, Ben."

He bent her legs back, opening her wide, and she began to yelp with each thrust as he went deeper and deeper.

Feeling her slick clenching around him, he could hear she was nearing her climax. He watched the look on her face as she strained for his cock each time he railed into her.

Reaching down to touch her clit sent her bursting over the edge again. He felt her convulse around him like a fist, coming like a geyser, and he tilted his hips to enhance her climax and bring on his own.

"Do you want my come?" he growled as sweat broke out across his back.

"Please…"

The way she begged sent him over the edge, pulsing as he spent himself in the tightest, sweetest embrace he'd ever felt.

As he did, she was moaning, wracked with the fulfillment of her orgasm settling over her in waves as it subsided. When the sensation of blinding triumph began to pass, he eased out of her and tried to relearn how to breathe. He couldn't believe how good it was.

"You have the most unbelievable, perfect body I've ever seen. Sonnets were invented to worship bodies like yours."

He looked mesmerized, settled between her legs as he watched her breasts sway while her breath kept coming in gasps. For a while they were suspended in sensations and silence.

The question of whether or not he'd expect her to get going was just beginning to cross her mind when he laid beside her and pulled her into his arms. Nestling her back against his chest, he kissed her shoulder before resting his chin in her hair.

"You're nothing like what I thought you'd be the day we met, Mr. Brooks. I never could have imagined this would happen."

Once she'd said it, she felt the hand that stroked her hip hesitate briefly. She shifted to look back at him.

"I didn't mean…"

"I know you didn't."

"Ben, about the night of the ball."

"Go on," he said, arching an eyebrow suggestively.

"About what I said to Margaret…" He laid back on the pillow and stared at the ceiling, knowing where she was headed. Mincing words was something he detested so thoroughly, but he didn't want to argue with her.

"I knew the way that the ladies would look at you when you walked in before I even saw how good you looked in a tux."

"I imagine when they find out I'm a felon it will clear the field for you. Though, I must say, I'm flattered you were jealous."

"You were jealous."

"Pshh, barely," he flashed his dazzling smile, and even now it made her whole body sigh.

"You already admitted it, don't try to go back on it now," she teased.

"Well, I rarely find myself jealous of someone like George Fletcher. It was fleeting."

"It galled you enough to demand to know wether I let him fuck me."

"I was upset on your behalf, Edie."

"Mmm, sure," she said, her eyes blinking lazily.

"I'll admit… I was jealous that any other man had ever touched you. If you promise to never let a man like that touch you ever again."

"What do you mean, a man like that? A member of the nobility?"

"A man who has no idea what to do with your body. You should be worshiped like Bastet," he said, raising up on his elbow to lean over her again.

"You know your history!" she said, beaming as she raised her palm to his cheek.

"My love is like a rising star, with beautiful eyes for looking and sweet lips for kissing. Your hand is in my hand, my body trembles with joy, my heart is exalted because we walk together."

It was a line of ancient Egyptian poetry. Ancient Egyptian society was a very passionate culture, and surprisingly romantic. She wanted to laugh, and smile, and meet his expectation by joking back that she knew where the poem was from, and some history about it, being the know it all she was. But when she went to speak, she felt the words trip in her throat.

My love, he said. She knew he was being cheeky, but she felt a tiny crack in her heart that it was still all a joke. It occurred to her, cruelly, that she wished it were real.

Sure, he'd said she should be worshiped like Bastet, the cat-like goddess of love and fertility. But he was just talking about her body, her breasts, her mouth. Her willingness, or responsiveness, perhaps. He approached leading her down the garden path to multiple orgasms with all the decorum of a colleague doing her a favor. He seemed to treat it as a matter of principle, and appointed himself as the right man for the job. Rightfully so, she couldn't argue with that. Two things were clear to her. He behaved as if he had a great deal of respect for her, and he was attracted to her in a way that made him act against his better judgment.

One thing even her mind couldn't play down was how angry he'd gotten in the library when he thought she suggested he was a quick lay. In actuality, she was referring to how promiscuous she assumed he was. He'd cared for her reverently, and been deeply hurt when she eluded otherwise. So it was clearly more than just a good time for both of them.

If this was the pang she felt in her heart at hearing him recite a silly poem after only knowing him for a week, she dreaded to think what it would be like to say goodbye once the dig on this tomb was done with. They'd already been making breakneck progress through the doors, and she hoped they would continue to do so. But another part of her didn't want it to all go by too fast. She was falling for Ben.

CHAPTER EIGHTEEN

BEN COULDN'T SLEEP. Many hours later, he was still gazing at her. Lashes fluttering, lips parted with rhythmic breath, hair splayed against the pillow like a waterfall.

He was in love with her.

She was going to blow through this tomb with the speed of a cyclone and the force of a butterfly. And then what? She'd get her book, and he'd go back to America, and she'd be a lecturer at the big, bad Oxford, or perhaps head a team at another dig, her choice of any dig on earth, probably. Maybe if he was lucky, he'd get an invitation to her wedding someday, to Rudolf Something-or-Other the Third. The thought alone made him curl his arm tighter around her waist before he realized it.

It was the urge to have his hands on her that finally forced him out of bed. Once he sat up, he saw the first light of sunrise cresting beyond the terrace.

They'd stayed up late together, lost in each other. The tense, frustrating days since they'd met had been lousy with high stakes, long journeys, and watchful eyes. Having to guide her into harm's way when she disregarded almost everything he said. Not being able to touch her, or hold her, or whisper what he was thinking about in her ear. One unwise hour with her naked beneath him on someone else's floor. All of their secrets slowly revealed to each other.

After all of that, being alone in his bedroom with her all night was surreal. Sharing all of themselves. It was some kind of magic. She was an Egyptian High Priestess, that much he could tell with no evidence, just by the way she had bewitched him.

He was sure she'd sleep in this morning. Which meant Ben had several hours he could not spend in this bed with her, and his mind wandered to the day before.

And he thought of the lotus.

Ben had his theory as soon as it happened, once they reached the bottom of the stairs and saw that the door to the tomb was closed. He knew it was the boy who was always sitting just at the edge of the oasis. Watching. No one on the team would have done it, and if they had, someone would have seen and snitched. That boy was always there, even when the rest of the crew was called off.

The only other place he'd ever seen that boy, other than lurking around the perimeter of the dig site, was on Market Street. The vendors would be setting up already, making the most of the early hours before the cool morning gave way to the baking afternoon sun. Especially today, when there was such an influx of tourists in the city abuzz with the news that the tomb had been unsealed.

Hopefully they'd make out pretty well, at least that's what Ben wanted for them, considering how very infrequently good fortune had ever hit this nowhere town. When thoughts of last night flashed in his mind again, Ben was sure he could make it to the market and back in time to wake Edie up with breakfast in bed.

He looked back at her one last time before he rose to bathe and dress, and he felt that familiar tug he always seemed to feel whenever he looked at her. A longing to be nearer that made him feel he should pull away.

Half an hour later, Ben descended the grand staircase to the lobby. Hair slicked back, his tweed waistcoat concealing his double barrel holster. He carried his duffle bag packed with all of his things.

When going to bargain at the market, you never know what you might need to have on hand to seal the deal. Once in Alexandria, there was no amount of money the merchant would accept for a particular pistol that caught Ben's eye. However, once the merchant had seen his American belt buckle, that was all it took. Ben walked away from the market that day with the pistol he coveted, and a length of rope holding up his pants.

He was ready to trade everything he had, including the shirt off his back if that's what it took, to get Edie's lotus back. The lotus he'd once stolen like an actual thief in the night in an effort to keep her safe.

As Ben strode through the lobby, he stopped to chat with Mesuda.

The sun had just begun to peak over the horizon as Ben set out down the red carpet of the winding limestone staircase at the entrance of the hotel. The lotus was sure to fetch a pretty penny at market, and if that was indeed the reason the boy had taken it, that would probably be his next move. He would want to be the first out to get that cash in his pocket.

Raven haired, golden skinned women wearing breezy linen were already up making flatbread as he walked through wafting scent of Egyptian spices. He found himself thinking of Edie even then, wondering if she'd be a meticulous gourmet chef, or wouldn't condescend to boil an egg. He could see her being capable of either and wouldn't hold her to the stuffy stereotype of always having servants wait on her hand and foot. He could just see her getting the idea in her head to make a coq au vin even if she'd never cooked before. She'd also be just the type of person to make it perfectly. He wondered if she'd ever had the notion, and then he caught himself in the midst of wondering.

He couldn't stop thinking about her. He'd met many women over the years in his line of work. Many had become companions in a manner of speaking, but he'd never been driven to distraction. In no time at all, they'd gotten tangled in a way that felt irreversible. It might be tricky to manage the sensitive subject of his obsession with her while navigating her full blown love affair with her career. One thing was for certain, and that was that Edie was going places. The last thing she needed was a petty thief tagging along. But then again… maybe a side kick was what she needed most.

Unfortunately, he knew her well enough to know that she'd more likely agree with the former statement than the latter.

It occurred to him, to his own satisfaction, they had actually made a pretty great team so far. He could see that he was helping her to get what she wanted, while also keeping her aware of what she really needed. She had a drive and a direction that he couldn't even remotely relate to. In fact, his own career had been built on being paid to achieve others objectives. He was known for getting the job done.

But Edie lacked experience in the world she strived to enter into. She could figure it out on her own, he was sure of that, and she could hold her own as well. But he could get her what she wanted faster, easier, and safer. He could take care of anything she wanted. He could take care of her.

It was amidst the unfamiliar territory of actually believing he could belong anywhere near Edie when the short stroll from the hotel to Market Street had come to an abrupt halt. He saw the boy standing near the table where he usually was early in the morning. But once the boy saw him, all of the answer was in his eyes. Ben's assumption was confirmed.

"Hey," Ben said curtly with half a smile. He meant business, but didn't mean any harm. The boy turned to slink away, attempting to avoid alarming his adult family members gathered around their table of wares. But as soon as he rounded the corner of the building, he broke into a run.

"Wait!" Ben shouted, and then again, in Egyptian. The boy ducked into an alleyway, and Ben ran to catch up.

"It's him, he's coming!" the boy shouted in Arabic.

"You're not in any trouble, I just want to ta—"

As soon as Ben turned into the alley, before he could see the lay of it, his vision went black in an instant accompanied with screaming, searing pain. He felt himself falling, but lost consciousness before hitting the ground.

Edith laid on a suspended bed of woven grass surrounded by sticky air, the scent of iris, and musky incense. Her eyes drifted open to fall on a golden chalice, and her body, unbidden by her, lifted slightly to peer over the rim to see the cup was full of wine.

Again, not of her own will, she began to move. A deeply tanned arm with long slender fingers bedecked in gold jewelry extended from her own shoulder to reach for the glass and brought it to her lips. Alarmed, she felt her head tip itself back and take the wine in a quick shot, feeling slightly floaty before it had even been downed, as if she was already tipsy. It was nothing like her own tiny sips.

Rising to her feet off of the swinging woven seat, she walked across the stone terrace toward an archway flanked by two guards. The breeze swept against her skin in a peculiar way, as if she wasn't wearing anything at all, certainly not the smart layers of linen, tweed and khaki she was used to. Though when she tried to look down to assess her outfit her head didn't move; she continued to look straight ahead. As she neared the guards, she saw that they were holding long staff. From them dangled incense diffusers that billowed a golden shimmering smoke. As she approached, they shifted their staffs from an upright position to their other hands, where they held the staffs diagonally so the incense diffusers were dangling in the doorway.

A vision! Edith thought, feeling rather dim. She was in a vision right now. Who was she? Was she Amnara? Of course, she must be. This was the smoke, the smoke that always ushered her to and from ancient times to see what had gone unseen for thousands of years.

Once Edith, traveling within the psyche of Amnara, entered the palace through the archway, her vision dimmed in the dark cool space away from the burning midday sun.

She approached a set of doors within the palace and saw Amnara's arms rise in front of her. She placed both of her palms on the door and held them there for a moment before the doors shifted and swung open.

She had put her palms on the doors just as Edith had done by accident when she was locked inside the tomb with Ben. And then, just like for Amnara, the doors had opened.

In the lamp light within the room she entered, she walked to a bathing pitcher and looked up to see her reflection in an ornate mirror encircled by golden snakes.

In the reflection, she saw a familiar site in the mirror even from within someone else's body. Amnara looked back at her with pale green eyes.

She turned to see a figure come into view from the shadows. A tall, muscular woman, bedecked in gold approached to stand before her. Her shining black curtain of hair swayed from underneath a queen's headdress, adorned with a cobra. The high side slits of her regal indigo linen dress revealed she had two dagger sheaths strapped to her thighs. Only one sheath held a dagger.

"Amnara," she said.

Suddenly Edith felt two sets of rough strong hands curl around both of her arms and yank her backward off of her feet.

Edith was jolted awake by the sensation of falling and yet, she didn't waste a moment.

"Ben!" she shouted as soon as she caught her breath. She looked beside her, and he wasn't there.

"Ben!" she shouted again as she leapt out of bed and ran to the bathroom. He wasn't there either. She walked to the doorway between their adjoining rooms.

"Ben?"

Edith looked around Ben's room and it was… empty. His room was cleared, and his belongings were gone.

Before her usual efforts to keep calm and carry on could prevail as they usually had, hysteria took hold in her throat.

When she saw the only personal belongings in his room were her clothes, her underwear, littered in a heap on the floor from the night before, tears stung in her eyes. He'd even taken the dig kit that he'd left in her room. He'd taken the dirty bandana from his nightstand. Everything.

Why?

Her heart pounded as her mind raced. What had she done? She was too chagrined to give a second thought to the notion that it could have been her who was in the wrong or could have driven him away.

Where could he find fault in everything that had happened between them? When would he even have the time, when he was so busy growling her name between spasms of release?

Though she refused to blame herself, her mind searched the night before. Had he said he was going somewhere? Had he mentioned anything? He'd been missing most of the day yesterday, and it turned out he was retrieving the cameras from the journalists.

Why are you jumping to conclusions? He's proven himself to you.

Some mild mannered part of her brain was on Ben's side. But the other part of her brain, the same part that had always assumed the worst, wouldn't hear of it.

Oh, he'd given her plenty of reasons to doubt.

He was a thief. A felon. A liar. He always carried guns. He always got what he wanted. Just what he wanted, she thought. He got just what he wanted out of you, and then packed up every last trace of his existence and left before you even woke up.

Stalking around the room, she looked for clues trying to quiet the doubt, desperately hoping somewhere deep down that he had left a note. A tear rolled down her cheek as she hoped that maybe he was just about to walk through the door.

But then, as her brain continued to pass over every interaction of the past few days, like fondling a shore of pebbles for a message in braille, a thought struck her. It raised prickly goosebumps from her ankles to her thighs that struck her spine like an electrical current.

He'd been out the day before searching for all of that camera equipment, but also to ask all of the crew, and all of the media, if anyone had seen the lotus.

He said no one had. But all she had on it was his word... the word of a criminal.

Do you trust me?

Damn, she thought. What if he had found the lotus? Would he rush back to give it to her? His words echoed in her mind, giving her the answer.

I won't let you go back.

It's dangerous.

Do you see what the visions do to you?

Next time it could be worse.

Her stomach dropped when it dawned on her.

I need something more valuable than treasure. I need a bargaining chip.

The key that opened the cursed tomb that could not be opened. He could take the lotus to negotiate reentry to America.

She chastised herself for even thinking to assume him guilty, but what choice did she have? This scheme was almost too obvious to even be attempted. Of course, he seduced her to get his way.

Edie, are you sure?

She shoved the words from her mind, his sweet, eager determination to secure her permission between all the spectacular orgasms he'd bestowed on her. She would not let it factor into her assessment of the circumstances she'd awoken to. Of course the swindler would make it look like it was her idea. All of the best con men do.

The bellhop at the front desk answered her phone call and informed her that he'd seen Ben going out early that morning, just before dawn, and he had said that he hadn't wanted to wake her, and to make sure no one disturbed the room.

Consistent with a getaway, Edith thought morosely.

If that were indeed the case, she had no hope of finding him. He could be anywhere. Although the key to the Cursed Tomb of Argo would certainly be an impressive trinket of memorabilia, her assumptions began to shift.

Upon further consideration, he wouldn't have done that. The only explanation for his abandonment would be that he'd gotten the lotus. And if he had the lotus, there was only one course of action that he would take.

He wouldn't have been able to negotiate with the lotus, as it wasn't discovered, but stolen. There was an undeniable paper trail as not only was insured through her family, but furthermore, Edith was about to be very publicly known as the person who unlocked the tomb with the lotus, as many witnesses would testify. That would hardly be the best way to get out of hot water with the law.

The most likely strategy to pursue, if she put herself in the shoes of a wiley tomb raider, would be using the lotus to get to the Collar of Queens, a much bigger trophy to be sure. Ben, and a nameless colleague with no connection to this project, were the only people who ever theorized the Collar of Queens lie with the mummy of the Weeping Viper. Without any other way to trace it back to any particular site, it could arguably fall under a jurisdictional gray area. Making it not only priceless, but free and clear of legal ambiguity.

She had already divulged that the lotus was a protective amulet, making this scheme even more attractive to a desperate man in search of a prize guarded by a deadly curse. At least this theory put Ben somewhere he could be found. In the belly of the tomb.

It was unfortunate for him, she thought as she bolted from his hotel room, that only she knew how to get past the third door.

Ben regained consciousness sitting in a chair with his head hanging low. He jerked his shoulder against restraints and realized his arms were bound behind him and his chest was strapped to the chair. His first thought upon opening his eyes was to look at the source of light, shallow windows just below the ceiling, to see the bright morning sunbeams. The quality of the sunlight suggested he must have been out for several hours now, and could only imagine what Edith would think when she woke up to see that all of his things were gone.

Why didn't he leave a note?

"You cocky bastard… ahh," he said under his breath before the sharp pain in his jaw registered.

You'll just stroll to the market, pluck the priceless artifact from the harmless little boy, and wake Edie with a warm baladi flatbread in bed, won't you? You fucking idiot.

He hung his head once again, baffled by his own stupidity. He couldn't believe he'd been so foolish. Of course it would look like he'd just abandoned her in the room on her own, or even worse, skipped town.

The single minded mission of getting that lotus back to her was so consuming he hadn't even thought through the plan of what he was doing. He was so sure he'd get back before she even woke up.

He was dying to see the look on her face when she realized he'd slipped the lotus around her neck when she wasn't looking. While banking on that fantasy he'd gotten himself into one hell of a tight spot.

It wasn't like him. She was making him dumber.

And now, she'd wake up alone, with all of his things gone, until... well, that brought his thoughts back to the present. Where was he, and how would he get out of here?

The pain registered again and once it did, it was staggering. He rolled his jaw knowing that's how he'd been knocked out. The skin of one of his arms stung like a road rash and he assumed he'd been dragged.

The boy had certainly taken the necklace. He may as well have been wearing it around his neck for how obviously it was written on his face. He began to look around the dimly lit, cavernous room he was in. Because of the placement of the shallow windows near the ceiling, he thought that the room must be at least partially underground. It was too large to be a cellar, but otherwise seemed like it could be the basement of some institution. When he looked closer and noticed the cots lining the walls, he realized it was a military bunker.

Then he began to notice what he was surrounded by. It wasn't just clutter. There were ancient artifacts everywhere. He spotted the chair that had entranced Edie during her vision on their first day within the tomb. No one had even reported it missing.

Could it really be what he was seeing?

Someone had already begun pilfering the tomb only days after they'd gotten it open. These artifacts were supposed to be cataloged to begin the restoration process. He looked to the side and saw the massive onyx sarcophagus they'd passed on the second day.

Ben was surprised to feel ire rise in himself about the rightful place of the artifacts. When usually he would have been fine with taking his payment and shoving off, unconcerned whether the tomb was disassembled and sold to the highest bidder one brick at a time.

Whoever had bribed the boy into stealing the lotus, whoever had intercepted Ben at the market, was ransacking the dig and it looked like things were already preparing to be shipped.

Ben was beginning to wonder if he would just be left here, and for how long, when the double doors he faced on the far end of the bunker opened to reveal a backlit silhouette of the portly culprit.

"Ben!" his voice boomed.

The voice of Ronald Pimsley.

"You..." Ben sneered through gritted teeth.

"Now, Ben. I know how this looks," Pimsley said, making a wide gesture with his hands as the double doors shut behind him with an audible click that echoed across the rows of folded cots.

"It looks like I've been sucker punched and tied up. And it looks like I'm in a bunker with thousands of years worth of stolen loot."

"Well, that's about the size of it, yes." Pimsley's tone was calm and congenial as always. But Ben had already known for many years by now that Pimsley was the kind of man who could be robbing you blind with a placid grin on his face.

When Ben was silent, Pimsley inquired.

"Well, don't you want to know why?"

"I already know why."

"Ah, yes. Because it was you who broke into my private study, wasn't it?"

"I knew long before that."

"Of course, that's why you would have broken into the study in the first place."

"Get these ropes off me Pimsley, get your thugs in here to release me now, or you'll regret it."

"I can't do that quite yet Ben, but you'll be freed soon enough. Well, free from the chair that is. But far from free in the truest sense of the word."

Ben issued a weary sigh.

"Okay, I'll bite. Why?"

"Because the French Foreign Legion will be arriving in a matter of hours to escort you to America where you will rightfully serve out your jail sentence."

"They can't do that."

"Yes, of course they can. You've violated the terms of your clemency."

"I have not."

"You have. By smuggling."

"What are you talking about?"

"You're going to take the fall for me in a big way, Ben," he sneered, as the gracious veil fell from his face and Ben saw the rare glimpse of his true nature surface. Seething greedy satisfaction.

"So, that's what all of this is. You're emptying out the tomb before it's even been completely excavated."

"I knew that you two were going to make trouble for me when you came to the gala. I thought you hated each other, which would have worked well to my advantage. Obviously that wasn't the case, as anyone could see. Soon after, I realized there was an opportunity in it. Knowing that you were the one who broke into my study just makes it all the more righteous for me to have you locked up for the rest of your life. I needed you two to get into that tomb for me. I didn't know how she would do it, but then she surprised us all. It's such a shame that I had to catch my best man smuggling goods." Pimsley's flashed with disingenuous sympathy.

"What will happen to Edith?" Ben's voice was low and vicious. Being a witness in Pimsley's fraudulent scheme would put her in a dangerous position.

"What will happen? You mean after I publish in my papers that she was sleeping with you, the incarcerated thief? She'll be the laughing stock of Egypt, she'll never work in academia again, much less archaeology."

"Is that all?" Ben asked.

"Yes," Pimsly said, grinning maliciously.

"That's your whole plan, no further details to share?"

"Well… yes," Pimsley said, still grinning maliciously, but his enthusiasm deflated a bit.

"Are we locked in here?" Ben asked.

"Yes," Pimsley said, now truly puzzled.

"Oh, good," Ben said blandly.

Suddenly, Ben shot to his feet, and slammed his back on the granite slab table behind him, instantly snapping the barrel chair into pieces. The splintered wood and unraveling rope fell to the ground in a heap around him. He sidestepped out of the debris easily, and began to slowly advance on Pimsley, who stood paralyzed with shock.

"You've got it all wrong, Pimsley. You know, I'm surprised that for someone who thinks so highly of their own intellect, you weren't able to piece it together. But I wonder… what do you think I was actually doing in your study?"

"Uh, I– I …"

Pimsley stammered, backing up as Ben came toward him.

"You're a petty thief, you were probably looking for jewels. Don't come near me, Ben, my guards will get worse than just your jaw this time." But Ben continued to prowl toward him like a tiger cornering his sniveling prey.

"Would I really look for jewels in your study? Oh," he laughed mirthlessly, "I love being underestimated. It's an invaluable element of my persona."

Still several paces away, he lunged at Pimsley, just to see him stumble back a few steps, and laughed again.

"I happen to know the French Foreign Legion will be showing up here momentarily. I actually had no idea that you had planned this little rendezvous, otherwise they would have been going straight to your private residence. But they never would have found you down here... that is, if you hadn't called them yourself."

"Wha- what are you talking about?"

"The charges against me have been dropped. They traded my measly old news case in favor of a much, much juicier target. A whale, if you ask me."

Horror washed over Pimsley's face as the realization hit him. That's what Ben was doing in his office.

"As a newspaper man, you know all about schemes like this, don't you? It's a set up. Plain and simple. I've been gathering information on you for years — and with the treasure trove of incriminating documents I found in your study, well... the evidence was, what did they call it? Staggering."

Ben had barked out the last word, making Pimsley jump.

"Poaching, grave robbing, libel, blackmail, and much, much worse."

Pimsley had stopped dead in his tracks as he tried to take in what he was hearing. Meanwhile, Ben had continued to gain on him. Now they were standing face to face, Ben towering over him, Pimsley trembling and red faced.

Ben's hand shot out to yank Pimsley in a handshake, as he clapped him on the shoulder with the other hand.

"Thanks for all the work over the years, but I think it's in my best interest for our professional relationship to be terminated."

"Arrgh!" Pimsley winced as the handshake increased in pressure that strained the bones of his hands.

"Oh, and if you get any bright ideas about launching a smear campaign against Miss Taylor... that is, before ownership of your publishing company is seized by the Egyptian government..."

Pimsley blanched to see a look in Ben's eye he'd never seen before — wild rage.

"Don't," he said sharply. "If I see her name in your newspaper — if I even see her initials in your newspaper — I won't even let you rot in jail for the rest of your natural life... I'll kill you."

Ben reached behind him to rest his palm on the cover of the onyx sarcophagus Pimsley was now backed up against.

"Now, I know I happen to be an extremely valuable international informant, but just for the trouble they've put me through, and how upsetting it all was to my mother... I'm not going to hand you over to the authorities on a silver platter. They'll have to find you themselves."

Ben grabbed Pimsley's collar and shoved him back into the sarcophagus. Pimsley's arms flailed madly as he was dumped into the deep stone coffin before Ben let the enormous top fall closed with a thunderous crack.

Ben turned, taking great strides toward the double doors, and as he stomped the length of the cavernous room he stripped off his waistcoat to reveal his double shoulder holster stocked with both pistols.

"They didn't even search me," he chuckled. "My final act as your consultant will be one last free piece of advice: never acquire henchmen on the cheap," he shouted back toward the tomb wherein Pimsley was shrieking for dear life.

He crossed his arms over his chest to retrieve both pistols, and aimed squarely at the doors.

Finally, he thought.

Bullets exploded from the barrels of both pistols as Ben fired, and continued to pull the trigger even as the hammers clicked impotently thereafter. Battered by so many rounds, the knobs fell to the ground smoking as the echoes of shots fired still rang off the aluminum walls.

"Ah," he sighed, "that felt good."

"But you — you have my keys!" Pimsley's muffled protest came from behind him.

"I know," Ben said, taking a deep, cathartic breath. "But, I really needed that."

He bounded up the stairs two at a time, spinning the cylinders as he reloaded them, and burst through the door at the top to find himself in a dingy office where Ingrid sat behind a desk, unimpressed.

He holstered his guns as she pointed her nail file in the direction of the corner where he saw his duffle bag.

"Thanks," he said, kneeling to sling the strap over his shoulder, and briefly wincing in pain.

"I'm borrowing Pimsley's car," he said, spinning the key around his finger after retrieving it from his shirt pocket.

"See ya 'round, Toots," he called over his shoulder on his way out.

"So long," she said, clacking her gum without looking up.

He rushed from the back office to find himself, just as he'd suspected, in the lobby of the military flophouse they had come to their first day in Argo. He picked up speed as he ran past the lounge where he shared his first meal with Edith.

Ben hopped into Pimsley's car and pounded it into gear with all the force of his raging adrenaline before speeding down the road. There was only one place that Edith would go. But he would try the hotel first, and hope to God that she was there. He tried to imagine a scenario where Edith stayed put in her room and didn't jump to the worst possible conclusion about him. Left cold by attempting to calculate the likelihood of that scenario, he drove faster.

CHAPTER NINETEEN

EDITH STOOD BEFORE the great stone doors eyeing the scene chiseled into its surface within the ornate border. She remembered, wistfully, the excitement she'd felt the first time she'd seen it, by contrast to how hollow she felt today.

There were so many occasions where she'd assumed the worst about him, and regretted it. Never in her life had she wanted so badly to be wrong. It wouldn't even bother her to look like a paranoid idiot. She would let him gloat.

It was too painful to bear that she'd fallen so hard for Ben, and was still capable of believing she'd find him betraying her in the depths of the tomb.

The closed door served as her proof that he wasn't there. The dash from the hotel to the Oasis had cleared the cobwebs of sleep, and burned off her anger, leaving behind only what she knew deep down: Ben wouldn't do this. He wasn't capable of what she'd maliciously charged him with in a brief and bitter moment of her own insecurity. By the time the door had come into view as she sprinted through the sand, she had already expected to find it closed.

Casting a long glance over her shoulder, she was forced to admit she was hoping to see Ben standing there, with his lopsided grin. She'd gotten used to having him by her side, despite how little she deserved the honor.

Yet, it was better this way she thought. How it was always meant to be. In a lighter mood she might have been amused to find herself in the exact circumstances she was hoping to contrive a week ago, and completely by accident. From the beginning it had been her plan to lose the crew, and embark on the last leg of this journey on her own. For all of the reasons it felt right. For the peril she'd be in, to put it squarely on her own shoulders without having any one else's fate on her conscience.

Even more meaningful, though, was how right it felt not just for the circumstances, not just for her career, and not just for this adventure. It was right for who Edith was her whole life. For her personal manifesto.

She would do this on her own.

It was on that thought that she finally squeezed her eyes shut and pressed her hands to the door. Dust unsettled around the entryway, and the doors swung open with a plume of golden shimmering smoke.

A numbness flooded her as the gravity of this confirmation took root — she was the key to this tomb all along.

With this realization came an avalanche of realizations. She was of Amnara's ancestry. She was of the Didia bloodline. She was from ancient Egyptian royalty; from a tribe of priestesses and healers. The lotus had been passed down for thousands and thousands of years and she was the first to make it here, the first in her family to solve the mystery.

She finally understood that this was bigger than her ambitions, bigger than her petty grudge against Oxford, bigger than her librarian's quest to find the Book of Light. The soul of Amnara, her ancestor, was trapped in this tomb with a curse. Not only her ghost, her remains, her possessions, the bodies of her loved ones; but also her story, cursed to be mistold throughout all of history.

This wasn't about Edith. This was about freeing Amnara, and telling her truth.

Edith heard the echo of her steps as she ran with a lit torch full speed down the stairs into the chambers, through the hall where she'd had her first vision. She continued to run the entire length of the corridor that led from the hall to the muraled catacombs they'd breached just yesterday. A melodic murmuring came from the final door at the end of all of the rooms and tunnels. The closer she got, the louder it became.

As she ran, with her heart pounding in her chest and her legs aching, the memories she shared with Ben were flooding into her mind. He was inescapable. As she fled deeper into the darkness, she could see more clearly that she had betrayed him. Though her memories reinforced that Ben could never betray her, with each step that fell in her flight, she betrayed him anew.

He hated the idea of her coming in here at all, she knew that he would never break her trust and come here alone. As she had done.

A new panic began to rise in her throat… if he wasn't here, then where was he? Where had he gone? What if he was in trouble? She thought of the Medjai, the desert rangers who he foretold would come after him.

Still she ran, driven by something else, overcome with a deep desire, a desire outside of herself, to finish what she started. The more logical part of her brain should have spoken up in her psyche, but her truest self that made those decisions had fallen silent. Despite how stubborn she was, she knew she shouldn't be here. It was true that it was dangerous, particularly to her, and that she shouldn't be alone.

Against her better judgment, or even the average person's common sense, she couldn't stop. The closer she got to the end of the hallway, the louder she could hear the murmurs on the other side of the door, the more she felt the urge to run and the less she thought about Ben.

She reached the final door at the end of the corridor and doubled over to heave air deep into her lungs.

There was still this odd pull, a magnetism that left her a bit queasy. It was a bit like the sensation of being in the dream. She was in her body, but controlled by something outside of it.

She was restless and couldn't wait to weigh her options all alone at the bottom of this tomb with no idea what dangers lie beyond this door. Without her usual calculated measure of which step to take next, she simply acted on the hunch that she had woken up with this morning.

On either side of the entryway, there were statues of Anubis, the god with the body of a man and the face of a jackal wearing an elaborate headdress.

The god of the dead.

Each statue that flanked the door had a hand holding a staff forward and another hand outstretched to the side toward the door. From the staff dangled an ornate copper cencer, a globe to diffuse the incense within, suspended from chains just as she'd seen when she read of the Didia. She saw these statues in her dream last night... but in her dream, the guards moved the incense-burning staffs to their other hand, pointing them toward the door. She peeked behind the statues, and sharply exhaled when she saw a slot behind the statue that aligned with the empty hands of the Anubis statue.

It was there just as she knew it would be.

Once the torch she brought down with her was secured on the wall, she carefully grabbed the staff from one of the statues. She shimmied a bit until she felt it was clear to be lifted out of its groove, and repositioned it to the other side of the statue to settle it into the slot at the base, letting the staff rest in Anubis' outstretched hand. Then she did the same with the identical and opposite statue. She took the kerchief from her neck, rolled it tight and tied the end in a knot, and lit it with the torch flame. Using her tightly rolled kerchief as a wick, she lit the incense burners.

The forgotten flaming scarf fell to the ground as the golden shimmering smoke of the incense billowed from the censers.

As if pulled by a vortex, the smoke began to swirl around the third and final door, and as it did, it illuminated hieroglyphs that appeared for the first time.

An opalescent shadow fell over Edith's eyes as the doors lurched open to reveal the treasure room.

The cavernous dome shaped room was lined with stories-high columns. Between each of the pillars were rooms stuffed with riches. Statues, furniture, vases, jewelry, chests full of coins. A series of steps ran around the perimeter of the room leading from the wall of treasure compartments, down to the sunken main floor. At the very center of the room, on an elevated platform, was the tomb of Amnara.

The tomb was a multitude of wonders… and yet, the discovery would not be the pride of Egypt. Edith would have awoken to see everything in the tomb was tarnished tin. There was not a speck of gold in the entire chasm. Edith's eyes had been overtaken by the pearly haze before the smoke had cleared enough for her to see any of it.

What she saw as the vision unfolded before her was the treasure room as it appeared three thousand years in the past. The way it looked the day it was sealed.

The toes of Edith's loafers dragged against the stone floor as she levitated, cradled by glimmering smoke, ushering her into the treasure room. Paralyzed and unconscious, the worst of Edith's visions were playing in her mind's eye.

She was surrounded by royal guards carrying in hoards of belongings, all made of tin, or clay, or other common place materials. Ramesses, deep grooves whittled into his face, shadows falling under his glassy eyes, looked on as the guards filed in carrying the belongings, stacking them in the compartments between the columns that lined the walls of the treasure room. He peered along the walls and seemed to inspect every guard as they came by.

He briefly looked down to the lotus shaped pendant he held in his hand, brushing his thumb over the pale green peridot stone in the center. But as a guard approached, he clutched it close to his chest, hiding it from view.

"That's the last of Amnara's treasure, Pharaoh," one of the guards said.

There was a man standing next to Ramesses who was dressed in the traditional garb of a royal high priest. He placed his hand on Ramesses' shoulder.

"Let us rest while the ritual proceeds. There is no need for you to cast your eyes upon this."

Ramesses patted the man's hand and they walked out together.

Edith could hear her heart beat as clear as a drum when she saw the final guard that entered the treasure room was carrying the book of light. He set it on a shelf underneath the casket before the vision warped in a time jump.

The star-shaped beams of sunlight shifted rapidly across the stone walls indicating a different position of the sun, which shone through the star shafts yet to be sealed. When Edith looked back to the center platform, she saw the mummy of Amnara set in the enormous coffin made to her exact shape. Her slender figure was wrapped tightly with fragrant strips of linen, arms strapped across her chest, to be bound and buried for eternity.

Through the entrance walked the woman from Edith's dream, the woman with one missing dagger. Dressed in plain clothes and void of her crown, she carried a bundle wrapped in purple cloth and tiptoed down the steps, across the main floor, and up the steps to the platforms to approach where Amnara was laid to rest. Edith noticed her throwing jerky glances over her shoulder intermittently.

At once the identity of the woman came to Edith, as she saw a gleam of gold within the bundle she carried. The way she was dressed in the dream, her tattoos, and the visions she'd seen.

It was Pharaoh's secondary wife, Teti.

Edith felt the pieces of the puzzle finally snap into place.

As a secondary wife, Teti's eldest child would have been next in line to the throne before Nefertari bore her son Amun. Edith looked on, Teti tossed the fabric aside and revealed the magnificent sparkling adornment she held in her arms.

The Collar of Queens.

It was magnificent in person; strands of gold beads in graduated rows from the top to the bottom, in the sloping shape of the neck and shoulders. In the final row were the missing stones from each of the other queens. Huge faceted settings of olivine, amethyst, feldspar, chalcedony, garnet, obsidian — all twinkling in the thin rays of the golden-hour light.

Then, as Teti approached Amnara's mummy with the collar, Edith saw the hieroglyphs on each of the columns that encircled the tomb. They illuminated, appearing to be backlit with gold, just as the door had before her she lost sight.

A scene of Ramesses proposing to Amnara, with her son in the background.

One of Amnara brandishing a dagger behind Ramesses' back.

The next scene made Edith recoil in horror. It depicted Amnara, with her son beside her, in her family's home as it was engulfed in flames. It was their public execution, she thought. One so shameful there was no surviving record of it anywhere in history. The corresponding hieroglyphs described the golden sparkling smoke coming from the house of magic as it burned.

She looked back at the mummy, realizing the body of the woman beneath the tightly wound linen would be burned badly. In the vision, her hand flew to her mouth, but alone in her own time she moved slowly as if underwater, as the treasure room filled with smoke billowing furiously around her.

Teti placed the collar on Amnara's neck and fastened it as she began an incantation in Egyptian.

"Your secrets shall die unspoken,

Your vengeance shall wither unborn,

This tomb shall remain lost to time,

With the magic of the gods in each stone,

I confine you to these walls to never be at rest.

Should your prison ever be unsealed and trespassed,

The daytime sky will blacken, and the ground shall swallow this tomb, and you with it."

Once the damning spell had been bestowed on Amnara's mummy, Teti wrapped the collar with linen to conceal it from the priests who would come in to seal the tomb. But Edith heard a voice, a familiar voice, echo against the walls that Teti didn't seem to hear.

"The tears I shed will show your stain,
My sisters will fight to know my name,
Though stones you cursed may bind me,
The legacy of the lotus shall set me free."

Teti finished her gruesome task, a malicious grin curling her lips into her cheeks, and whispered to the mummy, "You thought you would be queen, but now my son will be king."

It all came together, like so many moments before, huddled in a library surrounded by opened books and scrawled legal pads, one last brushstroke that completed an entire portrait.

Edith's eyes shot back to the column depicting Isfetheru and Ramesses.

He was going to marry her, that's why Teti had done this.

As Teti crept out of the tomb, Edith hurried down the steps, crossed the main floor, and ascended the steps leading to the casket. She stood one step below the platform, where the mummy, placed in the upright coffin, towered over her.

"How can I free you? I don't have the lotus." She darted her eyes around, apprehensive. In another time and place she would have thought it was silly, there was no one here to see her. The mummy certainly wasn't looking. Then, the familiar whispering voice echoed all around her.

"Read from the book."

She saw a tear beaded on the linen that wrapped the depression of the mummy's eyes. The linen wasn't wet, it wasn't coming from inside, but seemed to materialize from thin air. The tear grew until it dropped. Edith watched it slip between the stones of the floor, and looked back to the mummy's face where another tear was already forming.

Edith's eyes flew to the shelf within the platform of the sarcophagus. There it was, the Book of Light, it was still there, behind the canopic jars that had been placed there after the mummification ritual. She reached to move the jars aside, but her hand waved through them like a ghost.

Edith looked at her hand, and realized she was still within her vision. Her hand became blurred as her burning eyes teared up from the smoke that started billowing around her. Her next inhale snagged on a cough as the smoke entered her lungs.

Next time you have a vision, it could be worse. You might not wake up.

"Oh, no..." she whispered, between choking coughs. Her eyes drifted shut as her consciousness slipped away entirely from the vision... but was not regained on the other side where Edith lay motionless on the floor in front of the coffin, surrounded by smoke.

CHAPTER TWENTY

IN THE TIME it took Ben to run to Edith's room in the hotel and run out again, the sky was darkening at high noon. Even in his mad rush, it stopped him in his tracks to see the gray clouds swirling in a burgeoning cyclone directly above the tomb. From the steps of the hotel, he heard an ominous rumble unfurling deep underground.

All around him townsfolk were shouting with panic, eyes wild with fright, seeking each other and rushing to take shelter in their homes.

Ben leapt back into the running car, threw it into gear, and jammed the pedal all the way to the floor. He sped toward the oasis hoping the journey wouldn't be deceptively long as it had on foot. The shore was near by the time his tires had finally sunk so deep in the sand that the car couldn't go any further. Before it had even come to a complete stop, Ben burst through the car door and ran for the quay. He looked down at his boots sinking into the ground each time he yanked them free to take another step. When he finally scrambled onto the quay, he looked back to see the car pitching sideways in the ground as the sand claimed it.

"Quicksand," he panted.

He took one last glance at the work site as the last stragglers ran back to the city shouting at each other. The poles collapsed and the tents folded into the rippling ground.

Just beyond the worksite, he saw the Medjai descending a faraway dune. They would swoop in, he knew, and do what they could. But if he didn't get to Edie, there would be nothing they could do to stop the destruction. The Vipers Treasure, the Book of Light, the Collar of Queens, along with the pride of Egypt, Edith Taylor, would all be lost to the sinking sands.

Ben sprinted toward the smoldering tomb. Shimmering brown smoke streamed out of every crevice and seam gathering in an enormous roiling plume overhead. It mingled with the clouds circling above as they crackled with heat lightning against the blackening sky.

Once in the tunnels, he was running as fast as his legs could carry him through a spray of leaks that were springing in the crumbling limestone walls. Each step he took sloshed through a river that flowed toward the belly of the tomb. His heart was rioting and his lungs screamed in his chest as he pushed himself to run faster.

"Just hang on..." he gasped, "I'm coming..."

His desperate plea echoed back to him as he barreled down the final corridor. The tomb groaned and the ground trembled beneath him as the floor suddenly cracked, a fissure running from the ground to the top of the tunnel. The bricks shifted and the ceiling dropped an inch when settled. Ben had the terrifying realization that the entire tomb could collapse on itself before it even had a chance to flood.

His eyes burned from the gathering smoke, thicker the deeper into the tomb he ran. He tried to cast his deepest fears from his mind, still, he couldn't have imagined the horrific scene he came upon when he finally reached the treasure room.

Barreling in, he came to a stop in an astronomical circular chamber, a web of fractures wrapped around each of the columns that lined the perimeter. The cavities between each column were packed with treasures that were all that melting, thick streams of liquid metal oozing down the steps that encircled the main floor.

He spotted her right away, directly in the center of the wreckage. Boulder-sized chunks of the structure had begun to tumble into a black searing moat that was rising between the perimeter of the room and the center platform where Edith lay in a heap in front of a mummy sarcophagus. Ben's eyes searched the smoking molten pool around the platform that crackled on the surface revealing a glowing orange beneath.

"Edie!" He shouted, but over the sizzle of metal liquefying, the gales of swirling smoke, the roar of limestone crumbling all around them, he could barely hear himself.

"Forgive me," he whispered, and pulled his guns free from their holster firing three shots into the lava beneath. The gunfire pierced through the cacophony and he saw her head roll.

"Edith! Get up!" he was poised to shoot again, but she began to stir. He shouted again. "Edith, you have to get up!"

She sat up, bleary eyed, and began choking on a coughing fit. For the briefest moment, she took in her disastrous surroundings before trying to stand up, but stumbled back unable to lift herself.

"Edie, NO!" Ben shouted lunging forward, as she landed a few steps lower on the platform, closer to the rising moat of lava.

"Stay down!" He searched the moat frantically for a way to get across. It was too far to jump. She lay with her cheek to the ground, seeing Ben through tears welling in her eyes as she gasped for breath.

"I'm sorry," she croaked silently. She had done this.

Ben read her lips and shook his head violently.

"Edie, no, I'm sorry. Pimsley's men got me, I was … I'm sorry."

It was no use. She couldn't hear him.

"I should have left a note!" he shouted.

Her lips were moving again, but he couldn't hear her. She braced herself up on her palms, her head hung between her shoulders as she drew in a deep breath, and shouted as loud as she could.

"The curse is in the collar!" she screamed, then collapsed gagging on smoke.

"Edie," he said, dropping to his knees trying, uselessly, to get closer to her somehow. "You can do this, and you have to do this. You're the only one who can break the curse!" His hoarse voice cracked, and he was sure he'd scream until his vocal cords bled if that's what she needed. His fists scraped against the limestone as he searched desperately to find a way to get to her.

Edith looked up at the mummy, and dug deeper to summon a strength from within herself. She'd spent her entire life studying Egypt. These royals, these mummies, these tombs. If it killed her, she was going to make this right; to correct an inaccurate history.

Not only because she was the only person who could make it right, but because she could think of nothing she'd rather die for. The soul of an innocent woman, from a culture and a tradition that was so dear to her, was trapped.

She remembered the moment in her study, when she had asked for an answer... and quickly received it. Looking up, she stared into the face brilliantly painted on the coffin.

"Open!" she shouted, and watched the enormous solid stone cover of the sarcophagus creak open slowly. Edith scrambled out of the way just narrowly avoiding its massive weight as it fell forward.

Ben's jaw dropped, his eyes wide, as the cover of the coffin flung open at Edith's incantation, and it clattered down the steps, as the tomb continued to crumble.

The ground beneath their feet quaked with each crash of the enormous lid tumbling down the steps, each collision dislodging more enormous chunks of limestone from the columns and ceiling above, until finally it landed in the molten moat.

A colossal shift in his peripheral vision caused Ben's head to snap in the direction of the column to his side, and he looked just in time to see it falling forward.

Ben didn't think, he just ran toward the column, before the massive cylindrical boulders had even landed. Edith looked on in horror as Ben flung himself onto the crumbling column, and launched himself across the broken sections like stepping stones before they each disappeared, one by one, beneath the surface of the fiery lava.

Ben leapt from the final sinking chunk of stone a split second before it was swallowed by the pool of melted metal, just barely clearing the fuming moat himself. He hit the ground running, taking steps two at a time to meet Edith at the top.

She knocked over the canopic jars to get the Book of Light, still there, exactly where she watched it placed in her vision, after three thousand years. Her fingers could barely grip it, her hands were shaking frantically.

It was larger than any usual book, and forged in copper. The relief on the front depicted hieroglyphs of Isis, goddess of magic, surrounded by beams of light. It was an ode that reflected Ramesses' love for her, even up to the very end.

She began searching all over for a lock or a point of entry to open it, but couldn't find one. Meant to be sealed in the tomb and never opened, the design omitted a lock or key.

"How did you get in without the key?" Ben panted when he reached her.

"Ben, I'm the key," she said, her throat ragged.

Then she got an idea.

She placed the book flat on the ground between them.

They both startled as another column behind her rumbled, threatening to crumble. They scanned to the soaring ceiling of the treasure room as they both realized if any more columns fell, the roof would cave in completely.

Their eyes met for a moment, the gravity of their peril known but unspoken between them. She placed her palms on the book, just like she had with the doors of the tomb. The corners of the book unlatched and sprang open.

Everything stopped.

Their ears rang as the room fell perfectly silent. The smoke that had been swirling around had completely stilled, the shimmers suspended in midair. The columns and walls held steady, and the water rushing in from the corridor abated to a trickle.

Ben and Edith looked around them, shocked and shaken, then shared an elated glance, before their eyes snapped back to the book.

"Ben, the collar," Edith said looking up at the mummy.

"Right," he said, as she turned her attention back to the book, carefully turning the thin sheets of engraved copper.

Ben climbed to the top platform and faced the mummy. The ragged linen strips were hanging loosely around the collar, barely concealing it. He raised his hands, tentative for a moment, and then began to tug at the fabric, loosening the strips one by one.

"You know, it would be swell if you could calm down a little," he whispered to the mummy companionably. Edith laughed at first, looking up at him. He winked down at her, before grasping the last of the fabric to tear it away, revealing the gleaming jewels. Then her heart swelled with appreciation for him.

When they met, she scoffed that everything was a joke to him. Now she had become so accustomed to the levity his outlook brought to her life, she would feel it's absence acutely if she was ever forced to live without it.

Ben stared at the collar, at the rows of shining golden beads, at the faceted array of jewels. Even with everything at stake, and couldn't help but pause for a moment. He'd been hunting treasure, procuring artifacts, excavating tombs, and dodging curses for a decade.

He'd never seen anything like The Collar of Queens.

It was not only exquisite in design, but it was distinct for its immaculate condition. Swaddled in strips of linen, it had been sealed perfectly from all elements. The very first treasures to be stolen from tombs were jewelry, making each surviving piece special in its rarity. Additionally, the story behind it and its affiliation with this high-profile legend would raise its value even more. It would be outside the realm of what a private collector would even be allowed to acquire, but aside from that, every museum on earth would enter a bidding war to obtain it. It was without a doubt the most valuable item he'd ever come across.

He only paused for the blink of an eye, before gently removing it from the mummy and returning to Edith's side. She made to stand, placing one hand on the step beside her, and Ben helped her to her feet.

"I've found the incantation…" Edith looked around at the debris, at the crumbling tomb, at the cavities full of melting antiques. "…but when I say the words, we'll need to destroy the collar."

He looked down at the mournful look on her face and had to laugh.

"Look baby, I know you're passionate preserving history, but I think just this once—"

"But this was your treasure. The whole reason you were on this dig," she interrupted his teasing.

"Edie," he smiled, brushing dust from her cheek. "You're the treasure I found in the Cursed Tomb of Argo. All I need to get safely out of this place… is you."

She shot up to her tiptoes, to throw her arms around his neck and kissed him. Ben wrapped his free arm around her waist, rejoicing that she was okay.

"Edie," he said, breaking away from her lips, "I didn't leave."

"I know," she said, furrowing her brows, berating herself for mistrusting him. It was a mistake she would never make again.

"Look I know I'm irresistible, but let's get the hell out of here."

"Okay, okay, right," Edie said, giving her head a brief shake.

She gathered the book against her chest, closed her eyes, and after a deep breath, chanted:

"Soul to heaven, body to earth,

Cast away evil, uncover truth

Stop your tears, and break this curse!"

Her eyes flew to Ben as he threw the collar into the boiling lava that surrounded them, and wrapped her in his arms.

They watched as the collar melted, as if by acid, in a fuming sputtering swirl.

The moment the final golden bead was enveloped by the blackness, a blinding blast of light exploded with the force of a hurricane from the mummy's casket. The shockwave knocked out all of the bricks plugging up the star shafts, sweeping out with it every trace of shimmering brown smoke and dust through the tunnels and vents. The force knocked Ben and Edie clear across the room as they clung to each other to land roughly on the stairs before the tunnel.

In silence, they tentatively opened their eyes to see the tomb filled with sunlight that shined on all of the wonders of the tomb. All of the tin had melted into a molten puddle to reveal the treasures buried with Amnara were actually gold. The sunshine gleamed off of the valuables in a blinding sheen. At the center of the pedestal, the explosion of light had forced the casket to fall back flat. And when Ben and Edie looked up, now that the treasure room was brightly illuminated, the light reflected off the riches revealed that the ceiling was painted indigo blue with hundreds of shimmering golden stars.

A gust of wind drew their attention back to the casket, as they saw a slender golden spirit emerge from the mummy, and drift upward. A glowing phantom scene of an idyllic oasis materialized against the dome ceiling. A teenaged boy in a headdress with a sapphire scarab stood waiting, as the ghost of Amnara floated up and into his arms. When they pulled back from a centuries overdue afterlife embrace, they saw each other weeping.

"No more tears, Mama," the boy said.

Amnara looked down to see Edith.

"Thank you, Sister," she said, before she, and her son, and the oasis waiting for them on the other side, vanished. The soul of Amnara had finally been laid to rest

Edie and Ben stood to look around the room in shock with dazzled brilliant smiles on their faces and their eyes as wide as saucers. The opulence and splendor of the room sparkled from every corner and nook. Their elated eyes met for the briefest of moments before they turned on their heels and ran as fast as they could. Edie was holding the Book of Light, and Ben held her hand.

CHAPTER TWENTY-ONE

THEY ESCAPED THE final tunnel of the tomb and fell back against the door, pushing it shut. The pitch black sky had faded to a pale blue, and the afternoon heat had burned off the stormy clouds.

When she was able to catch her breath, Edie's eyes fell from the sky to settle on the horizon where she saw the army of Medjai along the ridgeline of the closest dune. Their leader who stood apart before the rest bowed slightly, before his men followed suit. Then he turned and led the desert rangers away.

It made Edith so proud to have healed an ancient wound for Egypt, her country.

She looked back at Ben to find his eyes fixed on her. He looked at her as though she was infinitely precious, as though she really was his treasure.

She leaned in to kiss him, and their bodies sighed with relief.

"Edie, I left this morning to try and find your lotus. I thought if someone swiped it from the dig site, they'd want to sell it first thing in the morning at the market. I didn't realize until I was hogtied that I'd taken all of my things with me and didn't leave a note, so the fault is all mine for that. But, I really thought I'd be back before you woke up. It was stupid, I'm sorry."

"Hogtied?" Edith asked, and Ben waved his hand dismissively.

"Still… I can't believe you came back here on your own. How did you realize you could get in without the key?"

"I had a vision in my dream last night. I was Amnara, and she placed her palms on the door and opened it with magic. I think I had that dream because… I think I am descended from Amnara and her family's magic tribe. I think that's why it was me all along that had to come and break the curse. She must be my ancient ancestor. Before my mother met my father, her family was of full Egyptian lineage going back hundreds, well… maybe thousands of years."

She sat quietly for a moment, looking down at where she brushed her fingertips against the sand dusted over the bricks.

"I'm so glad I solved the mystery, and found the temple, and recovered the Book of Light. I guess it's… worth losing the lotus for a discovery like that." Her words didn't quite match the grief on her face, as she tried to convince herself to be content.

One of his eyebrows shot up as he looked at her.

She blinked at him, then her jaw dropped when she saw him smirk. Her hand flew to her chest as she looked down and saw the pendant was there, around her neck.

"Oh, Ben!"

He laughed as she flung herself at him. Wrapping her arms around his neck, he fell back to land on his elbow, held her close to him with his other arm.

"How did you get it?"

"Well, that's where I went this morning. This boy has been sitting at the edge of the oasis, watching us every day, even when no one else from the crew was on site. I thought it had to be him, but I didn't want to let on and get your hopes up. I thought if he took it, he'd try to sell it at his family's market. That's where Pimsley's thugs ambushed me and dragged me into a bunker underneath your favorite bar."

Ben explained the scene within the bunker and his history as an international informant essential in bringing Pimsley to justice. Edith realized that was his true objective for this dig, before he'd even met her.

"I still don't understand why you came back to Oasis Argo after the night of the party. If you had already gotten your bargaining chip and turned in Pimsley. You didn't have to do any of this."

"I already told you I was going to get you that book."

Her eyes shimmered. Everything he'd done had been for her. He risked his life, his career, his assignment to bring down Pimsley — all to help her get the book. He got intercepted and beaten up by thugs trying to get her necklace back, and ultimately succeeded. He threw a priceless treasure into a river of metallic lava, a treasure that could have made him a very, very rich man. For her.

"Ben," she said, the words tripping in her throat, "I don't know what to say."

"Don't mention it…" His grin was boyish and dazzling, as it always was. But he had a mournful look in his eyes.

"So," he continued, trying to let out a sigh that stopped in his throat. "You'll probably be on the next ocean liner to England." He winced a bit, hoping he hadn't shown his entire hand when her head snapped to look at him. It sounded a bit less obvious in his head.

He tried to lighten up, not meaning to dampen what would be a joyous event for her, even though it would certainly be a devastation for him.

"All I mean is that by tomorrow, you'll be the most famous Egyptologist who ever lived. Just think of the copy." He made a broad gesture with his hand as he announced the headline "Edith Taylor Unlocks the Cursed Tomb of Argo; Solves the Darkest Mystery in Ancient Egypt; Discovers Oldest Illustrated Book In Human History. Hell, they'll need a three page spread just for the title."

He was making her giggle again. He could never keep a straight face for long.

"What about you?" she said quietly.

"What about me? I'm just some… filthy third-rate criminal," he said.

"Hey. You're at least a first rate criminal." She looked up at him, laughter in her eyes. He could almost feel his heart crack. Thinking of her sailing away to London and faking orgasms underneath another man for the rest of her life was a tragedy too overwhelming to bear. He just hoped it wasn't written across his face.

"I'm not even that anymore. I got my record cleared. I'm released from my arrangement with the French Foreign Legion. So now… I'm nobody," he shrugged. The way he'd said it was upbeat, imbued with possibility and mischief. But the words still landed with a thud in Edith's chest.

"Not to me," she said.

"Oh, yes I am. As I should be. You're incredibly intelligent, drop-dead gorgeous, polished and poised, and tough — I mean really tough. And now," he gestured to the book beside her. "You'll really be going places. You could have your pick of any university on earth. And you're definitely the life of the party, I mean, just get you in a library and — ow!" he exclaimed as she punched his arm, and they were both laughing.

"You can't say that Ben, I'm a lady."

His face straightened now, as he looked at Edith meaningfully. Letting what she'd said settle for a moment between them.

"Well, yeah," he nodded. He looked in her eyes and she understood what he was saying. He was saying he wasn't good enough for her. He was saying goodbye.

"Ben…" she said gently, placing the book on the ground beside her.

"Don't," he said sternly. "I mean it, do not thank me. It was an honor, truly. You did it all, I just watched. I just…" he scratched the back of his neck with a shake of his head. "I'm just trying to say, if you're ever in Egypt, or America if that's where I end up, I hope you'll… let me take you to dinner…or a drink, if it's what you want. Or, if there's ever anything you need, I mean anything, I don't care where you are —"

"Ben," she repeated, touching his cheek until he looked at her again.

"It's too bad you'll be going back to America."

"Well… it's not set in stone," he said, brushing his thumb over her knuckles.

"Because well… you've taught me a lot of things."

"Yeah?" he said, his spirits lifting a bit.

"Yes. You've taught me the secret to a woman getting everything she wants in life… is to have a big man get it for you."

He laughed and shook his head.

"I just don't know what I'll do without a body guard…"

His hand stilled on hers, as he froze waiting for her to continue.

"I've gotten so used to having one —and that was before I was destined for imminent worldwide fame. I'll need one now more than ever."

"Edie," he said, his voice rising with hope.

"I love you, Ben."

His eyes widened before he flashed her favorite smile in the whole world. His fingers sunk into the hair at her nape, his other hand drew her close by the waist, as his lips possessed hers in a kiss that was full of all the love he felt for her.

"So will you take the job?"

"Yes, baby, I'll follow you anywhere."

They fell into each other as he kissed her, and kissed her, and didn't stop kissing her.

She ended up in his lap, and they got lost in each other, not hearing the city below them break out into cheers that lasted well into the night.

EPILOGUE

IT TURNED OUT Ben was right about the newspapers. They were littered all over the luxury cabin, draped over tables and arm chairs and all other surfaces.

WOMAN SCORNED? THE TRUE
STORY OF THE WEEPING VIPER

OASIS ARGO SUDDENLY FRESHWATER;
INDUSTRY BOOMING

EGYPT MUSEUM BREAKS GROUND ON
NEW WING: AMNARA TEMPLE

NEWSPAPER TYCOON RONALD PIMSLEY RESIGNS
IN DISGRACE; MILLIONS IN PLUNDERED
ARTIFACTS RETURNED TO EGYPT

RISING STAR OF EGYPTOLOGY: EDITH TAYLOR

ACADEMIA DARLING "EGYPT EDIE" HAS LOVER WITH SCANDALOUS CRIMINAL PAST

Once again, Ben was hovering over Edie in bed, like the last time they'd been in a steamer, in a much less opulent room, in much less glamorous attire. And, just like that night, he was kissing her like it was the first time.

Edie was wearing a strappy black evening gown that slid over her curves with a beckoning sheen. Ben was wearing the bottom half of his tux; on top he had stripped down to his undershirt with his suspenders hanging at his sides. They'd fallen into bed after rubbing elbows with all of the big wigs at dinner. They were kissing and pawing at each other impatiently. His hand slipped under the hem of her gown all the way up her leg to her thigh where it found the hem of her silk tap pants. He groaned, and grabbed her thighs greedily.

"I love these things."

"Do you, really!" she said, delighted.

"Oh, god yes," he said sitting up, grabbing one of her knees to spread her legs and position himself between them. He leaned over to kiss her again as he slowly lifted the hem of her skirt.

"They always feel the same when my hand is up your skirt… soft, and silky, and thin," he said, kissing her neck as splayed his hands on her inner thighs, pushing them apart further. Her breath caught in her throat as his words made her heart race.

"But I never know what color they'll be. Like a pale mint julep…" Her skirt was gathered at her mid-thigh now; he pressed into her and she thrust her hips against him.

"Or golden, like a Turkish coffee... with cream," he said, planting kisses along her neckline before sitting up again, lifting her skirt up around her waist to reveal her underwear was a sweet red.

"Ah, cherry pie," he smiled devilishly. "Mmm..." he said, standing up and reaching for the button of his fly.

"Wait!" she said, and he froze. "Can we talk?"

"Yes," he said, clearing his throat and adjusting his trousers.

She blew out an exhale trying to focus as he stretched out beside her on the bed, propping his head up on one arm to look down at her.

"I keep forgetting where we're going, the past few days have been such a blur, and I need to write a letter to my mother. Tell me one more time before we ... go to sleep."

"Okay," he cleared his throat, and announced in his most diplomatic voice, "We are, at present, aboard the Arabic, a steamer taking us up the Nile river to Port Alexandria. There, we will board the RMS Lancastria where I will wine and dine you for two weeks until we arrive at Port Tilbury, in England where you will have very important meetings with very important people, and negotiate a very enormous salary."

She grabbed a fistful of his undershirt and squealed with joy as she pressed her forehead against his chest. He smiled into her curls.

"Thank you," she beamed up at him.

He grabbed her hand from his chest and kissed it before interlocking his fingers with hers. "You never forget anything, I think you just like hearing me say it" he laughed.

"What is it?" he said a moment later, as she studied him.

"I just can't tell if I like you better in a tux, or covered in dust," she said — but when she let go of his hand and raised it to brush his hair from his face, a glint caught her eye.

Edie's jaw dropped and she couldn't breathe.

She was wearing an engagement ring. A peridot surrounded by diamonds.

Her eyes were swimming in sparkles, and she'd never been so surprised in her life. When she looked at him, he was watching her with a huge smile on his face.

"Edie..." he said, as she looked back at the ring, and then back to him.

"Will you be... the Mrs. First Rate Criminal?"

"No," she sniffled, tears welling in her eyes "Say it properly."

"Yes, you're right, certainly," he said. He raked his hand through his hair, striving to be serious. "Professor Edith Taylor; Director of the Griffith School of Egyptology and Near Eastern Studies at the University of Oxford..."

She nodded, and the teasing left his voice as he took a tone she very rarely heard.

"I love you, Edie. Will you be my wife?"

She wrapped her arms around his neck as tears streamed down her face. He felt them land on his shoulder. He rested his chin in her hair and held her tight, laying back on the bed feeling tears in his own eyes.

"Did you steal it?" she scolded, lifting to look down at him with her wild curls falling in her face.

"No, I didn't steal it!" he said, highly offended, "Why do you always assume I'm broke? The day we met, I was being recruited as a treasure hunter. It's what I'm known for, in Egypt, the country dripping with gold."

"Because the day we met you were a small potatoes pick-pocket, stealing trinkets off of old ladies."

"Oh, that. That's just for fun. You have no idea how much time I spend on trains in my line of work, it's terribly dull. I only do it to people who talk down to service workers. And it's not stealing, really, I always give it back."

Then Edith's thoughts were flashing to the past. He'd bumped into the woman with a full length fur coat on the platform, deliberately so, to return the mother of pearl cigarette case. She'd seen him give back the general's oxblood embossed wallet. And she knew he'd only stolen George's wallet to steal her photo out of it, and then returned it to him before they left the gala.

"That's not true, I saw Masuda with the golden pocket watch when we were leaving the hotel."

"That wasn't stealing, it was redistributing. Everything I ever lifted from Pimsley I gave back to a native Egyptian. Mesuda is a fine young man, and he wants his sister to go to school instead of working as a maid at the hotel."

Edith sat up to gawk at him. She was astonished. He changed that young boy's life, and she'd been calling him a dirty thief for weeks.

"Benjamin!" she exclaimed. "You're… a great man. You're the most incredible man I've ever met. You're sharp and fearless. You know how to talk to anyone, from the noblemen at the gala to merchants selling dates in an alleyway. You never stop making me laugh, even though I'm an uptight know-it-all."

"Hey, you're loosening up," Ben said, blushing furiously. And she'd never seen him blush before.

"You're so handsome it makes me weak, your smile stops my heart every time."

"Stop," he said, rolling his eyes.

"You're the only man who's ever really seen me. You're the only man who's ever respected me as a person. I never could have done any of this without you. And I can't believe I've never told you until now."

"Yup," he said, sighing, folding his arms behind his head on the pillow, desperate to lighten the mood and halt her flattery. "Not until you found out I was rich. I knew you were a gold digger by profession, I just never pegged you as a gold digger in your love life. I liked you better when you thought I was a thief."

She punched him in the gut, feigning insult.

"Oof, there she is." They shared a fit of laughter.

"You are a thief," she said primly, holding her hand out to admire her ring and fluffing her hair with the other. "You've stolen my heart and I don't ever want it back."

"Okay," he said, admiring her. "I'll guard your heart, while I continue to guard your body," he said, raising an eyebrow as he reached out to grab her around the waist.

"Yes, you turned out to be an excellent body guard after all," she said, returning to lay beside him on the bed. Their laughter was muffled as their lips met, and they floated off in ecstasy as the steamer glided down the Nile toward their future.

IF YOU ENJOYED THIS SPICY MYSTERY ROMANCE FROM MAE LOVETTE, YOU'LL LOVE HER NEXT NOVEL...

A STEAMY MERMAID ROMANCE

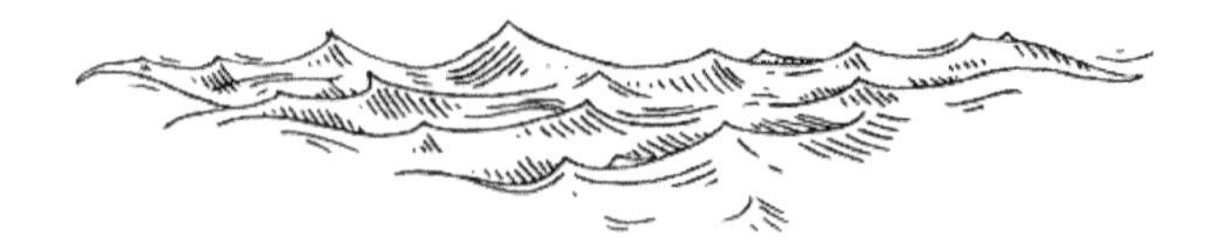

SCAN TO PREORDER

As I went out one evening,
And sailed out of sight from the land,
I saw her sit on a faraway isle,
With a comb and a glass in her hand.

Taming waves of long raven hair,
Her skin gleamed with shimmering scales.
Her cheeks were like roses; her eyes were like stars,
With her voice she bewitched the calm gales.

Once she dove into the menacing deep
The stormy seas beckoned to roar,
The winds did rage, the foam did rise,
And I never again saw the shore.

Heed the tall tales that warn of this song,
Though it may seem a heavenly sound,
For it leads all land-loving lads to their doom,
Who were only too eager to drown.

Come all ye merrily unmarried men,
That's living on land at your ease.
Beware the merfolk's comely charm,
And never incline to the seas.

ACKNOWLEDGEMENTS

The working title of this book was always "The Cursed Tomb of Argo." It didn't end up being the title of this book, but to me, it will always be the name of this story.

It was one of the very first book ideas I had scrawled on a flash card. My objective for my career as an author from the beginning, hypothetical as it was at the time, was to write lighthearted romance novels inspired by iconic moments of nostalgia. One such example that instantly came to mind was a brief shining season on the cusp of the millenia when my wildest fantasy was to be flung off the starboard side of a barge by the strong arms of a man I had tried to brush right out of my hair. Thanks to the age of oversharing, I was acutely aware that I had not been alone in such thoughts all those years ago.

The concept was this. What if the 1999 movie, The Mummy, was a romance novel?

Of course, The Mummy already was a romance novel. By the paranormal romance queen herself, Anne Rice: Pioneer of Sexy Vampire Fiction. The synchronicity doesn't stop there; her romance novel was also based on a movie, the 1932 Boris Karloff film, The Mummy.

I hope to have a prolific career as an author who offers satisfying love stories within comforting snapshots of the zeitgeist. I consider it very tidy that my first book isn't merely a romance novel that is inspired by a movie. It's a romance novel that is inspired by a movie, that was inspired by a romance novel, that was inspired by a movie.

So, I suppose I'd like to acknowledge Boris Karloff, Ann Rice, and Brendan Fraser. You rose from the dead, wrote out of spite, and ran like hell so that I could sip coffee in a comfy chair and write my little debut baby.

Next, I want to thank my momsquad. I met Rachel at a time in my life when I was not leaving the house. She introduced me to her friend Katie, and it was with the gentle, yet firm pressure only a sisterhood can provide that I reluctantly crept free of my comfort zone. Through block parties they befriended Katelynn, who eventually convinced her best friend Annie to join our strange group of women who hang out a lot, like a suspicious amount. Soon we found ourselves with the rarest of treasures in adult life — a circle of friends.

Each of them has been so supportive and encouraging about this dream of mine that feels very tender to share. Thank you all so much for being my village, and welcoming my boys and I into your homes, and hearts. I would not be the person I am without these women who I love like family.

I couldn't be where I am right now without my parents. My mother who made me a writer, and my father who made me a storyteller. Together they modeled a true love of reading, my mom who loves Sandra Brown, and my Dad who loves Stephen

King. They are so supportive of my strange gifts, and so proud of this slightly off-color achievement. But I know that they would actually be proud of any endeavor that meant something to me. I love you guys.

This book could not exist as it appears on these pages without my editor. It became so much stronger throughout revisions, and I am honored to have the insight which makes this completed work what it is. Also, I really appreciate the feedback: "I don't think a sack of hot coals is a thing." Your wisdom astounds me.

My cover designer brought Edie and Ben to life exactly as I had hoped. Book covers speak in a language that is only visual, and it can be the deciding factor in getting your book in front of its intended audience. The readership of romance novels are women who know exactly what they want, and the cover for Guarded Treasure perfectly communicates the steamy, light-hearted adventure they will discover between these pages. It has been such an honor to work with someone so incredibly talented, who was also gracious with myself, someone who doesn't understand commercial design at all.

My brand manager is fully responsible for keeping me pointed in the right direction. If I had crafted my master plan within the confines of my own mind, and without the aid of anyone else's insight, I am sure I never would have made it. Having someone to brainstorm and strategize with has been invaluable, but I am incredibly fortunate for this partner I had the honor of working with.

An author can't do this on their own any more than words can step off the page to publish themselves. Writing is only one part of the process. It's a critical part, I'd certainly say it's the heart of the process. However, if all I did was write the words... no one would ever get a chance to read them. Especially the era in which I'm publishing this debut novel, publishing a book is a business, requiring all of the branches of any other business.

When I think back on this 16-month experience, from the first day of research, all the way to where I sit right now writing the final page of this book, these are all of the people who come to mind when I think of who helped me get here. However, there is one person who I think of first, and foremost, as well as long after all the rest.

Sara. My sister, my best friend, my soul mate, my true north. You are so essential to this book that it feels very nearly a crime for my name to appear alone on its cover. Not just to this project, but to every step I've taken in my life. I can't take a step without you. Or, rather, I can't take a step without texting you twenty times, at a minimum, before, during, and after. Saying I could not have done this without you seems paltry, when the fact of the matter is I couldn't breathe without you. Thank you for loving me more than anyone.

From the bottom of my heart, I appreciate every single person who reads this book, and hope to have the honor of providing each and every one of you another delightful escape with each new book I am lucky enough to write in the future. Thank you.

ABOUT THE AUTHOR

Mae Lovette writes romance novels deep in the woods west of Chicagoland. She bakes pies and sews dresses and reads books. And in the evenings, she and Stuart the Cat curl up to enjoy their own happily ever after.

Visit Mae online and sign up for her newsletter at **maelovette.com** or find her on TikTok **@maelovettebooks**.

Printed in Great Britain
by Amazon

41369781R00189